Good For The Soul

by

Philip Rennett

Book 2 of the Path Finder Series

First published in Great Britain in 2025
by Pea Arr Books

ISBN: 978-1-7385747-1-1

Copyright © Philip Rennett 2025
www.philrennett.com

The right of Philip Rennett to be identified as the
author of this work has been asserted by him in accordance
with the Copyright, Designs and Patents Act 1988.

All rights reserved. No part of this publication may be reproduced,
stored in a retrieval system or transmitted in any form or by any
means whatsoever without the prior written permission of the
publisher except for the use of brief quotations in a book review.
Nor may it be otherwise circulated in any form of binding or cover
other than that in which it is published without a similar condition
being imposed on the subsequent purchaser.

Cover design by
Daniel Greenhalgh
cargocollective.com/danielgreenhalgh

Good For The Soul is a work of fiction.
Names, characters, places, and incidents either are the product
of the author's imagination or are used fictitiously.
Any resemblance to actual persons, living or dead,
events or locales, is entirely coincidental.

To Bridget

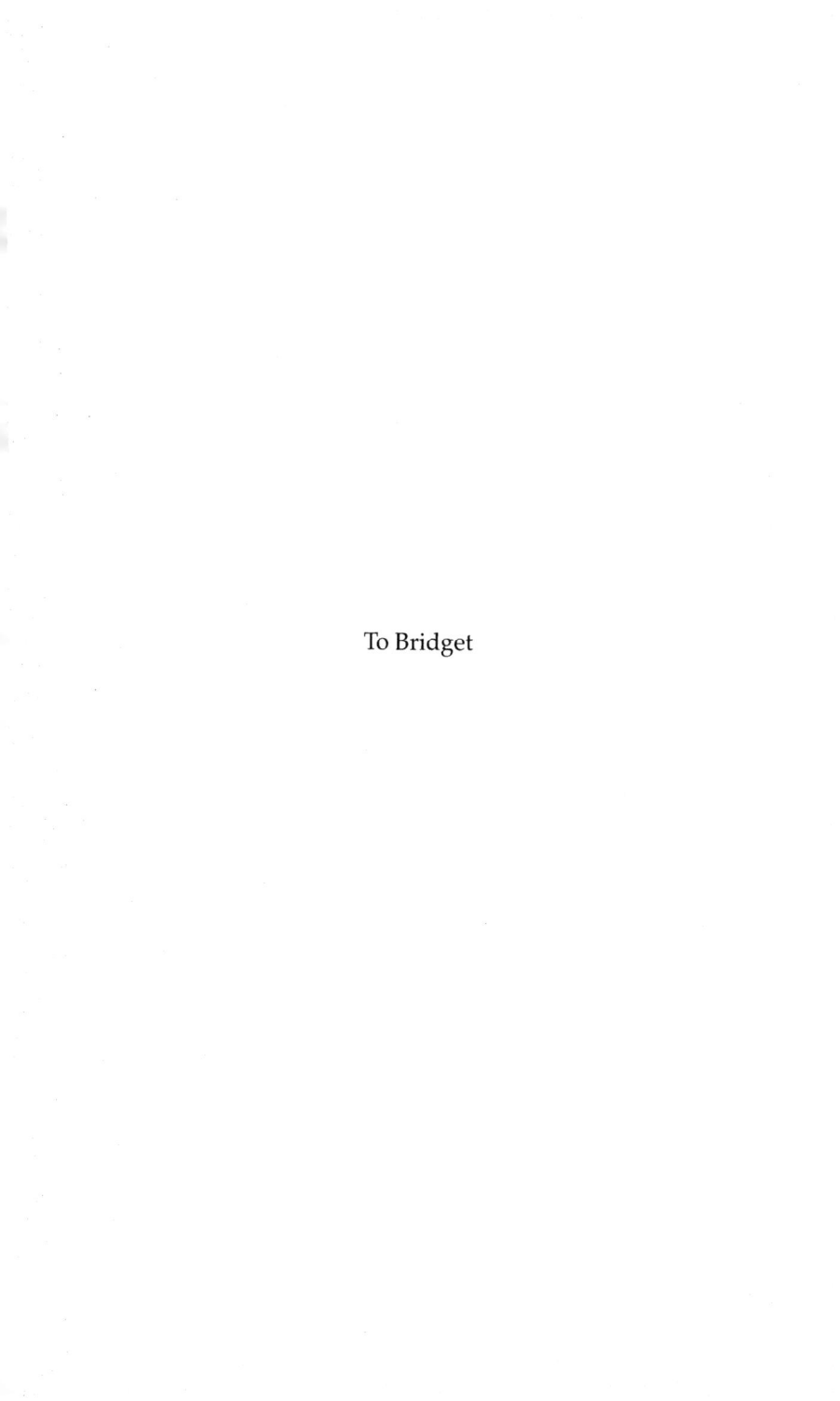

The Invitation

"How many people get shot every time they buy a cabbage? Do photographers never sleep? Have a day off? Die?"

Mindy looked down the hallway, put her finger to her lips, then pointed at the phone in her hand. Andrew Blackwell, former prime minister of the United Kingdom and currently unemployed, threw his parka and baseball cap onto the coat stand and carried two shopping bags into the kitchen, dumping them onto the wooden table.

"It's bang out of order. One of them shoved his lens in my face when... Sorry..." he said, finally noticing her look of exasperation and, eventually, the phone pressed to her ear. Mindy glared at him, grabbed her notepad and pen, then walked through the hall into the lounge and shut the door.

Blackwell checked his watch and ignored his phone. He had successfully avoided his mobile every morning for the past three weeks, determined to dedicate six hours to his memoirs each day before anything else. At least, it would have been six hours had he been an early riser. That had been the case in Downing Street; not so much in his own home.

Six months, he thought as he put away his purchases. Half a year since walking away from politics and into self-imposed oblivion. Keeping a profile so low, he was almost living underground.

Giving Damien Crockett, the new premier, his government and the country the chance to reset, just like he had planned. And the result? Abysmal failure. They hadn't filled the vacuum he'd left as he had imagined.

Rather than exciting policies, memorable events, a motivated electorate and dynamic economic initiatives, the Westminster Bubble had focused on its own navel, plodding along and waiting for the general election in two years' time. *Crockett must be banging his head against the wall*, he thought. *Welcome to my world.*

The result of the inertia had been a renewed interest in Blackwell, and that had increased the more he avoided the media. He had declined all interviews, documentaries, travelogues, and jungle stays.

Political editors resorted to reviews of his time in power - a period that seemed to grow in terms of achievement and credibility when compared to what had followed. Leaders of other countries, including the French, lamented his absence from the global stage.

The political party that had disowned him wanted him to make a glorious return - partly because of the current situation; partly because he may join another party and take supporters with him.

The internet was... well... the internet. The speculation about him making a return more sensational than the Second Coming had turned into a genuine hope. The clamour was intensifying. Hashtags and memes abounded. Petitions to parliament demanding his return had sufficient signatures after three days that the assembly was duty-bound to debate the resolution.

And throughout the six months, Andrew Blackwell had achieved something unprecedented. He had kept his mouth shut. He had no strategy to announce; no master plan to launch.

He was doing nothing, and the political elite and the marketing gurus were full of admiration. They thought he was a genius.

The genius stored the shopping and grabbed a beer from the fridge as a reward for his hard work.

As he did so, the lounge door opened and Mindy, his former assistant chief of staff at Number 10 and now his unpaid chief of staff, manager and fiancée emerged, looking pensive.

"Sorry about the interruption," he said. "Is everything okay?"

"I've just been on the phone," she announced, somewhat unnecessarily. "There's a three-day event in Ireland this coming week and we're invited."

"We always decline."

Mindy nodded.

"You might say yes to this one. It's a Global Conclave event."

"Ah. Billionaires meeting secretly to discuss big questions. What's the topic this time?"

"The world."

Blackwell sniggered. Mindy's face remained serious.

"I'm supposed to discuss the world?" he asked. "Have they had a cancellation?"

Mindy shook her head.

"It's vague because they don't know what you'll say. They don't care. They're intrigued. There's been no cancellation. You're the only speaker. No presentation needed. You'll chat. Informally, over drinks… dinner… They'll fly us out. Put us up. If they like what they hear, they'll work out how they can support you. Maybe take it to Davos. Take you to Davos. If they don't like it, they'll tell you and thank you for coming. Plus, they'll pay you for your time."

"I'm expensive."

"They'll pay you one million for three days, irrespective of the result. Plus the event will never be publicised."

"They have more money than sense." *And yet the money was not to be ignored.* "What do you think?"

"I think you hate being a fraud. All this spotlight, but nothing to share. A little cash input might be useful. Brainstorming with people you'll need onside can only help. And we get a few days in a mansion on the Atlantic coast. Peace Castle. Very posh."

"But are they serious?"

Mindy picked up her phone and handed it over.

"They've made a good faith down payment."

Blackwell looked at the banking app.

"You're right. Maybe it's time." He thought for a moment. "We'll accept the down payment. No more."

Mindy nodded. If this meeting leaked, the amount of negative opinion generated could be influenced by the size of the fee. Only accepting the down payment could limit the damage.

"You know who else will be in Ireland next week," she said.

Blackwell nodded.

"He'll be miles away in Clonbrinny, and he'll have plenty on his plate. I'll tell him once we're back."

"If there's anything worth telling."

The UK's former leader laughed.

"If we can't gather any gossip after socialising with six of the richest, most influential people in the free world, then we should be embarrassed."

Mindy tilted her head to one side - a clear sign she was back in work mode.

"It's a huge opportunity, Andy. We can't mess it up."

"It'll be what it'll be," he smiled.

"That's precisely what I'm worried about."

Confession

The door of the confessional in St Patrick's church, Clonbrinny, creaked open as the priest stepped in, closed it and settled onto his seat.

Before he could focus his mind, the penitent on the other side of the latticed opening decided there was no time to waste.

"Bless me, Father, for I have sinned."

The priest sighed.

"Let's cut to the chase, Margaret. Is it the usual?"

A gasp came from the other side of the confessional.

"How did you know my name?"

The priest stifled another sigh and whispered a quick, silent prayer of his own before responding.

"Your wheelchair is just outside the door, Margaret. Jimmy is sitting in the nearest pew, reading the Racing Post. Now, is it the usual?"

"I'm ashamed to say it is."

"Margaret, we have talked about this. Dreaming is not a sin."

"You say that, Father. But you came to me naked in my sleep and asked me to wash your cassocks."

"Cassocks?"

"I don't like saying bollocks in church."

Removing his glasses, the priest covered his face with both hands, rubbed his eyes, and - not for the first time - prayed for patience.

"We've spoken about this many times before, Margaret."

"But this one was special, Father. Dirty. It started when I caught you polishing your monstrance in the sacristy after Mass…"

Realising he would never get the next fifteen minutes of his life back, the priest put the earbuds in his ears, pressed 'Play' on his smartphone, closed his eyes, and relaxed at the start of Mozart's requiem.

By the time he reached *Rex tremendae*, Margaret would be drawing to a close, keen to catch the bus to the city to meet her younger sister for lunch. Thursday was roast day at the residential home. They would have a meal and a good chat, then Jim would return from the pub and they'd both come home again.

Sure enough, as the perfect cadence brought *Tuba mirum* to an end, he removed his ear buds just in time to hear, "And that's why I need to be punished, Father. No priest should ever suffer a sore bottom and a broken finger. Not even in somebody else's dream. Anyway, I'm sorry for these and all my sins."

Curious how whatever had happened had happened, but not so much that he regretted his musical interlude, the priest cleared his throat.

"A penance isn't a punishment, Margaret. It enriches life…"

"Then you should spank me, Father. Firmly. On my naked bottom."

The priest dismissed bending a seventy-eight-year-old over his knee and turned instead to the thought of penance.

"I think we'll go down a different route," he said.

"You said that in the dream."

Shuddering, he continued, "I want you to have a chat with God when you're ready to go to sleep. Thank him for his grace and mercy. Reflect on the wonderful things you've seen and done over the years. Ask him to remind you of those as you take your rest."

A moment's silence followed, then the sounds of movement as Margaret got to her feet and her walking stick clunked against the wooden surrounds.

"Thank you, Father, and bless you," she said, pausing for a moment before she opened the door. "You know, you're a lovely man when you're sober, but I think I prefer you when you're drunk."

And with that, she was gone.

The clink of coins tumbling into the collection box brought a warm flutter to the priest's heart. Then he sat back, replaced the ear buds, closed his eyes and pressed 'Play' once more.

Collection Time

The Phoenix Park Tech Zone is nowhere near and has nothing to do with the magnificent, 707-hectare Phoenix Park in the heart of Dublin, but that hadn't stopped the site's developers marketing the connection for all it was worth to potential customers across the world. The end had justified the means, with technology and software firms taking space in its impressive buildings and making it the home of their European operations.

In the reception area of one such eight-storey property, housing the European sales operations of three IT giants, the doors to the outside world slid open. Two men in suits strolled in and walked to the receptionist's desk, having parked their car in a zone for key executives, despite neither being a key executive in any global IT business.

The younger man, his untamed red hair and a cluster of freckles trying their best to cover his facial scars, looked ill at ease in formal wear. He stared at the desk as if he'd never seen one before, then wandered over to a waiting area. He helped himself to a free cappuccino and a *pain au raisin*, then sat down on a vacant seat and pulled out his smartphone.

The bigger man, by some considerable distance, placed his briefcase by his feet and smiled at the lady facing him.

She smiled back.

"You can't park there, sir."

"Sorry?"

"Your car. It's in the executive zone. You'll need to move it."

"Ah. There'll be no need. I won't be here that long. I'm just here to collect a payment from your finance department. Your facilities director, Mister Bingham, knows all about it."

"And you are?"

The giant pulled out a slightly tatty business card from his jacket pocket and placed it on the desk.

The receptionist looked at the card on the desk, then picked up the phone and dialled a number.

"It's Jane on reception," she muttered. "Is Mister Bingham there? I have a Mister Dunne from Yewowus Debt Recovery Services. He's collecting a payment…"

Mr Dunne leaned forward. "On behalf of Dexter Matthews Europe. Forty-three thousand euros overdue. Mr Bingham has copies of the court paperwork."

The receptionist gave the details, listened briefly, then hung up.

"I'm afraid Mister Bingham isn't available, but will call you once he's out of his meeting."

"That's grand. My colleague and I can wait."

"But your car…"

Brendan Dunne smiled. "That can wait too."

He picked up his briefcase and the untouched business card, then walked over to the younger man, who was busy on his phone. Having asked the other people in the area whether the building's owners also owed them money, he opened his briefcase, took out a flask, a box of sandwiches and a packet of crisps, then settled down.

The receptionist watched him as she picked up the phone again. Two minutes later, three men emerged from the elevator, one dressed in a suit and two in security uniforms.

The suit spoke to the receptionist, surveyed the waiting area, then walked across, flanked by his two associates.

"Are you fellas from Dexter Matthews?"

The man had a broad Dublin accent, Brendan noted. *This should be fairly straightforward.* He pointed at the food in his mouth and answered with a nod.

"You're wasting your time, boys. Mister Bingham is on two weeks' leave. This will be on top of his pile when he returns, but there's no point you waiting."

Dunne found the men's attempts to intimidate by flexing their fingers amusing. He swallowed his food and took a sip of his coffee.

"I was told Mister Bingham is in a meeting, and will speak to me afterwards. The forty-three thousand euros is way overdue. The court has ordered it to be paid." His voice rumbled and echoed around the atrium. "It may be peanuts to your business - in which case your reluctance to pay should alarm your other suppliers - or it's a big deal, in which case your financial situation may concern your tenants."

The suit looked around at the interested audience, then stepped forward and murmured, "It's not happening today. Do the sensible thing and leave now."

Placing his cup on the table beside him, Brendan looked at the three men. He first glanced at the name badge on the suit before meeting his eyes.

"It is happening today, Peter. We won't be going anywhere until it does."

He spotted his associate look up from his smartphone and give a slight nod, then took the business card he'd retrieved from the receptionist and held it out.

The man in front of him ignored it.

"No need for it, Mister Dunne. We already have your details."

"Look at the small print, Peter."

The man frowned, then took the card and read it.

"The other side."

The man flipped the card and blanched. Five words.

A Kay Eye Gee company.

"We're not from Dexter Matthews," explained Brendan helpfully. "But we bought the debt from them. They're lovely people. Family business. Very good at their job. We're from a debt collection agency that's part of the Kay Eye Gee Group. You may have heard of us?"

Peter nodded.

"Now, we'd like you to pay the debt, in full, to the bank details on the card, as per the court order. Once we have confirmation of payment, we'll be on our way."

"I'll need fifteen minutes."

"You've got ten."

"You know they won't work for us again because of this?"

"Frankly, they don't care. You're such bad payers. But you will use them again. They're good people, great at their job and excellent value for money. Just treat them right. You also owe them for work over the last three months in London, Frankfurt and Lille. You'll pay those outstanding invoices within the next week directly to them."

"Or else?"

Dunne smiled at Peter's bravado, surrounded by witnesses and with two security guards by his side. His smile transformed into a frown as he eased himself out of the chair. Witnesses weren't sure if he towered above the security team or if they shrank as he stood up.

The man's size pushed the air in the atrium away from him, rustling loose papers nearby. Adding to the drama, small clouds chose the moment to cross the sun and darken the scene.

"Or we'll be back. You now have nine minutes."

The three men scurried to the lifts and disappeared.

Brendan Dunne sat down once more and picked up his coffee.

The young man looked at his phone.

"I could just transfer the money now, you know," he said.

"Nah. Redirect it once it's arrived. We don't want them having second thoughts. And set off the fire alarm once we've gone, to discourage any such notion."

"Also, I've had a message. He wants another chat."

Dunne nodded and took another bite from his sandwich.

"We'll go straight there," he said, as he watched his colleague access the building's alarm system before returning to his Su Doku puzzle. "You got in quick."

The younger man grunted. "Network serial number on the display unit and a photo of a cat called Cloony on the desk. It wasn't rocket science."

Daniel Walsh

Jimmy Doyle sat down on the bus stop bench, next to his wife's wheelchair.

He closed his eyes and savoured the warmth on his face from the sunshine bursting through a gap in the light clouds, skimming over the nearby hills.

Margaret Doyle was busy on her smartphone, finalising the report. She'd started it in the confessional, once Father Aidan had closed his eyes and she could hear the faint music seeping from his ear buds.

Today's visit had been one of the better ones she made every fortnight to confess her sins and to monitor the priest's health. Jimmy had observed the priest was clean-shaven, had a ruddy complexion and his clothes appeared clean. She added she had noticed no smell of alcohol. His eyes looked bright - brighter than any time in the last three or four months. His mood was positive, and he remained focused on their conversation when he wasn't listening to his precious Mozart.

A former head of mathematics at Dublin University, Margaret - whose intellect was far keener than she let on - compiled a report after each confession. This was a favour for a former student, Kara Walsh, who was also the priest's concerned niece.

Kara's uncle hadn't been the same since Daniel - his twin brother and her father - had died in the goldfields of Western Australia three years earlier. Daniel spent much of his mining bonuses on drugs and alcohol. After a memorable all-night bender, he got into an argument with the huge bucket on a dragline excavator and literally lost his head in the Outback heat.

Almost everyone thought Daniel died at a Catholic mission in the Congo, helping to protect a congregation from a surprise guerrilla raid.

Having left Ireland for the role of facilities manager at the mission, Daniel neglected to inform anybody of his quick change in career path to a more lucrative and ultimately fatal position on another continent.

Anybody, apart from his wife Susan, who had seen modest monthly payments from Africa replaced by much larger amounts from Australia.

Timing is everything. News of his death coincided with news of the repelled guerrilla attack. The media in his home country were happy to create a story from an unverified assumption. The mission was about to issue a clarification when it noticed a significant increase in online fundraising. It elected to remain silent 'given the ongoing situation in the Congo and out of respect for the Walsh family in their time of mourning'.

A substantial donation to the family's fundraising web page ensured Susan's silence. In fact, as well as in fiction, Daniel died a legend.

Margaret sent the report by email, just before the bus squealed to a halt beside them. As Jimmy and the driver helped her onboard, a black sedan with tinted windows swept into the church car park. As the bus pulled away, she watched a large man emerge from the car and disappear into the church.

She picked up her phone once more and sent a text message, only relaxing and looking forward to the rest of the day after she had received an acknowledgment.

Next to her, her loving husband of forty years handed over the Racing Post and a pen. As much as he fancied himself as an astute gambling man, he knew his chances of success would improve if he left the decisions to his darling wife.

Take-Off

The jet stood at the far end of the only runway at the small regional airport. Its two turbofan engines were already warm from the flight across the Irish Sea.

Both pilots settled in the cockpit and the cabin crew of one waited at the foot of the steps as the executive van halted alongside.

One man stepped out and carried two suitcases into the plane, then returned to the van and opened a door. The two VIPs slipped out quickly and boarded the jet, their identity protected by large hooded coats.

Moments later, the air hostess followed, retracting the stairs and closing the cabin door behind her. The van pulled away, having prevented any observer in the airport buildings from identifying the passengers.

In the cabin, the air hostess double-checked the windows were covered, stored the coats and made sure her guests were comfortable and ready to go.

Five minutes later, having received permission from air traffic control, the jet launched into the blue sky and headed north towards Scotland.

Once the captain switched off the seatbelt sign, the hostess raised the window covers and headed off to prepare refreshments.

Facing each other in luxurious leather seats, Andy Blackwell and Amanda Abbott checked their surroundings and tried to contain their excitement.

"Were we followed?" asked Mindy.

Andy Blackwell thought through the carefully choreographed departure, which had involved the former prime minister's security detail, three identical vans and the vehicle wash at a supermarket petrol station.

"If we were, they deserve every photograph they took," he said. "I think we're fine."

Fifty miles into the flight, the co-pilot notified the authorities of a change in plan. The plane turned west and headed towards Ireland.

New Arrivals

The van took a left turn from the high street, driving alongside the hotel bar before swinging into the gravel car park at the rear of the building. The driver parked a good distance from the waste bins, glass bins, and the benches and tables of the spacious smoking section, marked by a row of traffic cones.

The side door slid open and the tall figure of Dave Westlake stepped out, keen to stretch his legs after the drive from the ferry terminal. Angus Grace emerged from the opposite side of the van, then Stuart Morris shuffled along on the seat behind him, leapt to the ground and trotted off to the hedgerow between the car park and the riverbank, where he threw up with impressive force, matched only by the accompanying retch.

Grace lit a cigarette, then took a couple of puffs as, more with curiosity than concern, he watched his retired former colleague try to catch his breath and control his stomach. "Always amazes me where it all comes from," he remarked. "You had next to nothing on the boat."

An ashen-faced Morris looked on the verge of replying, but another surge of nausea bent him double once again.

"And you certainly didn't eat or drink anything that colour," observed Grace, "Or with that smell."

He exhaled some smoke, then drew it back in through his nose to hide the stench.

Dave Westlake reached back into the van, grabbed a bottle of water, wandered over to his former sergeant, and handed it over.

"Have a couple of sips, mate. Might make you feel better."

Morris nodded his gratitude and rested on his haunches, while he tried to regain control of his bodily functions.

Neither man in the front of the van had shown any concern or interest whatsoever. The driver and van owner, David 'Coldfront' Davies, scanned the pub in front of them and the handful of vehicles in the vicinity before deciding the parking location was satisfactory.

"Late afternoon," he announced to nobody in particular. "We've done well." He removed the key, opened his door and set off towards the back to remove the luggage.

Simon Pope completed his text message and sent it from his smartphone, then copied it, pasted it, removed *'Give the dogs a hug from me. X'* and sent it to a second number. Gazing at his surroundings, he stifled an enormous sigh. He had no idea how the next few days would go and wasn't sure what constituted success or failure. He didn't know what he was doing apart from 'reporting on the situation', as the Garden Club had requested.

"You won't be in any danger," the regimental sergeant major had assured him on the phone call to explain the assignment. "You're just one of the many fishing groups they get every year. Just keep your eyes and ears open. Don't drink too much and send me the occasional update."

"But you've just told me this involves one of the most powerful gangland bosses in Ireland. A man with massive influence over politicians and the police."

"Possible influence. Yes."

"Someone with blood on his hands."

"Allegedly. No one has ever proven a case against him."

"Because of his influence."

"And the potential deadly threat he poses."

Pope had fallen silent. This wasn't the 'jolly with the lads' the RSM had suggested.

"Simmo, chances are you won't come across him or his people," the voice on the phone persisted. "This is a small town he visits. It's miles from his base in Dublin. Just sniff around a bit. If you see or hear anything that corroborates the request, we'll take it from there."

"You can't act now?"

There was a moment's hesitation.

"We fell foul of the Irish authorities several times during the Troubles, crossing a border that barely exists. Those times were difficult. Embarrassing. If this priest has an issue we can help to resolve, then we'll resolve it. We just need more detail before we commit. That's where you come in."

"So I can explain to the priest?"

"No. He doesn't have the card. He doesn't know we exist."

"Then who has the card?"

Another moment's hesitation. "Somebody else."

The memory of the phone call faded and Pope found himself in the hotel car park once more, the noise of luggage and fishing gear being dragged out of the van disturbing his reverie.

"Come on Simmo. These rods won't carry themselves!"

He opened his door and climbed out.

It's just a short break with the lads, he thought. *Keep your mouth shut and your ears and eyes open. You'll be home in no time.*

The guest reception area was at the end of the bar. Before the men even set down their luggage, five halves of 'the black stuff' were already lined up on the bar.

"Just a welcoming tipple after your long day," smiled the bar tender, brushing a stray lock of dark brown hair behind her ear so the newcomers could see how truly pretty she was. "We saw your van arrive. Enjoy your drink while I sort out the paperwork."

She noticed the pale features of the older member of the group. He'd been a handsome man, she thought. His quiet demeanour suggested his mind was elsewhere. She was right, as bar staff tend to be. He was trying to calm his churning stomach.

"Of course, if you'd prefer something else…"

"Do you have a glass of water, please?" Stuart Morris did his best to smile as he made the request. "I'm afraid I'm not feeling too well at the moment."

"Not a problem."

Already falling in love, as he did whenever he first met an attractive woman, Dave Westlake struck up a conversation.

"I thought stout was good for you."

"Most beers are," said the bartender, focused on pouring water into a glass and adding ice for good measure. "There are nutrients in them." She nodded at the full glasses on the bar. "More in that than most."

Westlake nodded in what he hoped would look like a thoughtful manner. "And does it help with any conditions in particular?" he asked.

The bar tender searched in her memory for facts from her tour of the brewery, then returned and gave the water to Stuart Morris as the others picked up their beers. "Decreases the risk of cardiovascular disease and increases bone mineral density. Allegedly. Apparently, something in the barley lowers cholesterol, reduces your risk of heart disease and protects against free radicals."

"Fascinating," said Westlake, not having a clue how beer protected against extremists. He turned toward his best friend, who was sipping the water, and patted his shoulder. "Heart disease preventer," he said, lifting his glass of beer.

"You should've been on these ages ago."

Morris nodded. "Increase in bone density," he replied. "So should you."

The woman smiled as the group laughed. She loved to see new characters in the bar. Gave her more of an insight into the world beyond Clonbrinny, and increased her desire to experience it while she was still young enough. She needed to alert her mammy about the new prospect - handsome and witty, but pale and not a natural sailor.

Peace Castle

The grand, castle-like mansion of Caisleán Síocháin, or 'Peace Castle', sits proudly on a high promontory overlooking the spectacular coastline of County Clare, a striking blend of fortifications and aristocratic luxury.

A long-standing symbol of Irish resilience and reconciliation, the estate passed in the 19th century into the hands of the Connellys, a prominent farming family known for their patronage of the arts. The mansion became a retreat for famous Irish poets, playwrights, and artists, many of whom found inspiration in its dramatic location and extensive wine cellars.

Unsurprisingly, the location, facilities and grandeur gradually attracted the attention of the great and the good. Early in the 20th century, the owners kicked out the arty types, who paid nothing and drank more than their fair share, and focussed instead on more lucrative markets. Despite the occasional blips, the mansion's attraction to the world's wealthy matched the pace of its modernisation and its eye-watering prices. The well-protected estate encompassed 350 acres of rugged coastline and lush parkland, including a private airfield. A nine-hole golf course blended seamlessly into the natural landscape, winding through ancient woods, and along windswept cliff edges.

A variety of peaceful walking trails cut through the woodland, many leading into a valley and along a small lake, or 'lough', which boasted an old, overly-large boathouse that was now used for hosting intimate gatherings and events.

It wasn't unusual for governments, global corporations or billionaires to rent out the entire property for vast amounts of money and this week was no exception, with the Global Conclave visiting for the fifth time in two years.

Andrew Blackwell and Mindy Abbott peered out of the windows as the pilots battled the coastal winds on their final approach. Atlantic waves tumbled onto the beach and crashed into the rocks, while the mansion sat imperiously at the top of the cliff.

Blackwell spotted three larger jets parked by the side of the small terminal. Two uniformed staff climbed into a small executive coach, which moved as the jet landed. As soon as the plane stopped, the hostess appeared with the large hooded coats. Moments later, the VIPs walked down the steps and into the coach, both suitcases followed, and the vehicle departed.

As per the agreed protocol, nobody said anything. The coach drove from the airport through the woods and stopped at the mansion's main entrance eight minutes later.

Still wearing their coats, both guests exited, picked up their suitcases and entered the lobby as their escort drove away.

Mindy paused, admiring the sumptuous surroundings.

The room exuded timeless elegance and opulence. The high ceiling featured intricate plasterwork and gilded mouldings. An enormous crystal chandelier, suspended from the centre of the ceiling, cast a warm glow that danced off the polished marble floor, even in broad daylight. Large oil portraits adorned the original dark wood panelling on the walls. A grand fireplace, with an ornately carved stone mantel, served as the focal point on one side.

At the far end, a sweeping staircase with a wrought-iron balustrade led to the upper floors. The first floor landing featured a large, arched window with stained glass accents, which, on a brighter day, would have flooded the lobby with natural light.

The reception desk was an antique masterpiece of polished oak with brass accents. By its side stood a polished brass luggage trolley. Even the desktop screen on the desk failed to detract from the historical charm. The overall atmosphere, Mindy thought, reeked of refined sophistication, with every detail carefully curated to impress. Everything was perfect, she reflected, apart from one thing. Nobody was there to greet them.

"Well, this is awkward," she observed. "It's not like we've arrived past midnight on an all-inclusive package."

"Awkward and embarrassing," agreed her partner, having hung both coats alongside several similar ones on the wall next to the entrance before rejoining her. "Check out the paintings."

Mindy walked up to the picture closest to her. The oil painting looked very old and expensive. It showed a middle-aged man in a military dress uniform, sat on a huge warhorse. *Holding a smartphone with a logo on the screen*, she observed. *With three electric vehicles in the background*.

"Oh, dear God," she said.

"Not quite." Andrew Blackwell stood at her side to get a better view. "But not far off. Aston Hail, founder and CEO of the global electronics and space technologies business of the same name."

Mindy was already on her way to the next painting along - a shepherdess amongst a flock of sheep, painted in the pastoral style, but with what looked to be chemical formulae painted in a clear varnish over the blue summer sky.

"Elena Marchetti. The cloning queen," she said.

Blackwell walked further.

"Tee Takahashi, software guru. Isaac Delemos, owner of the world's largest manufacturing business. Alexander Alcock, who appears to own several small nations. Evie Marsh of the Marsh Media Group."

"You know them."

"I've met them all - conferences, Davos and so on. I don't know them particularly well."

"Oh, I'm sure that will change over the next couple of days, Andrew."

Both guests jumped at the unexpected interruption and turned to see a handsome, tall man with short hair and a well-trimmed beard leaning against the entrance portal, resplendent in pristine golf wear. Emerging from the golf buggies in the courtyard behind him were the other members of the Global Conclave, each of whom Blackwell and Mindy recognised from their portraits.

"Show time," Blackwell whispered to his partner before stepping forward, hand outstretched and a broad smile on his face. "Aston! Good to see you."

Dinner Time

Back at The Fallen Hero, the new arrivals sat around a circular, dark wooden table in the dining area. They cleared space between the glasses they had collected over the past hour for the food that was on its way. Eventually, a healthier looking Stuart Morris stood up, gathered some empties and deposited them at the end of the bar.

"I'd have done that for you, you know."

Turning around, he met the gaze of a well-dressed woman in her fifties, who was carrying three plates of Irish stew - known as stew in Ireland - and had warm, sparkling eyes.

"I know," he said. "But the table didn't have space for the food."

Orla Brennan smiled as she walked past him and placed the plates in front of three guests at a neighbouring table. He watched as she turned and murmured to his four friends. They grinned at him before stacking the remaining empties and handing them to her. They still smirked as he settled back into his chair, having received a wink for his efforts as Orla wafted past him on her way back to the kitchen.

"What's so funny?"

"She was glad you got the glasses to the bar without throwing up in them."

Morris blushed slightly.

"Don't worry about it, Stu," said Dave Westlake. "At least you've made an impression."

"I reckon if you collect another 400 glasses tonight, Orla might let us stay a night for free," offered Coldfront. "Maybe two nights if you offer extras."

Looking at the confused expression on his older friend's face, Pope put him out of his misery with a succinct explanation.

"Her name badge says Orla. That's the name on the licence above the door, so she runs the place. The bar's filling; you can tell by the noise. She might need an extra pair of hands to help keep things tidy. And she gave you a look."

"A look?" Morris wondered how he'd lasted so many years in the police force when he apparently struggled to observe anything.

"A look," confirmed Coldfront. "And you gave her one back."

"I did?"

Dave Westlake put his hand on his friend's shoulder and nodded.

"Yes mate. You did."

"But..."

"But me no buts," interrupted Coldfront. "Here comes the food."

The group fell silent as Orla returned with three more delicious-smelling stews, followed by a young waitress carrying a couple of homemade pizzas. The men started eating, just as Margaret and Jimmy Doyle entered to celebrate a successful day in the city and on the racetrack with a slap-up meal and a couple of drinks.

Stuart Morris spotted the wheelchair, checked the direction of travel, worked out he was in the way and moved his chair. Margaret flashed him a beaming smile as Jimmy pushed her past and towards the reserved table nearby.

"Thank you. You're very kind," she said. "And you're having the pizza! A wonderful choice. I love pizza. Had a fantastic one in Egypt."

Morris returned the smile and brought a large, much-anticipated forkful to his mouth.

"Gave me my best shit of the holiday," Margaret said, then nodded at her husband. "He'll tell you."

Jimmy nodded soberly, which was some effort after a day in various pubs, watching the televised horse racing.

"Definitely," he confirmed. "Proper solid it was. Not like the rest. Very messy."

Morris shuddered slightly and stared at his fork for a moment, while the rest of the group waited for his response.

"After the day I've had," he announced, "That's the best recommendation I could've heard."

The pizza disappeared into his mouth, and Margaret squealed in delight.

"This is going to be a fun night," she declared, before ordering Jimmy to get her a pizza of her own.

Ocean Embrace

The *Ocean Embrace* suite at Peace Castle was everything Mindy had expected and more.

The suite itself was a luxurious blend of old-world charm and modern elegance. The floors were rich, dark oak, polished to a gleam. Antique tapestries hung on the walls, and a selection of rare books on Irish history and folklore stood on a nearby bookshelf. But the stars of the show were the triple-glazed floor-to-ceiling windows that framed the dramatic seascape of crashing Atlantic waves, rugged cliffs and endless horizon.

A huge four-poster bed draped in velvet and fine Irish linens occupied the centre of the room and faced the ocean. Plush armchairs by the windows created a perfect spot for morning coffee or evening drinks. The ensuite bathroom was a sanctuary of indulgence, boasting marble floors and a freestanding copper bathtub and a rain shower, lined with slate tiles and spacious enough for two. Both offered spectacular, unobstructed views of the ocean.

"Behold! The maxi-bar," announced Blackwell, looking into a large well-stocked fridge hidden behind a false bookcase.

"Leave that alone," instructed his partner. "I don't want you tipsy before dinner."

"Tipsy?" he answered, looking at the array of bottles demanding to be opened. "I'd be wrecked."

Mindy walked over and gently closed the door.

"Precisely," she said, putting her arms around his neck. "Besides, I have a couple of tasks for you before we head downstairs."

"Oh, really?" he smiled, wrapping his arms around her back and pulling her close. "And what might those be?"

She pulled his head closer and kissed him.

"Have a quick shower. You need it. Then sit down and go through the briefing notes again."

She let him go, turned him toward the bathroom, and smacked his bottom.

"I'm not leaving you in control of that bar," he protested.

"No need to worry," she replied, heading for the armchairs facing the Atlantic. "I'll be drinking in this view, that's all."

A thought occurred to him as he entered the bathroom.

"There were no staff with our hosts, did you notice?"

"They said it would be a dark event. I guess the fewer involved, the better."

"As long as we actually see some hotel staff. I don't want to be cooking my supper."

"I'm pretty sure that won't be the case. Now, hurry. We have one hour."

Waiting

Paddy O'Brien looked like Jesus, the priest thought, as he compared the photograph in the local newspaper to the alabaster crucifix on his kitchen wall.

In fact, Paddy was a dead ringer, apart from one important factor. The week before, Paddy had proved beyond all doubt that he couldn't walk on water by drowning in the Liffey.

According to the news report, he'd tried to do it the hard way - unconscious, with a broken arm and a fractured skull. The wall clock next to Jesus seemed to tick louder the darker it became outside the small kitchen window, muffling the sound of the rain while the dirty net curtain hid the raindrops on the glass. *Almost nine o'clock. Almost time.*

The priest reached across the cluttered table in front of him, his sleeve brushing a tattered postcard and knocking it to the floor.

He noticed his hand shake as it grasped the tumbler. The glass clinked against the knife on his dirty dinner plate. It had been good of Mary to drop off the stew. She had a sizeable family, but there was always food for Father Aidan.

The priest gave a silent, subconscious vote of thanks for Mary and her cooking. It wasn't Michelin quality, but it filled a gap. Even after drinking half the bottle, the whiskey's taste still caught him off guard.

Then, a face flashed outside the window, and glanced inside briefly before vanishing. Father Aidan gasped in astonishment. *Paddy?* The sudden, furtive knock on the back door stopped the fanciful thinking.

The priest silenced the radio's incessant chatter, set down his glass and stumbled to the back door as the insistent rapping grew louder.

Death stood outside - a tall, cowled figure, silhouetted by the light reflecting off the glistening back walls of the terraced houses across the alley. Death took a pace forward, dropped the hood of his waterproof and sniffed, eyes searching past the priest into the drab kitchen, searching for others who weren't there.

"What about you, Father?" chirped Connor Kelly, the youngest of the remaining Kelly brothers. The rain dripped off the fringe of his red hair and rolled to the tip of his misshapen nose - the only visible record of the bomb. Connor wiped the drop away.

"Hello Connor." The priest remembered the man from years ago; just a youngster, his hair combed carefully, smartly dressed in a crisp white shirt and a red clip-on tie, receiving and sipping the Communion wine. How age - and the family business - had changed him. Another soul drifting through troubled times, even though the real Troubles were history. Supposedly.

Aidan was only a few years older, but he remembered the Communion wine disappearing at the end of that service. Later that day, a cleric found five children in the cemetery. Vomit plastered the headstones. Young Connor wasn't there. None of the Kellys were. Nobody pointed the finger. There was no need. The reputation of his family went before him.

The man watched as Father Aidan swayed slightly. He smiled a tight, knowing smile as a familiar smell ghosted past his nostrils.

His eyes shifted towards the bottle on the table, then back to the tall, thin figure in the frayed pullover and dog collar in front of him. "He's waiting up at the church. You're alright, aren't you? Where's your coat?"

The priest took his overcoat off the hook on the back door, slipped it over his shoulders and stepped into the real world, closing the door carefully behind him. Neither man spoke as they walked through the untidy backyard and into the alley beyond. The sun had long gone, replaced by a climate better matched to the occasion. The rain bounced off the cobbles and ran in rivulets between them and into the gutter.

The priest held his coat tighter at the neck. "We don't see you on a Sunday as often as we'd like, Connor."

"That might be true Father." The youngest Kelly didn't even break step. "But I doubt it." A rumble of thunder rolled softly overhead. Connor Kelly stopped abruptly and thrust his head upward into the rain before settling his gaze on the wet priest. "Jaysus. That was good timing. You're a great double act, you and God."

"We've rehearsed a lot together over the years." Lightning lit up the alley and bathed the church up the slope in an apocalyptic glare. A loud crack of thunder followed straight after. The priest set off again at a faster pace, removing his rain-laden glasses in order to better navigate his way through the puddles. "But we haven't practised smiting sinners as often as we should have," he shouted, "So I'd rather not take the risk of being electrocuted, if you don't mind."

"Ha!" A brief look of consternation transformed into one of delighted bravado. Connor slapped the priest on the back and propelled him towards the sanctuary of St Patrick's. "If your sermons are as sharp as that, Father, I should pop in more often."

The church door yawned open in front of them, offering refuge from the storm.

The Conclave

Blackwell and Mindy walked down the stairs from their first-floor suite, across the empty lobby and along a corridor in the corner to the open door at its end. The dress code was 'smart casual', and both breathed a sigh of relief when they saw everyone dressed to a similar standard - the men all in smart shirts and chinos; the women in trouser suits or dresses.

Aston Hail was the first to spot them and announced, "Our friends have arrived."

Conversations and, to the visitors' surprise, the background music stopped immediately, to be replaced by a ripple of polite applause through the same system of hidden speakers. Andrew and Mindy strolled in, accepted a flute of champagne from the wine waiter, and greeted their hosts.

The classical music recommenced, but before conversations became too earnest, a gong sounded from the corridor and everybody sat around the circular mahogany table.

Blackwell sat between Italian cloning guru Elena Marchetti and the beautiful software billionaire Tee Takahashi who, he found out, had flown in from Japan the day before specifically for this event.

Mindy sat opposite, chaperoned by Alexander Alcock and Evie Marsh, and disappointed that the table was too wide for her to kick Andy if the conversation went awry.

She took a moment to absorb her surroundings. The relaxed opulence, like the rest of the place, did not disappoint.

Pristine white Irish linen covered the table and elegant silver candelabras stood gracefully in the centre, their flames flickering gently in the slight breeze from the corridor.

The tapping of a wine glass with a well-manicured fingernail caught everyone's attention. All eyes fell on Isaac Delemos, who blushed at the attention and swept back what hair he had in modest embarrassment before rising to his feet.

"Members of the Global Conclave. Honoured guests," he began. "I feel this is an auspicious occasion. We have tempted Andrew out of his hermit-like withdrawal from the world…"

The group smiled as Blackwell feigned to consider the notion, then nodded and smiled to acknowledge the fact.

"…and we can learn from him, to examine our own issues and, hopefully, to see how we may contribute to a better, more inclusive, more hopeful direction for humanity and our world. Andrew. Amanda. A sincere welcome to our group. Wherever the path leads, we're delighted you are both here to share the journey with us. Thank you."

Again, a polite ripple of applause filtered through the hidden speakers. Mindy hoped her face wasn't giving away what she was thinking.

They're so rich, they can't be bothered to clap, she thought. *Obviously, their time is worth more than the effort it takes*. She looked through the candelabra at Andrew, but he was chatting to Tee about his trip to Japan two years earlier.

Footsteps in the corridor announced the arrival of the starters, brought in on silver trays - smoked salmon, arranged delicately on each plate, the rich orange hue complemented by the green of the pickled cucumbers and fresh dill.

Four waiting staff gently placed a plate in front of each guest with a quiet and warm "Enjoy" before stepping back and allowing conversations to flow once more. Blackwell's shock at the American accents caught his face by surprise.

"My guys, Andy," said Aston Hail. "The usual staff are on holiday. Double pay for the week. Everyone you see working here is on the payroll, and I'd trust every one of them with my life."

"If your chef's as good as they are, Aston, we're in for a thoroughly enjoyable time."

Hail grinned. "Two Michelin stars, baby."

St Patrick's

St Patrick's didn't exude a warm welcome. Built some two hundred years earlier for a much larger, God-fearing community, the dank, austere surroundings and the hard stone surfaces didn't encourage the joyous celebration of Christianity or, more specifically, Catholicism.

Rather, the chilly, damp atmosphere, dark threatening corners and the sad visages of the various statues and figures in the paintings reminded visitors of how miserable their future would be if they didn't repent. It was a taster of damnation or, at least, purgatory. Like a hellish Crewe Station, where hapless souls would eke out their eternal life drinking weak tea and, even worse, spotting trains.

It was as if Ireland's patron saint had settled on providing the place with an eternity of misery and foreboding, avenging himself against the offspring of the raiders who had captured him and brought him from Britain.

"I'll sort them out," the sixteen-year-old in slave chains must have thought. "I'll give it six years, escape, nip back over to see the family, learn how to put the fear of God into people, then come back and wreak my revenge."

When he returned, his spin machine kicked into gear, claiming the young man had banished snakes from the island.

That there had been no snakes in Ireland since the Ice Age and that nobody really knew what a snake was, as they'd never seen one, was neither here nor there.

"He's good," they'd say. "Not seen a snake for ages. Or ever, for that matter."

Legend has it that Patrick lived until the ripe old age of 120, when average life expectancy was around thirty-seven. He had sown enough seeds of piety, fear and guilt in the local population to ensure he'd never be forgotten and that generations would feel they'd never be forgiven.

Understandably, being regularly scared to death about what would happen when you die, and striving to live a perfect and boring life as a result, had taken its toll on the local community around St Patrick's over the generations.

The church was now a place visited by the vast majority only three times in their life; when they were too young, too in love, or too dead to care.

Declan Kelly was not in the majority. He attended church more frequently than most, but not at the same time as other churchgoers.

The forty-something small, balding man with a big and deadly reputation didn't react when the church's door closed. He didn't so much as flinch as the storm unleashed another thunder and lightning combo close by, lighting up the church. He simply sat in one of the hard wooden pews, gazing contemplatively at the altar and the crucifix, absent-mindedly stroking the scar that ran down his right cheek.

The thing most people noted about the male head of the Kelly family was his proportion. His width appeared to match his height. Someone once joked that Declan was the only man people could look down on and look up to at the same time. He only said it the once. No one ever repeated it to Declan's face again, although he enjoyed the thought of others whispering it behind his back.

"Is God angry with us, Father?" The rain hurled itself against the roof and battered the windows of the church.

The priest stood, or rather swayed, with arms outstretched as a third man - the messenger from earlier in the day - frisked him a little more thoroughly than was actually required, before pushing him gently forward with a quiet "Thank you, Father."

Father Aidan took off his dripping coat and draped it over the back pew.

"Well, Father?" The head of the Kelly household turned and looked at the priest through hooded eyes.

The priest looked past him and gazed at the crucifix, drinking in a calmness that soothed his befuddled mind before answering. "What do you think, Declan? Does he have a reason to be?"

There was an audible intake of breath from the third man. Brendan Dunne, the original Hulk but without the humanity or the green skin, had been the Kellys' minder since school and nobody - absolutely nobody - answered one of his boss's questions with a question. At least, not without some form of retribution.

The younger Kelly - still a child inside, but in the body of a late-thirties man - sidled up to his brother, before bending down and whispering in his ear. Declan smiled slightly, creasing the scar into a gentle question mark, and turned around. "It's good to see you again, Aidan. It's been too long."

"Not long enough." The priest surprised himself with his own answer, but the drink and the fact that he was on home territory gave him a strength he didn't really feel. "I thought all this had finished."

Declan stood up slowly and examined the book in his right hand, turning it from side to side as if there was a secret opening just waiting to be discovered.

The gilt cross on the front cover lit up briefly, reflecting the lightning flash outside.

"You shouldn't believe everything you read or hear, my friend. That's always been your problem - ever since school. Too willing to believe." He flicked through the Bible's pages.

The priest swayed again as he weighed his next words.

"Declan, this has to stop," he said. "Confession is for sinners who genuinely want to cleanse their soul and to live a Christian life. I cannot continue to be party to…"

"Oh, but you can, Aidan." The step towards the priest was a small one, but full of threat and intimidation. "It's your duty." The priest tensed as the elder Kelly swung up his right hand, holding aloft the word of God. "Who are you to say who can and who cannot receive confession? Who are you to say who or what the Lord forgives?" A startling flash of lightning bathed the church in another brilliant light as a violent clap of thunder signalled the storm was right overhead.

"And how do you think your brother would feel if you denied a penitent? Could he renounce his sins before the end?" Still holding the holy book, the man some regarded as the most dangerous in Ireland let his last comment sink in, then walked past the priest and towards the confessional.

The priest felt a firm grip on his arm. The resolve he had felt just seconds before dissolved inside him, leaving a hollowness he knew only too well and which was hidden by one spirit, not filled by another.

"Come on Father," whispered Brendan Dunne.

Declan Kelly disappeared into Margaret Doyle's side of the confessional as the priest was half marched into the other side, where he sat numbly, fingering his rosary, waiting for more horrors to be downloaded into his conscience. The surrounds reduced the sound of the driving rain. He would hear everything clearly. Even the storm was no defence.

There was no escape.

On the other side of the box, Declan cleared his throat. "Bless me Father, for I have sinned…"

Outside the confessional, Brendan Dunne stood guard like Cerberus at the doors of Hades. Connor sat in a pew and rested his feet on the back of the one in front, flicking through a battered hymn book and chewing absent-mindedly.

At the other end of the church, high among the shadows of the choir stalls and half hidden by a pillar, Kara Walsh sat motionless behind the cloaked video camera, perched on the small tripod.

Help Me

Father Aidan watched from the church porch. The brake lights flashed twice before the car turned right, crunched out of the car park and disappeared into the misty gloom towards Dublin, the centre of the Kelly's criminal fiefdom.

The storm was spent, leaving a miserable drizzle in its wake. Clutching the elder Kelly's gift of a bottle of whiskey, the priest stepped into the rain and made his way slowly to the alleyway and on towards his house. As he stumbled without seeing, his feet sloshed through the puddles.

He had no recollection of his journey home or how he came to find himself at the kitchen table, soaking wet, staring at the full tumbler. The clock continued to tick and the Paddy O'Brien lookalike continued to stare mournfully at him from his cross on the wall. All so normal. Aidan looked more closely at the crucifix.

"What are you looking at?" He made his way over to the sink and wiped the rain off his face with a dirty tea towel, before picking the Christ figure off the wall, searching for meaning in the face.

He returned to his chair and laid the crucifix on the table.

The clock ticked even louder. He picked up the glass and raised it to his lips, before holding it up in a mock toast. "To the glory of God. Bottoms up."

The whiskey roared like fire down his throat, rekindling memories, feelings, fears. He sat for a moment, the tremors surging through his body. The table melted in a blur of tears. The glass smashed into the wall and a sweep of his arm sent the bottle crashing onto the floor.

Clonbrinny's priest sat shaking uncontrollably as the tears continued to flow.

"Help me."

The crucifix rested on the table; the clock ticked on the wall and the spilt whiskey soaked into the worn carpet and into the edge of the faded postcard.

Outside, protected from the elements by a hooded waterproof and looking into the kitchen from a safe distance, the priest's niece wiped a tear from her own eye. A car pulled up at the end of the alley. She slung her bag over her shoulder, retraced her steps and climbed in, before the driver switched on the vehicle's lights and pulled away.

The Opening Statement

By the time the Conclave had demolished the braised Irish lamb with Colcannon mash, followed by the Irish cream and honeycomb parfait with Irish Sea salt caramel, the diners were drunk or well on their way.

The wine, combined with the ex-politician's good humour and natural charm, helped to dispel any remaining formality in the room.

At the end of the meal, the group waited for the chef to appear to receive his recorded applause, then moved as one into the lounge, where a fire crackled softly and the scent of fresh-brewed coffee and Irish whiskey filled the air.

The chatter around the dining table had covered updates on each Conclave member's business interests, intriguing gossip about other global figures and comment on general world developments.

Andrew and Mindy had stayed mostly silent, offering opinions only when requested, unwilling to hog the limelight their hosts obviously cherished.

Despite their power and fame, they're desperate to impress each other but equally keen not to be seen to be doing so, thought Mindy.

There's insecurity here. It's probably one of the few times they doubt they're the biggest ego in the room.

Blackwell's thoughts bounced between the points on Mindy's briefing paper and wondering who in their right mind thought cutting up their own food and creating forkfuls was beneath them.

Wearing identical outfits daily, some people save time and energy by not dwelling on trivial matters, he thought. *But Tee, Elena and Evie had taken that philosophy to a whole new level.*

Now that everyone had settled into the plush leather armchairs or the velvet sofas arranged carefully around the fireplace, it was time for the spotlight to fall on the former prime minister.

It was Aston who introduced the change. "So, Andy. It's been some six months, huh?"

Blackwell took his cue. "It has, Aston. I guess you all may know some of the story. I'll start at the beginning, in case any of you have been on another planet until recently."

The group smiled good-naturedly while Blackwell sipped his Irish coffee.

He held the glass in both hands, looking at the liquid and swirling it around for a while, as if reflecting on all that had happened.

As he did so, Mindy glanced at those looking on, reading genuine interest, vague amusement and something approaching contempt in their faces.

"It all began when I sent the German Chancellor a photograph of a sausage."

For the next forty-five minutes, Blackwell spoke about his breakdown, added some colour to the official account of what happened when he vanished in the Midlands and explained how the root cause of events had been germinating during his two years in Downing Street.

After a brief hiatus for the group to refresh their drinks or use the restrooms, he talked about the last six months and his reasons for avoiding the public spotlight.

He outlined his change in outlook - something he had talked about at the time of his return - and reflected on the impact of those words and his subsequent actions, or rather inaction, to an international audience.

Finally, he touched on the development of his work in progress, a global philosophy whose adoption might influence - some were speculating revolutionise - world affairs and international politics.

He concluded by thanking the group for the opportunity to speak to them.

"This is the first time I have spoken about the last six months. I'm humbled by the interest you have shown in what I've had to say." He looked at each of his hosts as he spoke.

"Your own experiences will influence what you make of my musings. Look honestly and openly at your world. How is it being affected right now by actions and movements outside your control? What could happen to it tomorrow? Next month? Next year? And how do you manage those events? Now think about the lack of control globally. How could society work for the benefit of all and what needs to be done worldwide to effect that change? Find the answers and you're on your way to working out how can you contribute, both for the good of humanity and to promote and protect your own legacy. Thank you for your time."

What surprised Mindy most - apart from Blackwell staying on track, hitting all the key points and holding the group's attention - was the lack of applause, manufactured or otherwise, at the end.

Had Aston forgotten to press the button? She looked at the surrounding faces. *Damn, they were good poker players.* Everybody remained noncommittal. Not a smile; not a frown. No head shakes or nods. Just silence. *And what did Andy make of it?*

Blackwell looked around and grinned.

"I've worn you all out," he said and, before anybody could respond, continued. "There's a lot to take in. You may recognise some of my truths. Maybe some are yours as well. I've spent six months thinking things through with nothing to distract me. I'm nowhere near working out what needs to be done and it would be great to hear your perspectives on what you feel should happen from here."

He stood up, walked to the door, and turned.

"After a long day, opening up to you, my friends, has been a relief but emotionally draining."

Mindy made her way to the door, delayed by hugs with each of the hosts, who stood as she passed them.

"Think about what I've said," Blackwell continued. "Discuss it amongst yourselves. If you have questions, either as a group or as an individual, I'll be delighted to explore answers with you tomorrow. Thank you for a first class evening." And with that, he swept out of sight, followed by his fiancée, and pursued by delayed applause from the hidden speaker system.

Meeting Maggie

As the noise in the bar grew louder, and the musical entertainment for the evening conducted a soundcheck, everyone in the dining room agreed to remain there.

The plates and cutlery on the table had gone, replaced by many empty or half-full glasses, and Margaret and Jimmy had joined Pope and company at Margaret's self-invitation.

"It's always nice to meet new people," she explained. "And sometimes it's nice for them to meet us as well."

She quickly learned that most worked at, or had recently retired from, a large food warehouse; and the van driver owned a small taxi business.

The group had decided early on that revealing the military and police background of its individuals might be unwise. As a warehouse operative, Pope spent time on the journey explaining an order picker's and a forklift truck driver's jobs, so that each man could talk about his fake career.

"The key is to base what you say in fact," he told the three policemen, as if they hadn't spent their entire careers finding holes in statements made by suspects and witnesses. "If you're asked anything you can't answer, just say it's beyond your pay grade and refer it to me."

The reason for the trip was straightforward; to celebrate Stuart's return to good health and his retirement.

At least, that was the belief of four of the five, and it was essentially the truth. Only the trip's organiser knew differently, and even he felt his undercover mission would have zero impact on those around him. At least, for now.

Margaret explained she had retired from the university on health grounds following the incident that left her in the wheelchair.

"Fortunately, I've had this good man by my side for four decades, in sickness and in health," she said, reaching over and squeezing Jimmy's hand. "He's looking after my every need."

She paused and looked around the table.

"And I mean… Every. Need."

She stopped for another second, savouring the looks those five words prompted.

"And in return, I do favours for him."

Jimmy nodded enthusiastically.

"She's very good at picking winners," he explained, "And other stuff as well."

Leaving it there and remaining enigmatic, he announced he would get the next round with today's winnings, took the order from the group and left for the bar.

Keen to move the conversation on from where it might well be heading, Pope blurted out a question.

"What does Jimmy bet on?"

"Oh, the horses mostly. That's where my skills lie. I also help him with other bets, but he's not so willing to take advice there in case it has him betting against his own team. It's an emotional thing. That's the reason we never bet on the dogs. Greyhounds like to run; not to race. We've seen how they're treated…"

Pope just nodded and pulled out his phone.

"Well, Margaret, you've just made a friend for life there," said Westlake.

Pope showed his new friend for life pictures of his two dogs.

"Fred and Ginger. Both rescues," he said.

Margaret beamed as she looked at the photographs.

"How lovely," she said. "We have a rescued brindle girl called Bella. She's six. Who's looking after yours while you're living it up over here?"

Pope swiped the screen twice to a photograph of Pippa with the dogs, her bright smile beaming at the camera lens.

"What a beautiful girl," exclaimed Margaret. "Is she smiling because of you or the dogs?"

The group assured her it was because of the dogs and that Pippa regarded Pope as something of a charity case. Somebody offered odds on the locks to the house being changed by the time Pope returned home. Another suggested a new man - or possibly a woman - had already moved in. Pope simply blushed and laughed.

"Well, I think you're a bunch of green-eyed monsters," observed Margaret as Jimmy settled back next to her. "I think Simon delights her. If not, Jimmy could offer some tips."

Blissfully unaware of the turn the conversation had taken since he left for the bar, Jimmy responded as helpfully as he could about betting. "Oh, I think Maggie's best placed for that. She's a genius at turning little things into big results, just by studying past performance and using a pencil."

He looked stunned as the wall of laughter hit him.

Breakfast At The Hero

The Fallen Hero wasn't the only hostelry in Clonbrinny. The small town on the banks of the Liffey had more than the average number of pubs, inns and bars, which, in Ireland, seemed to account for every fourth building. However, the Hero was the largest, relatively speaking.

Each of its four guest rooms could easily accommodate one business traveller or a couple on a romantic weekend. With a little imagination and the judicious use of the limited space, it was even possible to use each of the largest two rooms, over the bar area, to house up to six people.

These guests were on a budget; happy to sacrifice almost every comfort, strip themselves of their dignity, and remove every vestige of privacy in order to have more money for beer. They were fishermen and golfers. And every week, a group or two would fall like lemmings into the Hero.

Breakfast that morning was one for the history books. At least, it would have been if there had been someone there to record it. Nobody turned up. The doleful bell of St Patrick's announced the eighth hour of the day. Sinead smoothed down her apron and entered the small dining room, armed with a notebook for the orders and a couple of smart one-liners to fend off the comments that invariably came her way from groups of lads off the leash. She required neither.

The cereals remained untouched. The orange juice jug was still full. Not one piece of cutlery was out of place on the pristine white tablecloth.

The sassy waitress-cum-bar-manager-cum-owner's-only-daughter pursed her lips, brushed away the stray lock of hair placed fetchingly on her face, and sauntered to the opposite window, overlooking the car park. The van had gone. These lads were serious about their fishing.

She turned on her heel and made for the kitchen, feeling a little disappointed.

There was always a thrill chatting with a new group; feeling their eyes on her; fielding the comments from the brave ones and seeing how many would be cowed by a flash of her eyes. And there was always the chance of meeting someone special. It wasn't every job that brought in fresh prospects every week. And she didn't intend to stay all her life in The Fallen Hero; thirty-odd years was plenty.

Sinead had been looking forward to seeing the tall one again... Dave... after last night. They had passed in the corridor as the group had staggered back to their room accompanied by a lot of swearing.

He had given her such a nice, apologetic smile for someone with such a strange haircut. His eyes were the thing, though. The smile had started in his beautiful, hazel eyes and had held her, caressed her, for an age that lasted all of a second.

The smell of bacon caught her nose, and she hurried on. Her mammy wouldn't be happy, having cooked enough food to feed a small army. She already knew what the Snack of the Day would be in the bar that lunchtime. And "If your rod's as big as your mouth, you should have no trouble catching fish today" would have to wait for another time.

She almost bumped into his chest before she realised he was there. One of the new guests, casually dressed in a grey sweatshirt, neat jeans and a pair of cross trainers.

A flurry of apologies on both sides erupted and then stopped just as abruptly. He looked concerned, a frown creasing an already troubled countenance, dark hair all over the place and tousled unfashionably. With glasses, and if the scars had been on his forehead, he'd have been the dead spit of an ageing boy wizard.

"I overslept… sorry… is there still time for breakfast?" He looked past her into the dining room, sweeping his right hand over his hair, attempting to bring a semblance of control.

Sinead eyed him speculatively, then smiled. "Breakfast ends at nine, so you're grand. Your mates have gone out, though. Have they left you behind?"

Simon Pope stepped past her and made straight for the jug of orange juice on the side table. He poured a large glass and knocked half of it back in one gulp. "I don't fish. Waste of time. Is there a menu? Ah, thanks." He sat at the table, accepted the proffered card, took another gulp of juice, and squinted at the selection. "Just egg on toast, please."

"No sausage? They're local. The bacon's good too and…"

"I'm fine, thanks, but my friend might fancy some." Before she could reply, the giant with the strange hair and a big grin appeared at the doorway.

"Did somebody mention sausage?" Dave Westlake asked. "Things are looking up." The policeman strolled past her, never losing eye contact, even when dropping two sugar cubes into the cup of tea poured for him by his mate. It should have been four cubes, but he missed with two as he continued to gaze into her eyes.

"Got a sweet tooth?" she asked.

"Think I might need to build my strength up a bit. Best have fried egg and beans too," he replied.

Sinead smiled. "I'll sort your sausage," she said. Maybe this morning wouldn't be a write-off after all.

Going Fishing

The first day of fishing didn't get off to the best of starts, courtesy of Angus Grace. Handing responsibility for breakfast to David 'Coldfront' Davies hadn't been the best of plans - unless breakfast heaven was a large bag of cheese and onion crisps and a can of lager in the cramped confines of a van, sliding around the treacherous corners of the narrowest roads in the world.

"Why cheese and onion, Coldfront?" Grace reckoned the more blame he could shovel onto the driver, the less would stick to him. "They should at least have been smokey bacon. And lager?"

"Alcohol is necessary for a man so that he can have a good opinion of himself, undisturbed by the facts." Davies heaved the steering wheel to the left, bashing some low-hanging branches as the van lurched around the bend. "Finley Peter Dunne said that," he added. "And we're fishing, so we'll need all the opinion assistance we can get."

The rain played a drumroll on the roof and battered the front windscreen, turning the dark and alarmingly big trees on each side of the road into a blurred wall of impending doom. Everybody grabbed hold of something as the rear end slid across the road towards a ditch, before Coldfront turned into the skid and straightened her up.

"Careful! I nearly spilt my pint!" The near spill of beer affected Davies's driving more than a nun with a baby in a pushchair crossing the road.

His van slewed to a halt. A bait box toppled from its precarious position on top of a pile of fishing kit onto the seat next to Stuart Morris. The group's senior member, by twenty years, turned from his reflection to watch the unfolding chaos. The van was a confusion of arms, legs, slopping cans of lager, annoyed faces, and crisp packets. *Like Picasso's 'Guernica'*, he thought, *but with more colour*.

He stared impassively at the box wedged beside him, hauling his mind back into the present from a future he dreaded. "That box nearly killed me," he observed to nobody in particular.

"Pity it didn't, you old sod," commented Grace, unaware of how close he was to the truth.

"Sorry lads." Davies checked to make sure everyone was alive, then picked up the handwritten instructions left for them at the pub. He thrust the sheet in Grace's face.

"Just down here, I reckon. Farm should be on the right. Jimmy said he'd be waiting at the stile next to the gate."

Angus tried to match the sketch map to the nightmare that had been the last fifteen minutes, but the roads flowed together in his memory and, in truth, he hadn't a clue. The idiot behind the wheel boasted the most accurate sense of direction ever known to man. As it was his van, he had every right to drive it however he wanted, especially as he was an expert.

Davies had kept them all awake the previous night, slurring driving anecdotes from his army years while they tried to sleep; each story wilder than the previous and not ideal conversation for an Irish pub. They hadn't believed Pope's warning that Coldfront was called Coldfront because he created depression wherever he went. They did now.

Grace didn't like to think about his army time. Few did. He glanced up, then nodded.

"Yep. Go steady, though. She's not a Warrior."

Coldfront grinned at the reference and crunched the van into first gear. "Once more unto the breach, dear new friends…"

The van lurched forward and headed towards the farm that appeared, along with Jimmy Doyle, sixty seconds later on the right.

The Breakfast Farce

Pope pushed back from the table, relaxed in his chair and burped, gazing appreciatively at the empty plate. The belch was still reverberating when Sinead re-entered the room to collect the dirty plates a moment later. She felt herself warm slightly.

Seeing her blush, and realising the cause, Pope sat up nervously, which caused the waitress to blush even more. He cleared his throat, keen to break the silence, but with nothing to say.

"Did you enjoy your breakfast?" Sinead smiled as she set about the detritus on the table. She passed in front of the window, the outline of her body fleetingly revealed through her blouse by the daylight beyond.

Breakfast! Of course, breakfast. "The breakfast was very nice. I liked the eggs." *Idiot. Say something else. Fill the silence.* "So, what do you do around here?"

"I'm a waitress and the bar manager and the receptionist." Her look said it all.

"Sorry, what is there to do around here? Besides the fishing, I mean." Pope reached for his cup of tea and kept his head down, hoping she didn't think he was the village idiot.

Maybe she thinks they don't take me fishing in case I eat the bait, he thought.

Perhaps he doesn't go fishing because he eats the bait, she thought, eyeing him speculatively. *After all, he's drinking from a cup with nothing in it.*

She wondered how long he would pretend to drink from the empty cup. Pope considered jumping through the window into the car park, then running away, and never coming back. The telephone ringing in the reception area interrupted their thoughts.

Sinead walked out to take the call, just as Westlake, resplendent in his new walking gear, returned to the dining room and saw his mate banging his head on the table. The police officer knew when someone was choking. Pope's bright red face confirmed it.

Shouting for help, he raced around the table and pulled his stunned friend to his feet from behind, kicking the chair out of the way. He linked his hands together, knuckles pointing into Pope's sternum.

"Clear!" he roared, confusing medical emergencies as he lifted his hero into the air. Pope's feet belted the table, sending crockery flying, just as the bemused waitress and her alarmed mother raced through the open doorway.

Morning Sunshine

By the time Andrew Blackwell woke up in the Ocean Embrace suite, Mindy had showered, dressed and was sitting with a fresh coffee, looking out at a becalmed, sparkling Atlantic. She turned as she heard him stir.

"Morning sunshine," she said. He paused, remembered where he was and why, then sat bolt upright in bed.

"What time is it? Have I missed anything?"

"We had a message from Aston." She held up the suite's electronic tablet. "They're golfing. We can catch up with them or meet up for lunch in the old boathouse later."

Blackwell pottered over to the coffeemaker and brought a flat white and a couple of fresh pastries to the window, where he sat down in the second armchair. He spent a minute absorbing the stunning panorama, while organising his thoughts on the previous night.

Mindy had been right to suggest sleep rather than reviewing events straightaway. Making sense of something while tipsy was never a good idea.

Aston Hail had requested they leave straight after the speech. Mindy suspected the members wanted to discuss the content between themselves and agree on a joint position before responding. Certainly their poker faces had given nothing away, but the session this afternoon would reveal all.

"Thoughts?" she asked.

"I slept well. Much better than I expected. It was a relief to get things off my chest." Andy sipped his coffee. "Today will be interesting. Was I just the evening entertainment or might they get involved? And is their involvement something we want?"

"I guess we'll find out soon enough."

Mindy stood up and paced the room. Blackwell stayed silent, watching her every move and quietly offering a prayer of thanks they had found each other again personally, after years of working professionally. Eventually, she sat down and stared at the waves tumbling almost apologetically onto the rocks below. She picked up a notepad and pen from the table and wrote something down.

"I guess we will," she said. "I'm feeling hungry again. Fancy some breakfast and then a walk? Sunshine, fresh air, no photographers?"

As she spoke, she handed over the notepad.

Room bugged?

Blackwell could have kicked himself. Their hosts were big fans of data. They had to assume someone was listening.

"Splendid idea. I'll grab a shower."

Mindy watched as her fiancé stood up and walked off to the bathroom completely naked, and fervently hoped that any recording was only capturing audio.

Reaching The River

The gentle stroll down to the river was more like a yomp across the Falklands. Soaking wet clumps of grass emerged through the sea of mud and cow pats; tempting landing platforms made treacherous by the rain that, mercifully, had eased off to a light drizzle.

The field angled steeply down to a barbed wire fence; the riverbank beyond reached via a stile that had seen better days.

Even the cows refused to set hoof in the field, huddling together at the top edge, seeking what pitiful shelter they could find by the overgrown hawthorn hedge. The fishing party did its best to avoid the worst of the conditions by stepping tentatively from clump to clump without falling or dropping any of the kit.

Most hesitant of all was Stuart Morris. He was a fishing novice and a reluctant one at that. Horrendous, hypothermia-inducing weather; slippy, break-your-neck grass; then sitting next to a raging, drown-you-in-an-instant torrent for hours. He could think of better places to be. By the time he struggled to the stile, the others were already staking out their positions alongside a lethargic stretch of water. Morris took stock, checked his heart rate, and clambered over onto the narrow bank.

They were on the outside of a bend, facing a lush forest that bordered the river's edge. To their left, the farmland skirted the bottom slopes of the hills that led to the mountain beyond. In the distance, shafts of sunlight pierced the breaking clouds, bathing the hills in a warm, mottled glow and illuminating a flock of birds - lapwing, judging by their flight - as they rose into the air before settling just as quickly in a neighbouring field.

The noise from the road and farm above didn't reach the bottom of the valley. Nothing impeded the view of nature at its most glorious, or disturbed the tranquility.

Morris soaked it all in. The last ten minutes were a bad but inconsequential memory. The drizzle had gone and the prospect of warm sunshine was hastening towards them as fast as the clouds could scurry out of its way. This was why he was here. The great escape from daily life, now that retirement had made daily life unbearable. Almost.

A huge fart ripped through the silence; so loud it almost echoed down the valley. The others stopped what they were doing and turned in surprise.

"What did you expect after that breakfast?" smiled Morris, half expecting a startled rabbit to flee from the nearby undergrowth. "Where do you want me?"

Resisting the temptation to retort "As far away as possible," Jimmy wandered over and gestured, rod in hand, beyond Morris to the riverbank. "Park yourself over there. I'll set you up."

Morris grabbed a spare fishing seat and opened it up close to the edge of the bank. Settling in, he examined the stretch of water in front of him, then turned to see his former colleague Angus Grace walking towards him with a rod and bait box.

"Why does the old man get the best swim?" Grace frowned, not looking best pleased, but with a twinkle in his eye.

"Come on. It's his first time," replied Jimmy without turning around. "You'll never get him out again unless he catches and catches well."

"After that fart, I'm not sure I want him out again."

Morris felt a warm glow inside. A splash on the water caught his attention. Two swans had landed to check out the strangers, dragging the sunshine in behind them on their flight downstream.

Grace plonked down the bait box and prepared the hook and line for the challenge ahead. The others tried to clear the swans away without resorting to throwing a can of valuable beer at their inquisitive heads.

"I'll show you how to cast," he told Morris. "The secret is to give the fish every chance to move towards the bait. No need to reel it in. Let the fish come to you. When you feel a tug, give me a shout and I'll show you how to land it."

Ten minutes later and glorious sunshine picked out the varying shades of greens that swamped the valley. Blue sky chased away the clouds towards Clonbrinny and the first few midges ventured into the bright light, dancing just outside the tree line on the far bank.

The group settled down; the silence only interrupted by the call of a woodland bird or the gentle whirr and plop as a line was cast. Jimmy checked everybody was happy and returned to his own swim. Now, he could enjoy the tranquility of the surroundings and savour the prospect of catching his tea.

The Talk Of The Town

The sunshine enjoyed at the river pierced the dull clouds over Clonbrinny just as Westlake and Pope embarked on their day of exploration.

Pope halted on the edge of the pub car park and glared malevolently at the sky; his face was still a darkish shade of pink; the amazed - then amused - looks of his hosts embedded in his memory.

Westlake caught up with him and unslung the half empty rucksack he had just loaded onto his back. "Told you the rain was going," he said. "Waterproofs in the bag, then catch me up."

He dumped the bag at Pope's feet and marched on, out of the car park entrance and left, down the main street. The sunlight reflected off the wet tiles of the terraced houses opposite and lit up their dull, red brickwork, but the change in weather did little to brighten his mood.

All he'd done was try to save a mate's life; a man who was choking to death. And now, a sparkle in the waitress's eye and the smile that played around her mouth told him he was going to be the talk of the town.

Westlake stomped on through the puddles, putting as much distance as he could between himself and his embarrassment.

He passed an old couple, standing on the pavement and chatting to the local butcher, who leaned his thin frame against his battered shop doorway, casually sharpening an evil-looking knife.

The conversation dropped for a second as Westlake walked past. He caught a slight smirk play across the meat man's face. *Surely he can't know already*. He muttered a curt "Morning" and received civil nods from both men and a big smile from the old lady in response. *Nah. It only happened ten minutes ago. Word wouldn't be out yet.* He shook his head slightly and strode on.

The old lady watched him leave, then turned back to the butcher. "Do you think he's one of the lads from the Hero?"

"Oh yeah," came the reply. "And here comes his mate. The one who drinks air." The old couple turned to follow the butcher's gaze up the street, and locked onto the lanky figure of Simon Pope striding towards them, wrestling waterproofs into the open rucksack.

Parting Of The Ways

Westlake passed the row of terraced houses on his right, then stopped at the bottom of a lane that led up to the town's church.

St Patrick's peat-black bell tower dominated the skyline and the small surrounding graveyard. The newly promoted police sergeant shuddered slightly. Not being a fan of austere religious buildings or graveyards, he turned to his left and the much more acceptable vista on his side of the road.

Over the dry stone wall and down at the bottom of the sheep field, a large stream, swollen by the recent rain, flowed happily along the foot of the wooded hills on its opposite bank.

The sight of the flock took him back to the search for the missing prime minister in the fog-bound West Midlands just over six months ago.

What a wild few days that had been. Life changing for several people.

Almost life ending for Stuart Morris. The man - his best friend - was still struggling to recover, not so much from the heart attack sustained while arresting potential terrorists who were actually foreign warehouse workers; more from the shock of retirement.

Hopefully, this break would be a catalyst for him.

Help him realise that life was more than police work, estranged family and divorce. Give him some ideas to fill his comfortable, police pension-funded future. Positive, exciting reasons to get up in the morning.

"You look a million miles away." Pope had finally caught up. "Where were you?"

"In the back of an ambulance. Just hoping this break's going to be worth it."

Pope leaned on the wall and took in the view. "Last night wasn't a bad start once he'd recovered from the ferry. The landlady liked him and the locals were good fun."

Westlake nodded. "Let's hope the introduction to fishing maintains the momentum," he said. "Anyway, there's your church, although why you're interested in checking it out is beyond me."

"Call it professional interest, following my earlier career," lied the former Church of England minister. "Always good to see what the competition's up to. Are you coming?"

Westlake resisted the urge to shudder again and shook his head instead.

"Not my cup of tea," he said. "I'm heading down the road for a look at the lough."

"Fine. Catch you up soon."

Westlake took the rucksack and hoisted it onto his shoulders. Pope watched him set off down the road, out of the village. From an Afghan firefight to an armed stand-off in his garden to a hike on a damp day in Ireland, the relationship between the two men had been anything but boring. Pope looked forward to when it might be. It would be a welcome change.

Hopefully that phase had already started, but Pope didn't believe it. Not just yet.

The Beach Review

Mindy debated a post-breakfast stroll versus returning to bed. Andy may have slept well, but she had been awake since five and had slept only fitfully through the night, having first made notes on her smartphone of everything she could remember from the conversation over dinner.

This was her fiancé's gig, she knew that, but while the potential benefits were considerable, so was the potential downside.

As the former prime minister's assistant chief-of-staff, she was used to firefighting when events didn't go to plan. Doing so effectively meant imagining worst-case scenarios and having strategies in place to handle any that actually occurred. Her notes could prove helpful later.

Blackmail, that kind of thing.

Blackwell's time in office had its fair share of problems, but Mindy's crisis management skills had significantly reduced their impact on his premiership. Until, that is, he'd disappeared, triggering a Whitehall leadership crisis. She had smuggled him back to London and then helped to thwart two assassination attempts. All in the space of five days.

"Are you cold?" asked Blackwell, feeling her shudder as they walked hand-in-hand along a woodland footpath from the mansion towards the coast.

"I'm fine," she smiled. "Do you think we're okay talking out here?"

"Probably, but wait until we're near the sea. Wind and waves will make things tricky for any eavesdropper."

They walked in silence until breaking out of the trees and onto the gravel coastal path where the sounds of the sea, the birds and the breeze overwhelmed the relative quiet of the woodland. A signpost nearby showed a route down to the beach. Following a brief descent down concrete steps with a handrail, they rested on a flat boulder by a rocky outcrop, shielded from the wind and any onlookers on top of the cliff.

"So," started Mindy. "Yesterday was… let's say… memorable. Today will be the same."

"True," nodded Blackwell. "Were we the after-dinner entertainment or are they really interested in what we had to say."

"No doubt we'll find out later. At least we'll have some useful feedback on your *Path Finder* ideas, even if we're back in London by tonight."

"I want more, but I'm not sure what 'more' entails, and I'm nervous that there may be conditions."

Nervous, thought Mandy. *I've never heard him admit to being nervous before. Apart from asking to marry me.*

The views of the ocean and a passing flock of birds gave her an idea. She leaned against him and held his arm.

"Remember the last time we sat on a beach, talking like this?"

For a moment, his brow furrowed, then his eyes widened, and he smiled.

"Brighton. Just after I'd become an MP," he said. "And just after I'd left the vast majority of the party conference delegates hacked off with me."

Mindy laughed. "A few were intrigued."

"You being one of them."

"And look where you were just a few years later. Leader of the party. Leader of the country. And it all started with you telling your truth by the seaside to people who felt uncomfortable or who thought you were a joke."

Blackwell looked out across the vast expanse of ocean. Sunlight caught the crests of the waves before they plunged back into the sea.

"And then we grabbed two bottles of cheap fizz, sat on the beach near the hotel, and you told me where I'd gone wrong, in excruciating detail."

"And what you'd done well. You listened, did what I suggested to improve, and now look where you are."

"Back on a beach, sat alongside you?"

Mindy laughed.

"Well... yes. But you're also raising revolutionary ideas with some of the world's richest and most influential people. Even if they don't like what they hear. Even if the discussions make them uncomfortable, dismissive and angry, they'll remember what you said."

Blackwell nodded. When he'd accepted the invitation, he knew there'd be risks, however receptive or otherwise the Conclave turned out to be. But time was passing. He had been in a rut, deciding what he was trying to say and who needed to hear it. This path had appeared from nowhere and, with Mindy's approval, he'd chosen to take it.

The key was to maximise the upside and minimise the downside. Despite the guarantees given to him, both Mindy and he expected that news of this meeting would break. The media would have a field day, unless they had a plan in place to mitigate the impact. The good-faith payment he had received was already in the coffers of four charities, so nobody could accuse him of doing this for the money. If a member of the Conclave went rogue, Mindy had enough in her notes from last night to make things awkward for them.

Whatever happened today, something had to give.

"Come on," he said, standing up. "Let's have a wander along the shore and build an appetite for lunch."

"Good idea," smiled the woman who had appointed herself his assistant all those years ago on Brighton beach. "I'll use the time to give you some suggestions for this afternoon."

Blackwell laughed and hugged her tightly.

"Some things never change," he said.

The Church Visit

Pope looked up at the church, waited for a farm truck to pass, then crossed the road and headed up the lane towards God knows what was coming next.

The temperature dropped as he walked through the creaking gate from the car park into the church grounds; the crunch of footsteps on gravel replaced by a more muted step on the graveyard's flagstones.

The air took on a vague but discernible scent of damp earth and moss. Many of the headstones, weathered and crooked, jutted from the ground as if a seismic movement had forced them upwards, their inscriptions hidden under lichen or barely readable after centuries of wind and rain.

Pope's eyes scanned the untidy ranks and fell upon a tidier, more orderly area, which suggested more recent burials. He stepped off the path and made his way between several tall trees scattered among the graves, the creaking branches and rustling leaves accompanying him as he walked across the thick grass.

The church loomed ever closer, its stone walls covered in patches of dark green moss. Despite the movement of the trees, the air grew heavy and still. The three rows of more recent graves, clean and pristine with sharp lines and clear inscriptions, were a welcome oasis of relief.

Fresh, or at least reasonably recent, flower arrangements adorned some, providing a remarkable splash of colour within the gloom and decay. Rosary beads draped over the edge of other headstones, the colour of the beads complementing or contrasting with the stone. Some graves carried a small teddy bear, or a limp balloon at the end of a fraying and faded piece of ribbon.

Pope moved slowly between them, honouring the dead by reading their epitaphs and acknowledging them at least for a moment. At the end of the third line was a larger family plot, marking the resting place of two brothers and their sister. They all died in their teens, two on the same day and the oldest brother, four years older, a couple of years later.

The plot's size and headstone inscription suggested more Kellys were to follow.

Kelly.

Pope retraced his steps, back to the second row. There it was. Martin Kelly. Old enough to be the kids' father; died after they had died, but not buried in the same plot.

Must be a different family, Pope thought. *Plenty of Kellys in Ireland.*

He surveyed the graveyard once more, listened to the faint caw of a distant crow and shivered slightly as a chill breeze caught him unawares. At least, that's how he explained the shiver to himself.

Westlake was right, he thought. *Graveyards were nobody's cup of tea.* He returned to the path, looked longingly at the car park gate, then turned left, pushed on the heavy wooden door and stepped into the church.

The scent of stale incense caught him by surprise and he struggled to focus on anything in the dim light that filtered through the narrow stained-glass windows, throwing muted shades of reds, greens and blues onto the worn flagstone floor.

Pope gave himself a moment to get accustomed to his surroundings. Rows of dark wooden pews stretched out before him, flanked by tall thick columns supporting an arched ceiling that disappeared into shadow. At the far end of the nave, part-illuminated by a soft candlelight, stood the altar, draped in a simple white cloth with a golden crucifix suspended behind it. Beyond the altar, Pope could just make out the faint outline of a choir loft, with the grand organ pipes high above the centre and, he imagined, the organ itself just below.

The silence was profound. Thick walls muffled outside noise, eliminating worldly distractions unless - that is - some sightseer wandered in when you had more heavenly matters on your mind. Pope noticed the pale faces of three people in different pews, all staring at him. He nodded to them and sat himself down in a nearby side pew, putting the nearest column between himself and the local flock. The change in location revealed faded murals of saints and angels on the walls, the figures looking as subdued as their original colours.

On the far side of the church in a small alcove, Pope could see the Virgin Mary standing vigil over a row of votive candles. Some burned steadily, others sputtered in their melted wax and the rest were long since extinguished. He couldn't decide if the Madonna looked sympathetic or bored stiff. A sudden movement caught his eye. He watched a woman emerge from the confessional box against the opposite wall, well hidden in the shadows, and walk over to the candles. She picked up a new candle in its holder, used a taper to catch the flame from another, lit hers and set it with the rest.

Uneasy looking on, Pope watched an older man enter the confessional and close the door. Assuming the other two people in the pews were also waiting, it would be a while before the priest finally emerged.

Pope grabbed a couple of threadbare kneeling cushions to improve the comfort of his seat. There was a reassuring calmness here; a peace he hadn't realised he'd missed. A sense of being sheltered from the trials and tribulations of day-to-day life.

He checked his mobile phone and was quietly pleased. Because the thick walls prevented the signal from penetrating, the internet's temptations remained unavailable to him. He settled back into the stillness of his surroundings and waited.

Fishing Reflections

Two hours in and the fishing trip was turning into every other fishing trip. Early success for Angus Grace and Coldfront, each catching a roach, which generated some animated discussion over whether it was the same fish before returning it to the water, possibly for the second time. Then nothing for a couple of hours, testing the patience of everyone along the bank apart from Stuart Morris.

Jimmy noticed the older man had taken his line out of the water and was simply staring at the flow. Putting down his own rod, he strolled along the bank and sat down next to him.

"I feel we won't be making a fisherman out of you, Stuart," he said.

"Nah," came the reply, "Don't get me wrong, Jimmy, I'm enjoying myself. But that's down to the scenery and the tranquility. Watching the lads catch the roach put me off fishing for life."

"Oh?"

Morris let the silence drift for a while before answering.

"This might sound daft, but I have a lot in common with that fish."

That did sound daft, thought Jimmy, but he passed no comment. *Let the fish come to you.*

"As I see it," Morris continued, "That fish was just getting on with its life. Not a care in the world. Then it sees a tasty morsel, goes to grab it and the next second it's fighting for its life on a riverbank. Has no idea if it's going to live or die until it's bundled back into the water."

For the first time, Jimmy considered the roach's viewpoint. It wasn't something he was going to share with his regular fishing buddies, or his wife, for that matter.

Morris was getting into his stride, taking his new friend's silence as encouragement to go on.

"It reminded me of last year. One minute I'm working. Next minute I'm in the back of an ambulance, barely able to breathe and with an enormous weight on my chest. Then, I have an operation that changes my life forever." He hesitated; not sure where to go with his train of thought. Reluctant to offer any more background.

"So. What happened to you… We're doing the same to the fish?"

"If you were a roach, and you faced something horrific during your daily routine, how would you pluck up the courage to do anything again? We're changing its life completely. Just for the hell of it."

Jimmy nodded in what he hoped was a thoughtful fashion. He silently prayed for an intervention, but the others focused on their lines, having caught some of the conversation and not wishing to catch any more.

He considered swimming to the opposite shore, then vanishing into the woods beyond. Eventually he stood and stretched, then bent over and put his hand on Morris's shoulder.

"You're okay though, right?"

Morris smiled. "Thanks for asking."

Jimmy patted him on the shoulder, muttered "Good talk" and wandered back to his kit.

Morris inhaled deeply, chuckled softly, then leaned back in his chair and closed his eyes.

Clouds were gathering once again - this was Ireland, after all - but he was genuinely enjoying the day and wouldn't mind another in this beautiful setting. No rods next time, though. He'd leave the fish alone.

Much like he'd done today.

First Contact

"Jesus!" Pope woke with a start and grabbed the hand that was gently shaking his arm. It took him several seconds to remember where he was and to realise he was lying down on the pew.

He released the hand and looked into the kind, amused eyes of the priest, part-hidden by the candlelight reflecting in the holy man's spectacles.

"Not quite," said Father Aidan. "I was on my way out when I heard you. Are you alright?"

Pope sat up and rubbed his face, unsure what to say.

"Sorry. I must have fallen asleep. Only popped in for a quick look. We arrived yesterday. My friends are fishing. I'm supposed to be walking with a mate." Pope checked his watch. "But he's had 90 minutes start on me. God knows where he is by now." Pope bit his lip.

"God probably does," smiled the priest. "Look. Are you here for confession? It's just that I have visits planned to homebound parishioners…"

"Oh Lord, no," said Pope, before wondering how many verbal blunders in sixty seconds would make a new world record. "I'm not Catholic, Father. Just like to visit old churches. I'll leave."

Pope stood and shook the priest's extended hand.

"Catholic or not, confession's good for the soul," assured the priest, noticing a look flitting across the stranger's face that suggested dark memories and inner pain. He removed his glasses to get a better view of the visitor.

"If you want to talk things through, you're welcome to return."

Pope hesitated a moment, wrestling with his own demons.

"I appreciate that. Thank you. Maybe I will."

He walked out of the pew and past the priest towards the door.

"I'm Father Aidan, by the way," the priest called after him.

Pope turned and nodded. "Simon Pope," he said.

"Pope!" The priest beamed. "Good to meet you, Simon Pope. I'm glad you found peace in this place. God bless you."

Pope nodded again and walked out past the gravestones and down the lane, then back along the road towards the pub for lunch. He heard a car crunch over gravel in the church car park and turned, just in time to see the priest pull up at the junction, then drive off in the opposite direction. The same direction that Westlake had taken to leave the town.

Caught In The Storm

Dave Westlake was lost, though he hated to admit it even to himself. He found the lough underwhelming - a large puddle, its only redeeming quality a misty veil obscuring its monotony - prompting him to climb a nearby hill.

He reached the summit just in time to greet the mother of all rain clouds, approaching from the other side. This settled swiftly over the surrounding countryside, unleashing a deluge, blocking the entire view and causing sudden disorientation. He wasn't that bothered, swathed in a set of newish black waterproofs, the jacket's cowl of a hood keeping the worst of the rain at bay.

Moving off the summit gave him a little protection from the weather.

Unable to identify any landmarks from the ascent, he continued downhill but in a sweeping slalom route, to reduce the gradient and the chance of any fall on the increasingly slippery ground.

Not long after, he came across the remains of an ancient farm track heading down the hill and followed it, confident he'd soon arrive at something more substantial and modern.

As the rain beat an impressive rhythm on his waterproofs, Westlake focused on maintaining his balance on slopes getting more dangerous by the minute.

Finally, the old track morphed into an old road with remnants of tarmac forming an archipelago as puddles banded together. The road was barely wide enough for a horse, never mind a petrol driven vehicle, and visibility remained poor in all directions.

Eventually, Westlake stopped to get his breath and leaned against another dry stone wall - although this one was incredibly wet. The wall marked the boundary of a small, derelict church, with a graveyard of ancient headstones surrounding a large, turfed patch of ground. This had no gravestones on it, other than a stone monument in its centre. Westlake noticed a small metal sign on a post further along the wall and he walked over to check it out.

'This parish remembers the 98 men, women, and children lost here during the Great Famine's first year. Pray for them and pray for those who buried them here before moving on.'

Despite his warm waterproofs, Westlake felt a sudden chill. Clonbrinny's church graveyard had spooked him. All graveyards did. They were silent witnesses and immutable proof of the outcome waiting for everybody, despite everyone's best attempts to avoid or ignore the issue.

But this was another level.

Squalls, part-hidden by the storm, slung dark wraith-like shapes across the burial ground. To Westlake, these were the restless, anonymous, abandoned souls, unwilling or unable to leave their last resting place, raging against their fate.

He shivered and hurried away, stumbling into puddles as he did so and only feeling in control again when the old lane widened and regained form as a proper road.

This started at a gate that led into a field where sheep huddled quietly in the pathetic shelter offered by an enormous boulder deposited during the last ice age, standing in defiance of this storm as it had thousands of others across the millennia.

None of the animals uttered a sound, but stared malevolently at the dark spectre walking by on the other side of the gate, who wondered why they appeared to be blaming him for their sorry predicament.

Westlake hurried on his way, spurred on by the downward direction of travel, the robustness of his path and the thought of an Irish coffee by the fire in the pub lounge, hopefully served by the girl he'd met so memorably over breakfast.

Second Contact

Back at the hotel, Pope changed, washed, then headed for the bar. Quiet bars always unsettled him. This one was close to being very unsettling, especially when it had been so busy the night before.

The television was on in the far right corner, but nobody was watching. There was nobody at the pool table. The two fruit machines glittered and flashed, but there was nobody to attract. All the customer tables were tidy and clean; not a chair out of place. Pope sighed to himself and checked the lunch menu on the blackboard. There appeared to be a lot of breakfast items on it.

Sinead was behind the bar, emptying the glass washer and stacking the glasses on the shelves. She caught sight of him in the large mirror she was facing and gave him a bright smile.

"Feeling better?" she asked.

Pope smiled back and nodded, reluctant to return to the incident at breakfast.

"Excellent," she said. "Shows what a good sleep can do for you."

She giggled at the confusion on his face. He'd only been awake fifteen minutes and the news of his power nap in the pew had already reached The Fallen Hero. She put him out of his misery.

"Dermot heard you snoring when he left confession. He couldn't wait to get here and tell us."

Pope grimaced. "He didn't have a camera with him, did he?"

"A smartphone."

Pope grimaced again.

"Have you seen them?"

She shook her head. "The eejit hasn't a clue how to use the camera, never mind in low light conditions. You were lucky."

Pope sat on a bar stool.

"The priest woke me up. Lovely man, even when I blasphemed three times in a minute."

Sinead laughed.

"Father Aidan's a top man, but he's up and down. Depends on how much he's had to drink."

Pope leaned forward, his forearms on the bar.

"Sounds an interesting character…"

Sinead pointed towards a girl Pope hadn't seen earlier, in the corner, working on her laptop and eating a sandwich.

"She might tell you more. Kara Walsh. The priest's her uncle."

Pope waited until his bacon sandwich and mug of coffee were ready, then carried them to a table close to Kara Walsh, where he could watch the television while eating. The news programme showed a public demonstration in the Far East turning ugly, followed by an election event in Eastern Europe turning ugly. He heard the clatter of the keyboard from behind him stop. She was eating, watching the news or watching him.

"Do you mind keeping your leg still?"

Kara Walsh was watching him. He turned round to look at her. Late twenties, short hair and an attractive, slightly annoyed face.

"Sorry. Nervous habit."

Pope dug his heel into the carpet. Behind him, the keyboard clatter resumed. Two minutes later, the twitch started again, prompted by the aftermath of a shooting in America. He heard the keyboard stop.

"TV is clearly not good for you."

Pope laughed. "I'm sorry. The news isn't good for me."

"The news isn't good for anybody."

"Fair point."

Time to grasp the nettle. He turned his chair so he could look at her without doing some damage to his neck.

"My name's Simon."

"Kara."

He nodded towards the laptop.

"Working on anything interesting?"

"No." She closed the laptop. "Just a draft report."

"What's it about?"

"Just an update." She paused for a second. "How's your break going?"

"Not been here 24 hours and I've lost everybody. Some have gone fishing. No idea where. I had planned a walk with another mate, but lost him when I ended up falling asleep in the church."

"St Patrick's?"

"Don't know. Just down the road. It's old. I'm a sucker for the old ones. Just something about them. Wandered in for a mooch around. Sat in a pew. Next thing, the priest is waking me up. My snoring is alarming his flock."

"Father Aidan?"

"That's him. Nice guy. About six feet tall? Glasses? Dark hair? Looks like a rabbit in headlights?"

Kara smiled and nodded.

Pope left it a second before continuing. "He saw the funny side. Asked if I was there for confession. I wasn't, so he politely kicked me out. Do you know him?"

Kara nodded again. "You're right. He's a lovely man." Then, again, changing the subject. "Your first night must have been a good one."

"Yesterday was a long day. Not at my best this morning."

"So. Were you drinking out of the empty mug, or trying to save your mate from choking when he wasn't?"

Pope threw a quick glance at the barmaid. Sinead didn't see him, or pretended she hadn't.

"Are there any secrets in this town?" he asked nobody in particular.

"Not with ICARUS," Kara replied, before catching herself. She checked her watch. "I have to go."

Pope watched her stand up. "Work beckons?"

"Afraid so."

"Well. Thanks for the chat."

"No problem." She walked past him toward the door to the toilets and the car park beyond. "And stop watching the news."

A minute later, he heard a vehicle drive past the side of the pub.

He looked through a window onto the road at the front of the building and watched her small black car drive away.

Pope turned back to his meal, aware he was being watched from the bar.

"Scared her off?" asked Sinead.

"Work beckons. What's ICARUS?"

"Oh, it's part of the community website. It tells us what's happening," she said, then turned to serve an elderly couple who had just entered the room from the front entrance.

Pope settled down to his bacon sandwich and watched the television, but saw nothing.

He'd told the RSM that he wasn't a spy. The last few hours had proved it. His profile was much higher than the stipulated target of 'low'.

He'd met both the priest and the man's niece as directed, but had failed to gain either's trust or to learn anything of note - although he'd check out the community website.

It was time to report to the Garden Club, although it wouldn't be as helpful as they were expecting. Still, there was time yet.

He could make an even bigger mess of things. He was sure of that.

The Cottage Confession

The Kelly family home didn't seem big enough to accommodate five children plus the parents, thought the priest as he parked his car in the lay-by opposite, next to the lough. The size of the terraced cottage was diminished by the large body of water at its front and the steep slopes of the hills behind. Its only protection from floods or avalanche appeared to be the small, tidy front garden with its neat picket fence and the longer garden to the rear.

He emerged from the car with his briefcase, and looked at the other five cottages in the row, all empty, each appearing more dilapidated than the one before.

Such a pity, he thought. *And such a wonderful, peaceful location.*

He walked up the short path across the well-kept lawn to the front door. The key was under the second pot. Knocking on the door, he entered and called out to Clodagh, just in case she had found the gun again.

"I'm in the front room, Father, watching the horses," came a weak reply. "Get yourself a hot drink and then join me. I'm not armed, but I have the biscuit tin."

The priest walked down the small, dark hallway past the stairs and into the kitchen, pausing, as always, to pray for the man who took his last breath there all those years ago.

Clodagh's husband had died unexpectedly, although not as unexpectedly as the three children who had died before him.

Aidan Walsh tried to remember the father of his school friends, but could only recall the black-and-white image with the defiant face and the staring eyes that the local police, the Gardaí, had released to the papers. He remembered laughing and rolling down the hills in the school summer holidays with the Kellys and others from the cottages. Mr Kelly would call them all in for tea. But when he thought of the man's cheerful shout from the end of the back garden, he could only picture that police mugshot. Those eyes…

Aidan wondered how many victims had looked into those eyes. Probably the last thing they had ever seen. He sighed. No wonder it was so tough to pray for Martin Kelly. It was a waste of his time and God's time.

The extended kitchen was a lighter, airier space with brighter walls and modern appliances, but Clodagh had insisted on retaining the original floor. He suspected he knew why.

He made himself a tea, noting the kettle water was still hot, and walked into the front room. Clodagh looked away from her beloved horse racing and smiled, a warm greeting that belied her frail condition.

"Thank you for coming, Father. It's so good of you."

He sat down in the armchair close to her wheelchair and put his mug on the side table between them.

"It's good to see you up again, Clodagh. Are you feeling any better?"

The smile waned, and the wrinkles on her face deepened.

"I had the doctor here this morning with the latest results." She picked up her coffee, took a shaky sip and placed it back on the coaster without spilling a drop. The priest smelled the whiskey in the coffee, and Clodagh had never been a drinker. "I'm glad you're here, Aidan."

Aidan. She hadn't called him that since he went into the priesthood. He reached out and held her hand. She took a firm grasp of his and he could feel her trembling. *No matter how ready you think you are…*

"Me too, Clodagh. Shall we begin? Then we can talk afterwards if you like."

She squeezed his hand and nodded; tears welling in her eyes.

He let go of her hand and reached for his briefcase, took out his stole and kissed it before hanging the long piece of decorated purple silk around his neck. When he was ready, he took hold of her hand again and gave her an encouraging smile.

"Bless me, Father, for I have sinned. It has been two weeks since my last confession. These are my sins."

The priest nodded and closed his eyes.

"And brace yourself," said Clodagh. "This one's going to be a doozy."

The Evolution Of Power

Declan Kelly knew the road like the back of his hand, but the ferocity of the storm and the lack of visibility forced him to take extra care as he drove alongside the lough towards his mother's house.

He swung around the left-hand bend, went past the farm lane on his right and stopped at a viewpoint lay-by one hundred yards further on. Not to admire the view, though; the rain ensured that was available to nobody today.

A hundred yards further down the road stood the row of six terraced cottages, the homes of farm workers for decades and still intact but empty, except for the furthest house in the row. The Kelly family home for several generations and still his mother's home.

No amount of cajoling could persuade her to move to a more modern, more spacious, warmer house.

Her soul was here, inextricably linked to those who had gone before, to the hills, to the mountains beyond and to the water. It had taken a while, but her oldest surviving son had finally accepted this was a battle he would never win.

With very little need to do anything apart from offering slightly above the valuation, he had purchased the other five properties. The reason was simple. To protect the life his mother loved and wanted to live.

There had been a plan to do them up for friends and the wider family to use when visiting, but Clodagh said no. She liked her own company, loved the solitude produced by the departure of neighbours, and could only tolerate others in small doses.

Instead, Declan planned to renovate and sell the five he'd bought, or operate them as holiday rentals, but not the sixth house. A small park area would replace it, including a bench or two that travellers could sit on to admire the view and savour the peace that his mam so enjoyed. A fitting tribute to a wonderful mother.

Today there was a car already parked outside the last house. The priest's car. Declan would wait. He hated meeting familiar people in unfamiliar surroundings. Made him feel vulnerable. Not in control. He was, however, pleased to see the priest was there. Yes, it was Aidan's job, but many would have forgiven him for neglecting Clodagh, especially in this weather.

Many people - probably everybody else Declan knew - would have given the Kellys a wide berth when provided with the most miniscule opportunity to do so. Credit to the man for turning up. And credit to the man, he mused, for protecting his own family by doing what he did.

Declan had a reputation as a hard, callous bastard, but he knew his reputation meant nothing to the priest, his former schoolmate.. He never saw fear in the priest's eyes. Never heard his voice tremble. And as much as that disturbed him, he respected it. Violence wasn't power when it came to this priest. Knowledge. Reputation. Family. Those were the keys to this relationship. And the fact they'd known each other since their infant school days.

Declan worried about his mam. Fretted about her and her health. In his darker moments, he feared how he'd cope and what he'd do when she passed away.

His visits to her were frequent, but not at regular times and never out of duty. He wanted to be with her whenever possible, to cherish the diminishing number of moments they'd have before the inevitable. He thought about the afterlife and wondered what hell would be like. Despite his regular confessions, he suspected he'd find out in due course. And heaven? He prayed for heaven for Clodagh, but wondering if she would make it ripped him up inside. Not that she'd done anything wrong - not in his eyes, anyway.

"Those McGills. Someone should take them down a peg or two," she'd sniffed after being upset by a snide comment after church one Sunday, when Declan was only ten. A week later, the McGill family drove off from church, but failed to stop at the T-junction at the bottom of the lane. The car smashed through the wall on the other side and careened through the sheep in the field beyond, slewing to the left and toppling onto its roof, just before the large stream. The rest of the congregation heard, but could not see, the commotion.

"God moves in mysterious ways," was his mother's only comment on the matter, although Declan spotted the twinkle in her eye.

Somehow, events had escalated from there, each benefiting the Kellys or bringing misfortune onto others. Clodagh commented little on anything that happened, unless it involved quietly but fiercely defending her family against any insinuations that came their way.

If it wasn't a twinkle in her eye, Declan thought, then there was steel. And over the years, with the unspoken approval of his mother, the eldest surviving Kelly child quietly evolved into a powerful criminal overlord. At least, that's what everybody else thought.

And that mattered more than almost anything.

The Catalyst

By the end of the confession, the priest's brain was mush. Like many in his vocation, he found it fairly easy to forget the vast majority of confessional detail almost as soon as he heard it. That was the only way to keep your sanity. The key was that the penitent had confessed and received absolution, not the sordid, morbid, or plain weird activities that preceded that event. With two decades in the priesthood, Father Aidan had heard it all.

At least, he thought he had.

Clodagh looked upset and exhausted after finishing her confession, as well she might, and was watching him apprehensively, waiting - hoping - for absolution. The problem was, the priest wasn't certain she needed it. Not for everything. He stood up and paced the room, then looked out of the front window, through the pouring rain and across the water, trying and failing to gather his thoughts.

"Father?"

He turned to look at her, but didn't see a frail, dying old lady in a wheelchair.

* * *

He saw the same woman, but younger and sitting on a sofa, smoking a cigarette and drinking from a tumbler of whiskey.

The room was much darker, the light from the standard lamp and from the television throwing sharp, black shadows onto the walls. She wasn't watching the television, though; she was staring hard at the sweating man in the armchair who was.

"You know who killed him, don't you? Bobby Brennan? Years ago, and Orla and Sinead are still at their wit's end. God help them."

Martin Kelly's eyes remained fixed on the television. He took a large slug from his own drink and winced slightly as he swallowed the fiery liquid.

"I don't know what you're talking about."

Clodagh looked at her husband of twenty years and wondered what had happened to him; where the man she had adored had gone off the rails and turned into this monster.

"You never do, do you? When that bomb caught our kids. When your eldest son died in fear. You pled ignorance, didn't talk, didn't rage or even cry. Did you actually care about them?"

Again, the eyes never strayed, but the voice had a distinct, threatening edge.

"Never throw my kids' deaths at me. Or Bobby's. They were not my doing. And never presume you know how I'm feeling; what I'm thinking."

If the edge was meant to cut the conversation short, it failed miserably.

"The bomb that killed Liam and Freya was meant for you. And if you hadn't got Seán involved in your stupid…"

"Enough!" His furious glare caught her by surprise and the shout made her look at the ceiling, hoping her remaining sons were asleep and couldn't hear the simmering row.

"No Martin, it's not," she said, conveying a calmness she didn't feel.

"Declan says you've been talking to him. He's only fourteen, and he's already scarred for life. You're not taking him from me as well. I'll make sure you don't."

Her husband stood, somewhat unsteadily, his face sweaty and flushed.

"Yeah?" He took two steps and towered in front of her. "How?"

Before she could answer, he was out of the door and into the hallway. She grabbed the knife she had hidden between the sofa cushions and followed, then stopped. There were no footsteps heading up the stairs. Instead, she heard the door to the kitchen open and a chair scrape on the flagstone floor.

Clodagh imagined he was going into the garden - his favourite place to calm down. He looked like he needed some fresh air. Given what had happened to their family, maybe they all did. Then she heard a surprised groan, followed by a crash and a thud.

Her first instinct was to rush in, but that lasted no longer than another step towards the door. Given what had happened over the last few years, she had no wish to jeopardise her own life or those of her sons. She tiptoed to the cupboard, gently removed the gun from behind the hidden partition, and crept into the hallway.

The kitchen door was slightly ajar, but the light wasn't on and there was no sound. Clodagh walked across to the foot of the stairs, and hid behind them, resting the gun on the bannister to stop the shaking and pointing the muzzle at the kitchen beyond without exposing herself to any immediate danger.

A full minute went by in complete stillness and silence.

"Help. Clo…"

The voice was weak and frightened. The words followed by a grunt of pain, then a long, low moan.

"Clo…"

She crept to the door and pushed it open, handgun still pointing forward.

Martin was flat out on the floor, staring up at the ceiling; his breathing shallow and fast; a kitchen chair lying next to him on its side. The back door was still locked with the key on the hook. She stared out of the window but could see no movement outdoors, just her dim reflection staring back at her.

Clodagh watched him in the gloom for a few seconds, then returned the gun to its hiding place and picked up the house phone on top of the cupboard. She lifted the handset but pressed her other hand down on the cradle, then dialled the emergency number and waited a few seconds.

"Ambulance please... Kelly... The Cottages, Lough Road, Clonbrinny... My husband's collapsed; he's in a bad way... Martin Kelly... Barely conscious and struggling to breathe... I think he's had a heart attack... Quickly please...Thank you."

She replaced the handset and looked at it for a while before walking into the kitchen and turning on the light.

Her husband barely moved. His face was still sweaty but now very pale and his lips were turning blue. Between his urgent gasps, he whispered.

"Help... Please..."

Clodagh walked around the kitchen table, knelt down by him, and stroked his hair. He had cracked his head on the floor as he fell. There was no blood, but a contusion on the side of his right temple was already starting to swell.

"The ambulance is on its way," she lied. "I told them it's an emergency."

The reassuring news calmed him down for a while. She rested her arm on a chair for support and waited. Neither said a word, the ticking of the clock on the wall the only noise to disturb the silence.

Gradually, the gasps became shallower, more desperate.

His face contorted in a mixture of pain and panic as his body spasmed once, twice, and for a third time.

"Please... Clo..."

Clodagh stopped stroking his hair and knelt closer to him, so her lips were close to his ear.

"This," she whispered, watching his eyes spark for a moment, before dulling forever. "This is how it ends."

One last gasp and all was still.

Clodagh stroked Martin's hair for a couple more minutes. They had enjoyed some wonderful years together, raised five beautiful children, and she thanked him for all of that. It was everything else she couldn't forgive. She stood up, using another chair to push herself upright, and leaned against the sink, gathering her thoughts.

That's when she noticed a slight movement in the hallway.

"Mammy?" said fourteen-year-old Declan, sounding scared.

* * *

"Father?" The priest refocused. The old lady sat in front of him and daylight flooded the room once more. Outside, the storm rattled the garden gate, and the rain battered at the front window.

"Clodagh. You were not responsible for your husband's death. The medics would not have reached him..."

"I didn't give him that chance, Father. They would never arrive. Five minutes... fifty minutes... would have made no difference."

The priest saw the pain and desperation in her eyes. She had probably saved countless lives through her decision, including those of her remaining sons. He could have told her that, but he didn't.

Best play it safe and leave it to the big man, he thought.

He walked over, knelt in front of her wheelchair, and clasped her hands in his own.

"God, the Father does not wish the sinner to die but to turn back to Him and live."

Not that the latter's going to happen, both thought independently.

"He loved us first and sent his Son into the world to be its Saviour," he continued. "May He show you His merciful love and give you peace. Give thanks to the Lord for He is good."

The old lady's frail body rocked gently as she leaned forward, touching the priest's forehead with her own

"His mercy endures forever," she murmured.

The priest took a moment.

"Your sins are forgiven," he said, feeling a strange relief of his own. "Go in peace."

Clodagh pulled back and looked at him, her anguish replaced by a joyous beam.

"Thanks be to God," she said, happy tears in her eyes. He reached for the nearby tissue box and handed it to her. She dabbed away the tears and put the used tissue in a small wastebasket. "Thank you Aidan. You've made an old woman very happy. Now, let's have a proper drink to celebrate."

The Request

The celebration lasted as long as it took to savour a couple of sips from the glass tumblers.

Clearly, the old lady had something else on her mind.

Now that her soul was in a better place, she wanted to talk about someone else's.

She looked at the priest as he gazed at the whiskey swirling in a micro maelstrom at the bottom of his glass.

"I haven't got long, Aidan."

The priest's eyes remained focused on the tumbler.

"I know."

"I need you to do me a favour. Once I'm gone."

The priest took another sip of the 12-year-old malt, then set his glass down on the table.

"I need you to look after Declan."

The priest picked up his glass and took another sip, larger than the others. Some may have described it as a gulp. And everybody would have understood why.

"I'm not saying it will be easy, Father, what with all the illegal goings-on and the violence and everything. But he has a kind soul if you strip all that away. It needs saving."

The priest wondered why Clodagh didn't view violence as illegal, but decided not to push the point.

"Does he talk about those things, Clo?"

"No Father. He talks about his businesses, and how well Connor's doing for a lad with his condition. But I hear the rumours and the Gardaí pop round now and then. They say they're checking how I'm doing, but the conversation always turns to Declan and one of them will sneak off for a look around."

The old lady took another sip from her glass.

"Does my son come to confession still?"

"I can't say, Clo."

"I'll take that as a yes. Oh, don't worry," she said, noting the consternation flit across the priest's face, "Your job and your chances of reaching heaven remain intact. You haven't betrayed the Seal of Confession. If he hadn't been, you could have said so, but you didn't."

Father Aidan considered the logic and simply shrugged. Clodagh's eyes narrowed, and she took in his discomfort.

"Say nothing, but you know what my son's been up to," she said. The rain attacked the windowpane with a renewed fury, breaking the tension in the room but not, fortunately, the glass.

"You were great friends once. Declan, you and your brother, God rest his soul. You know there's a good man inside."

"There was a good man, Clodagh."

"I think you'll be surprised."

"You don't think I've tried?"

Clodagh hesitated, caught in the priest's sudden glare, struck by the plaintive tone in his response and recognising the fear and frustration behind those five words. She held his stare until his eyes turned back to his glass; the silence broken by the storm and the sideboard clock, each tick more important than the last, counting down to her last breath.

"I've lived here a long time," she murmured. "This home holds a lot of memories, good and bad… terrible, actually…

When I remember them, I see my family, my beautiful children. I try to remember the fun times and the laughter, but sometimes I can't help but remember the overwhelming sadness and tears… so many tears…" She took another sip of her drink and saw his eyes lift to meet hers. "And do you know what? In most scenes that play out in my head…"

"I'm there."

"You're there," Clodagh smiled.

The Passage Of Death

Declan ended the call to the doctor, dropped the mobile onto the seat beside him, and slammed the steering wheel with both hands. The storm barely covered his howl of furious rage and anguish, although it seemed to quieten a moment, unsure of what it had just heard, before continuing unabated.

He gripped the wheel tightly, trying to get a similar hold on his emotions. His mother was going to die soon and no power on earth was going to stop it. His protection of her was going to fail. He would never see her again; never talk to her; laugh with her.

He considered himself head of the household after his father's death, despite being fourteen. He'd looked after them all. Defended them. Protected them. But his mother was always there. Supporting him. Encouraging him. Spurring him on to ever greater achievements. His muse. His confidante, to an extent. And all that was about to disappear.

Declan felt vulnerable, alone, anxious.

He had tried hard to look after her in this life, but had he done enough to protect her in the next?

A movement through the rain disturbed his train of thought. He saw the priest leave the house, close the door carefully behind him and then run, head bent, to the shelter of his car. Moments later, the car drove off into the mist.

Declan started his car, intent on reaching Clodagh and making the most of whatever time was left. He checked his wing mirror and gasped. Floating through the downpour from the lane to the abandoned church, a dark shape shifted from side to side.

He watched as the spectre grew in size, moving towards him and with greater purpose. There was no time to waste.

He put the car in gear and careered down the road, slamming to a halt in the parking slot just vacated by the priest, half-hoping the latter's recent presence might deter whatever demon was behind him.

He scrambled from his car, then sprinted up the path, avoiding any backward glances. He fumbled for the door key, cursing the priest for being conscientious despite the weather, praying it was in the right place and murmuring "Amen" when he found it.

Trembling, he unlocked the door, rushed inside, and slammed it shut. Ignoring the concern and the questions from his ma, he closed the front curtains, grabbed the crucifix off the wall and crouched next to her, muttering a Hail Mary as he did so.

Hiding her surprise at the tears and the fear in his eyes, Clodagh put her arm around his damp shoulders and stroked his head. She opened her mouth to speak, but he looked at her glowing face and shook his head violently from side to side, putting the crucifix into her hand and clasping it with his own, shifting position slightly to look at the door as the storm reached its climax with a deafening roar.

Death drifted through the storm, paused to view the house, wondering who had rushed in, then shrugged its shoulders and stomped off down the road.

Westlake wanted to reach the warm, dry pub before his waterproofs decided enough was enough and let in the rainwater.

Five minutes passed by with nothing happening in Clodagh's home, aside from the ticking of the clock. Outside, the wind and the rain subsided. Declan squeezed his mother's hand, stood up, moved cautiously to the front window and peered between the curtains. Nothing. Just his car and the weak sunshine breaking through the clouds and throwing its rays onto the lough. The demon had vanished.

He turned to face his mother; her face a mixture of concern and amusement.

"Son," she said, "You look as though you've seen a ghost."

She pointed at the bottle of whiskey the priest had left beside her.

"Get yourself a glass and tell me all about it over a little drink."

"Mammy. Should you be drinking right now?"

Clodagh laughed.

"Oh, I think so," she said. "It's not like it's going to kill me."

Open Doors

The van whipped into the car park and crunched to a halt as close to The Fallen Hero as possible.

The return was earlier than expected. Heavy rains had raised the river level alarmingly quickly, forcing a swift evacuation. Unfortunately, not swift enough to avoid complete saturation.

The weather and the departure had been so bad that it wasn't just Stuart Morris who had serious doubts about his fishing future. Everybody had.

The rain had eased off enough to transfer the soaked kit into the hotel's storage area. The reason for the dehumidifier and the tumble dryer in the room had not been clear beforehand. It was obvious now.

An hour later and everybody had showered, changed and were sitting in the bar alongside Pope, munching bacon sandwiches, drinking Irish coffees and swapping hard luck stories from the morning's adventures.

Jimmy Doyle had sat in his car and watched them depart the fishing site before setting off back home. *Interesting.*

Despite the raging storm, neither of the van's front doors or the sliding side door were closed until it moved off. There was more to this group than he'd originally thought.

Jimmy knew the reason the doors stayed open.

Everyone in Clonbrinny knew the reason, because everyone in Clonbrinny did the same thing. And ICARUS was always there to remind them, in case anybody forgot.

He pulled out his smartphone, clicked on the community website, typed a few words and pressed send.

The Old Boathouse

Nestled by the tranquil shores of a small lough, the old boathouse had kept its original charm. The exterior of stone walls with moss and ivy clinging to the cracks blended the structure into the surrounding landscape.

"Impressive," muttered Mindy, as she and Blackwell emerged from the tree-covered hillside and followed the path that skirted the water's edge.

As they walked towards the large, refinished wooden door, it swung open without a sound, revealing a tastefully designed interior that blended tradition with hi-tech comfort.

"Facial recognition," whispered Blackwell, pointing towards a CCTV dome camera fixed discreetly just under the eaves. "We might be the first here."

Mindy hung her coat in the cloakroom just inside the building and walked into the main room. Large windows flooded the room with natural light and provided stunning views of the surrounding hills and woodland, with the small lough's serene waters lapping against the shore just outside.

The grain of a long oak conference table matched the exposed, polished beams, while ergonomic chairs guaranteed comfort during meetings of any length. Blackwell headed to the bar and catering area, noting the advanced technology along the way.

He poured two mugs of fresh coffee and brought them over to the table, along with a couple of warm pastries.

"You're sitting in my seat."

Both swung around to see Elena Marchetti silhouetted in the doorway, with a smiling Evie Marsh standing just outside, gently shaking her head.

Blackwell and Mindy exchanged glances, wondering who had fallen foul of the global clone queen.

Marchetti pointed at Mindy. "You need to move."

Mindy bought some time by taking a bite of her pastry, dropping small crumbs onto the table and the chair, and then sipped her coffee.

"I think you've dropped something outside Elena," she said, as Marchetti marched towards the table, then halted, momentarily confused.

"Manners," Mindy continued helpfully, gazing into her accuser's face. "You must have misplaced them." She took another bite of her pastry, dropping more crumbs as she did so.

Blackwell watched, wondering how red the Italian's face could get. Two more figures appeared at the doorway - Alexander Alcock and Isaac Delemos. Alcock coughed politely, breaking the silence but not the tension.

"Apologies, both," he said. "There should be name cards. Seating was the subject of intense negotiations during our first visit to this wonderful place and has remained the same since. Plus, Elena had an absolutely shocking game of golf this morning."

"Golf!" exclaimed Blackwell, so loudly that the women engaged in the staring contest jumped and turned to look at him. "Oh Elena. That explains a lot. Let me tell you about the game I played during my leave of absence. One guy - they called him Coldfront because whenever he approached he created a low depression…"

As Blackwell recounted that memorable day, Evie made herself and Elena a coffee. Alcock showed Mindy where she and Blackwell could sit, and Delemos produced a brush and pan from a cupboard and removed the offending crumbs.

By the time Aston Hail and Tee Takahashi walked in, conviviality had replaced acrimony and amusing golfing anecdotes filled the air. More importantly, for Elena at least, everyone was in their allocated position around the table.

Mindy's smile reached her eyes, but her mind was a whirl.

Marchetti's unexpected, angry reproach suggested their hosts were not as genial or as respectful as they had initially appeared. They had been at the mansion for around 24 hours and had barely discussed the important stuff.

Was Andy the afternoon entertainment, or somebody to be taken seriously? For the first time in a very long time, she felt nervous.

Attack And Defence

The promised return call from Government Communications Headquarters (GCHQ) arrived much sooner than expected. About 70 hours sooner, and only two hours after the former regimental sergeant major - the current head of the Garden Club - had sent the original request.

"What the hell did you send me?"

"I have absolutely no idea," replied the RSM, partly alarmed, partly curious. "That's why I sent it. But I guess you're about to tell me."

"I checked it out over lunch on my laptop at home and it's a good job I did. GCHQ and the Club would have been badly compromised. It could have been a national disaster."

The RSM shifted in his seat.

"How so?"

"On the face of it, it's just your standard community website. One of the links is for ICARUS and it's the only link that is password protected. It looks like basic password protection, but it's more than that."

The GCHQ contact gathered her thoughts, wondering how to explain what she'd encountered to a layperson.

"Imagine you're entering an exclusive nightclub and you have to knock on the door before you do anything else."

"Or click a link?"

"Exactly. But before you go in - before you even give the password - the doormen leave the club, come out to you and give you a full body search, take the keys to your home and gain control of all your assets. Only then do they check you're a pre-registered guest and not a threat to them. If pre-registered, then fine. If not, they deny you entry, but they retain control over you, your possessions, and your life. They can do what they like whenever they want."

"Sounds a bit over-the-top for a community web page."

"I guess it depends on how keen you are to deter the wrong people from trying to access it."

The contact couldn't contain herself any longer.

"Pete. It's brilliant. Genius. And it's frightening. The moment the visitor clicks, the ICARUS landing page loads and starts a zero-day browser exploit. Here's the killer - if there isn't one, it actually creates one either in the visitor's browser or in one of the browser extensions. The exploit makes the visitor's system believe it has a vulnerability, then ICARUS takes advantage of it! It downloads malware, which grants remote access to the machine and escalates privileges. Automated scripts disable security systems, access and copy data, and take full administrative control of the visitor's system and any network beyond."

The RSM preferred the club analogy and resolved never to visit one with such a strict admissions policy.

"How do you know all this?"

"Because it took over my laptop."

"Who's behind it? And what's it doing on a community website?"

"No idea. It's light years ahead of anything I've seen before. The source code is heavily encrypted, and I can't get close for fear of getting too close. It could be booby-trapped as well. Once this thing has you, it may never let you go. Fortunately, it let me go pretty quickly. Two minutes max."

"But it only reacts to approaches? It's not proactive?"

"All I know is if you fly too close to it, you'll crash and burn quickly. Like the guy who flew too close to the sun."

"So it's a defensive measure? It's protecting something?"

"Yes, but the same programming could wreak havoc with a bit of tweaking. Who knows? That may already be the case."

The RSM ended the call, promising to find out as much as he could. He started writing a text message, then scrubbed it, selected the number instead, and put the phone to his ear.

The GCHQ contact took her personal laptop onto the balcony of her fourth-floor apartment, checked there were no pedestrians on the pavement below, then dropped it. Her insurance would cover a new one.

The First Move

Coldfront's account of his confrontation with an angry swan was interrupted twice - first by a tired, damp Dave Westlake who had dumped his waterproofs in the drying room before making his way to the bar and ordering an Irish coffee and a bacon sandwich.

Two minutes later, the door opened again and Pope returned from taking the RSM's call, looking thoughtful. He caught sight of Westlake and walked over to him, just as Sinead placed the order on the bar.

"I'll pay for that," he said, "And another Irish as well, please."

The barmaid headed back to the coffee machine.

"Apology accepted," said Westlake, wolfing down his first sandwich. "What happened?"

"Fell asleep in the church." He held up his hand to ward off any comment. "Don't bother, I've heard them all. The priest woke me up, but I was about ninety minutes behind you by then. I came back here when the rain returned. The lads got washed off the riverbank. Arrived an hour ago."

"It's going to be a long, messy night, then."

"Maybe not." Sinead set the second coffee on the bar. "It's quiz night. That'll keep you occupied, but don't expect to win. It's good craic though."

"We won't win," grinned Westlake. "Care to bet on that?"

"What's the wager?" asked Sinead, leaning forward so Pope could tap the pay system with his card.

"If we lose, I'll take you out somewhere. Your choice."

"But if you win?"

"I'll take you out somewhere. Your choice."

She reached over and shook his hand, holding his gaze a touch longer than one would normally in polite society.

"You're on," she said, almost skipping down to the other end of the bar where other customers were waiting.

Westlake turned to Pope, a triumphant smile on his face, and heard the comment he'd heard several times before.

"Oh mate. She'll have you for breakfast."

Open Discussion

Much to Mindy's delight and surprise, the roundtable discussion with the Conclave was going better than she had expected.

Andy's speech the evening before had touched a nerve, or maybe it had merely confirmed what some of the group were already thinking.

Evidently, discussions had extended late into the night, and then resumed on the golf course.

Aston had summed up his feelings succinctly.

"Sometimes I feel like I was messing in the sea on an airbed and accidentally caught a gigantic wave I wasn't expecting," he explained. "People watched me and I rode it home. Suddenly, I'm the best surfer in the world. Any wave, any height, anywhere, I can master it. People admire my achievements, but…"

His voice faded as he contemplated his wild ride of business success and considered the good fortune he'd had along the way.

"But you know you got lucky and that events outside your control could change that fortune at any moment," reflected Alexander Alcock. "We're all in the same boat."

The London-based venture capitalist sipped a coffee and collected his thoughts.

"I've made a career out of moving markets and building businesses. Heck, I've even tried my hand at taking over industries and the occasional small nation," he smiled. "I've made a lot of money, I've lost a lot of money and many times the outcome has been outside of my control. Every time it scares me." He nodded to emphasise the point. "Deals used to be a buzz, but now it's different. The more expertise and experience I've gathered, the more I realise I'm not in control. I don't like that feeling."

Mindy wasn't sure whether to fill the silence that followed, but Isaac Delemos saved her the trouble.

"We share a common problem, my friends. People regard us as too big to fail, but we know that is wrong. As Andrew explained, we are captains of ships at the mercy of forces more powerful than our own. But we cannot be too honest about our fortune. That will frighten the markets; create chaos; destroy our businesses and our reputations. The question is, do we have the imagination and the capabilities to create a political, economic and environmental movement that will deliver a greater, fairer balance for the world's population, without jumping off a cliff ourselves?"

"And the willingness?" interrupted Tee Takahashi, looking down at her tablet. "It's a huge, expensive, long-term challenge and will probably not occur in our lifetime. It requires a massive effort on our part and for relatively little reward. International bodies and national governments must support this initiative; they will take credit for its achievements. At best, we will be footnotes in history, or the new system could fail and our corpses will be the scapegoats."

The silence hung heavy for several seconds until the Japanese software guru voiced what the rest of the Conclave were thinking.

"Can we really be bothered?"

Mindy felt depressed. Even the light outside seemed to fade suddenly, the bright blue sky reflected in the waters of the lough transforming into a dull grey as clouds massed across the hills on the far shoreline.

Blackwell walked over to the bar in the catering area, poured himself a whiskey on the rocks, and stood at the panoramic window, absorbing the scene outside with his back to the group.

"I know the answer to that. I thought about that for three months," he mused, almost to himself. "The answer is no."

"Then why are we here?" Isaac Delemos asked, but out of curiosity, not exasperation or annoyance.

Taking another sip of his drink, Blackwell returned to the table and sat down.

"Wish I knew," he smiled. "I wanted to know if you see the world as I do. I have my answer to that, but I'm also interested in your thoughts on necessary actions, possible solutions and how you might help to get humanity into a better, maybe a more honest place."

Mindy watched carefully as the body language around the group changed. Most people sat up straighter and leaned forward, apart from Aston and Evie, who sat further back in their chairs, deep in thought.

"Whether you're bothered is not the question," Blackwell continued. "The scale of this challenge is too big for the world to contemplate, never mind the Conclave. Consider this an intellectual exercise - much like the Bolsheviks did with communism. Lenin and his friends were busy pontificating in Sweden when the women in St. Petersburg rioted over the lack of bread. The Bolsheviks got lucky; the world, not so much. But this is a bit of fun. I'm more interested in your ideas than anything else."

"So it's a mega project we need to break down into smaller steps?"

"Each of your empires is a mega project. You've all done it before. What's the ultimate aim? What are your objectives? How do you recognise and respond quickly to problems or opportunities on the way?"

As Blackwell finished speaking, he noticed a hum emanating from the room's edges. Two large electronic whiteboards lowered into place, and each of the Conclave placed their tablets on the desk.

Aston cleared his throat.

"Thanks Andy. We'll take it from here. Dinner at eight in the hall?"

Blackwell sensed Mindy's hand tighten on the armrest of her chair and put his own hand on top of hers as he rose.

"Thanks Aston. And good luck everyone! We'll see you at eight."

Quiz Night

Friday nights were big nights because Friday nights were quiz nights. It seemed as if the entire population of Clonbrinny relished a bit of brain work. The overcrowded bar and lounge were full of good natured banter, cracked by the occasional cackle of laughter that carried into the residents' dining room.

The lads had left the bar late in the afternoon to get themselves ready and to take a break from excessive drinking and Coldfront's tales from the riverbank.

Stuart Morris and Dave Westlake had taken more care than usual over their appearance, much to the amusement of the others. For the first time in five months, the ironing board and iron emerged from the hotel bedroom's wardrobe.

Even Simon Pope felt good, despite the challenge of learning more about a website that threatened to destroy civilisation, according to the RSM. Pope hadn't understood the club bouncer analogy, because the RSM hadn't quite grasped it before relaying it.

Now, noting with satisfaction that even Stuart Morris had a smile on his face, Pope shelved the mission for the night. The former police sergeant had struggled since retiring from the force on health grounds and it was good to see the effect this break from normality was having on his mental health.

Not much had been normal recently, Pope reflected. Ending up as friends with a broken prime minister; surviving two assassination attempts on the same day and reuniting with his former fiancée had just been the start.

And now, tasked with keeping a low profile on this, his first reconnaissance mission, every person in the pub was sporting a sticker related to the breakfast incident.

Feeling the sensible action was to cut and run, Pope had gone with his instincts and embraced the new-found fame with good humour. After all, no self-respecting spy would attract so much attention.

And besides, he wasn't the centre of attention on the stickers. That would be the expert first-aider Dave Westlake, now famous for his imaginative mash-up of the Heimlich Manoeuvre and defibrillation, when all Pope was suffering from was a major case of embarrassment.

Now, the embarrassment was Westlake's, faced as he was with stickers on all sides saying '*However red I look, stay away from me*' or '*Caution: first aid-free zone*' or '*I'm not choking*'.

A smiling Sinead even had a special one for Westlake himself, which, to his credit, he accepted and wore with pride. '*Danger. I'm a first-aider.*'

Margaret and Jimmy Doyle entered just as dinner was almost over, with two helium balloons tied to Margaret's wheelchair to ensure everyone noticed her and avoided her chair, however chaotic things became.

"As a former mathematics teacher, I have concluded we need to split into two teams," she announced, with the confidence that came with the three gins downed before leaving the house. "Quiz rules state a maximum of four people to a team, so one of you fine gentleman will have to join my husband and myself. Somebody will walk through that door at some stage and join my team. They may be a quiz genius or a waste of space. The suspense is delicious!"

"Count me in," grinned Stuart Morris. "Jimmy helped me catch no fish today. It's only fair I help him get no points tonight."

"Grand!" shrieked Margaret above the general laughter at the gentle jibe. "Join us when you're finished. We have a table reserved near the quizmaster. Bring drinks with you." The couple moved away, the balloons bouncing off assorted heads as they weaved through the crowd.

The group resumed their meal, with the conversation focused on which team would beat the other, if not win the overall competition. Drink had loosened Coldfront's control over his unsociably-competitive instincts.

"We'll smash you," he asserted.

Morris shrugged.

"He's not bothered," said Angus Grace, his mouth full of stew. "The quiz isn't the game tonight, is it, pal?"

Morris shrugged again.

"I clocked him earlier," continued Grace after swallowing his food. "Checking out the tables while at the bar. It's everyone for themselves with four exceptions - a table for Team Margaret and Jimmy because of the wheelchair; two for residents - so we'll have one of them; plus one more, also near the quizmaster."

"And who's that for?" frowned Coldfront.

"Team Landlady," crowed Grace.

Coldfront threw his cutlery onto his plate and, unable to think of anything to say for once, stared at Morris, who had the courtesy to blush before picking up his drink, raising it in salute and leaving the table.

"I have something to win," he said, waving farewell.

Dave Westlake watched him go, pleased to see the swagger back in his former boss's walk; his shoulders no longer hunched.

There was life in the old dog after all.

At that moment, Sinead walked in to help clear the plates. She didn't look his way, but he caught sight of her sticker. *'You can only squeeze me if I can knee you in the balls first,'* it said.

Others wore the same message, but only Sinead mattered. Both of them knew they were winners that night, no matter what happened in the quiz.

The Awkward Moment

Orla Brennan was already settled at her table by the time Stuart Morris reached his, carrying a tray of drinks for his team. The landlady had dressed up for the occasion, wearing a blue skirt with a white blouse, topped off by a silver necklace and a radiant smile. She cherished her weekly night off, and there was the chance that tonight could be more memorable than usual.

"Why Margaret, you didn't tell me you had a secret weapon," she said, her eyes sparkling.

"Oh, you know me Orla, happy if any waif or stray wants to jump aboard. Problem is, I won't know if he's any good until afterwards. He could peak too soon."

Everyone laughed except Morris, who distributed the drinks and contemplated suitable replies, before realising the opportunity had gone.

Jimmy closed his eyes and shook his head slowly from side to side in mock disapproval.

"You two…" he said. "Behave."

"Never," they responded in unison, and both tables laughed again.

The bar clock ticked towards the start time of eight and the crowd around the bar settled down at their tables while the quizmaster distributed the required papers and pens.

The two tables reserved for residents filled up, with Morris's friends arguing over their team name and who should write the team's answers.

"If I'm doing the writing, then I'm deciding on the name," declared David 'Coldfront' Davies. "We're the Fishing Flops, because it's true and will remain true no matter what happens tonight."

"Bravo!" laughed Margaret Doyle, captain of Mag's Magicians. Other tables announced their team names to the quizmaster and his assistant.

Simon Pope was about to comment on the noise level and the fervour in the room when both crashed. His friends looked at each other, unsure what was happening and why; wary of doing or saying something when the change in volume level might signal the start of the quiz. Then he caught sight of the landlady's stony face as she looked towards the bar. He turned and saw two men ordering drinks and searching for seats at a table.

"There's not a seat big enough for that lad," murmured Dave Westlake, looking at the big man buying the drinks.

"There's not a seat for either of them," observed Coldfront, surveying the tables between him and the bar.

The smaller and younger of the two men surveyed the room before turning and talking urgently to his associate. The latter nodded, perched on a bar stool close to the door, and sipped a pint of orange juice.

The younger man waved at the quizmaster and pointed at Margaret's table.

"Permission to join Mag's Magicians?" he asked loudly. "Brendan's happy to watch."

The quizmaster looked at Orla, who looked at Margaret. Stuart Morris noticed Jimmy tense up and Margaret's face look fleetingly solemn, before she flashed an apprehensive smile.

Orla took the microphone off the quizmaster and looked hard at the younger man.

"There's a space, Connor, but if there are any shenanigans like last time…"

Connor Kelly looked embarrassed. He swayed from side to side.

"I just want to take part, Orla. That's all."

The landlady looked beyond him to Brendan Dunne on the bar stool, silently seeking and receiving a subtle confirmation that he would intervene should any problem occur.

Stuart Morris looked at his four friends next to him and received a similar confirmation. He turned and winked at Margaret, who waved Connor over. As the new team member reached the table, Morris stood up and shook his hand.

"Hello. I'm Stuart."

"Connor. I am… very pleased to meet you, Stuart."

Morris sensed the man's smile was real enough, but there was an awkwardness to his speech that suggested there was something amiss.

Connor also greeted Jimmy with a handshake, then leaned over and embraced Margaret.

"Thank you, Margaret."

She patted his freckled cheek.

"Now don't you be letting me down, young man. I want to win this one."

Connor smiled. "I'll do my best."

The quizmaster took the microphone and cleared his throat.

"Welcome to the Thursday night quiz, everybody. Eight rounds of ten questions, with a drinks break after four. No arguing with the quizmaster over the answers. Extra points to any team who buys me or my wonderful assistant a drink at any time."

The announcement cut through the tension like a knife.

"Any questions, apart from whether I know who my father was?" He waited for the laughter and the catcalls to fade away. "Okay. Good luck everyone. First round. General knowledge."

Brendan Dunne settled back and relaxed.

There didn't look to be any issues. The welcome from the stranger had been a nice touch. Maybe the lad would enjoy himself.

If he did, then so would Brendan.

The Split

Dinner at Peace Castle was not as convivial as the previous evening's affair.

The food and drink held their own, and there was yet more automated applause for the chef. The atmosphere around the table, however, was thin - much like the feedback on the brainstorming session offered to Blackwell.

"We discussed the possibility of a global political party," outlined Aston between mouthfuls of the main course. "Agreeing and campaigning on the same issues, so that a vote wherever in the world is a vote for the same thing. Just a focus on moving towards a global system, but with agreed adaptations to deliver national benefits. We'd promote arms de-escalation; resolve conflicts peacefully; coordinate healthcare research and drug distribution; and develop the global powerhouse, focused on clean energy and shared research."

Hail waited for the plates to be cleared and the arrival of the dessert before continuing.

"We'd demand the conscientious management of finite resources; create an environmentally friendly global transport infrastructure; and raise education standards across the board, sharing teaching and IT resources. There'd be specific regional development programmes for agriculture."

"Sounds a great start," enthused Blackwell, even though a sixth-grader in a remedial class would have come up with a similar list. In fact, so had he just three months earlier.

Mindy detected the slightest impatience in his voice, even as she feigned interest in the development of artificial intelligence in Elena's cloning applications.

"And what did you move onto from there?"

Hail had three spoonfuls of profiteroles before answering, relishing the spotlight and keeping his guests waiting.

"I'm afraid I can't divulge that, Andy. Proprietary information. You understand, I'm sure."

Blackwell wasn't sure he'd heard correctly.

"Proprietary, Aston?"

"Yeah. Yeah. We came up with a name for the political party. Alexander has a cool idea for the brand identity. I have a research team compiling a proposal to bring the concept to market via a …"

Blackwell couldn't help himself. He laughed.

The Conclave looked surprised, apart from Delemos, who seemed embarrassed.

"I'm sorry Aston. I was just looking for some feedback on my thoughts. Maybe some ideas. Now I learn you're moving things forward, but you won't tell me how?"

Hail wiped his mouth with his napkin and shrugged.

"Andy. Each member of the Conclave is a potent combination of visionary and pragmatist. You came to us with a concept. Helped us to realise what's been staring us in the face for years. It's like you said in the boathouse…"

Blackwell's disembodied voice floated through the invisible speaker system.

"…how do you recognise and respond quickly to problems or opportunities on the way?"

Aston Hail leaned on the table and smiled.

"I guess we respond quickly to opportunities."

The Halftime Break

The halftime break in the quiz gave everyone the chance to have a breather, grab a drink and, in the case of the British guests, to get to grips with a kind of pub quiz they had never experienced before. Coldfront, in particular, was fuming.

"In Lady Chatterley's Lover, what was the occupation of Mellors the gamekeeper? Who wrote JK Rowling's Harry Potter books? What sort of questions are they?" he asked, with more than a hint of despair in his voice.

"Fun questions," answered Morris. "They keep people interested; give them a giggle."

"And then you get what does the HTTP status code 418 mean," moaned Coldfront. "And what was the first video uploaded on YouTube, and who uploaded it."

"Yeah," mused Morris. "We got both of them."

Time seemed to stand still. Morris enjoyed the stunned silence before clarifying.

"I say we," he started, then looked over to the bar, where his new teammate was sharing a laugh with his huge friend.

"I can't make the lad out. Very bright in some areas; but not good in others. That question about American football teams with a bird in their name? He suggested Chicago Bears. When he realised what he'd said, I thought he was going to kill somebody… or himself. He was so mad."

To their credit, nobody laughed out loud, although Coldfront bit hard on a beer mat to stop himself.

"He also suggested the sport where players use a tennis racquet is squash," continued Morris, curious to see if Coldfront was actually going to cry.

Distracted, Pope asked, "What does HTTP status code 418 mean?"

"I'm a teapot."

Coldfront creased up and stumbled towards the toilets. The others grinned as they watched him go.

"Seriously?" asked Pope.

"Apparently, it's a humorous error code where the server thinks it's a teapot, so can't brew coffee. Go figure," said Morris, as his drinks order arrived. "I'm going to chat with Jimmy. See if I can find out more about our tech prodigy."

"You might need a few more like him to catch us," crowed Angus Grace, forgetting all about pride coming before a fall.

Margaret was in deep conversation with the landlady, who threw an occasional, anxious glance in Connor's direction. Morris put the tray on the table, placed a pint in front of Jimmy, and came straight to the point.

"What's Connor's story, Jimmy? I feel there's something going on. I'm just not sure what."

Jimmy leaned in and kept his voice down. "Connor is a Kelly. Brother of Declan, who has a terrible reputation. Be very wary of any Kelly around here. The big lad is their minder, Brendan Dunne. Be even more wary of Dunne."

Morris took a drink of his Irish coffee. "And Connor?"

Jimmy looked thoughtful before answering.

"There were five Kelly kids about twenty-five years ago. Their dad, Martin, he was a decent man, but he got caught up in the Troubles. One Sunday, the family was getting ready for church. The kids were messing about by the car. There was an explosion. It really sent Martin off the rails."

Jimmy looked up and noticed Connor heading back.

"Two kids died. Connor has what they call an acquired brain injury. He's in his late thirties but hasn't really grown up. Very sharp, but can have trouble understanding, and that's frustrating for him. Loses his temper easily. Brendan's with him most of the time. To keep him out of harm's way. Brendan was the kid who dragged him and Declan away from the burning car. Watch out, he's coming back."

The men laughed as if sharing a joke as one of the two remaining Kelly brothers sat himself down and accepted the proffered drink.

"What's so funny?" he asked.

"I was just telling Jimmy, my friends couldn't believe we'd got the tech questions correct. Their faces were a picture."

Connor stared at the floor. "It's about the only thing I know anything about."

"It's an excellent area to be an expert in nowadays."

"I suppose so," agreed the younger Kelly, "But it'd be nice to remember that a bear isn't a bird before opening my mouth."

Morris smiled at the comment. "I was about to say the Baltimore Orioles, so I got the bird right; not the sport."

"Ah, we've all got a few of those in us," interrupted Jimmy Doyle, who held up his drink. "A toast," he proposed. "To quiz cock-ups."

"To quiz cock-ups," echoed the other two, clinking their glasses.

Margaret turned her wheelchair back to the table and picked up her own drink.

"What are we toasting?" she asked.

"Cock-ups," answered Connor.

Margaret raised her glass.

"Of course we are," she smiled, with a knowing glance at Stuart Morris.

Ocean Reflection

Armed with a torch each, rugs, flasks of coffee, two mugs and a bottle of whiskey, Blackwell and Mindy retraced their earlier walk through the woods to the coast and headed down the steps to the beach.

Neither said a word. The discussion at dinner lingered, but that wasn't the reason for the silence. The warm hues of sunset over the Atlantic's western horizon reflected off the water, presenting a scene of incredible beauty and tranquility, but the stunning low-angled light also made walking a dangerous pastime.

Eventually they found the flat boulder close to the rocky outcrop, which had sheltered them that morning. A minute later and they were sitting together on one rug with the other wrapped around them, savouring the fortified coffee.

The deep orange, pink, and gold had almost disappeared, chased off by a sky transitioning from soft purples and blues to an inky darkness as night fell. Mindy soaked in the view and took a deep breath.

The air was crisp and carried the fresh scent of saltwater. A light breeze made her grateful for the rugs and the coffee. As the twilight deepened, faint starlight flickered, then formed recognisable and not-so-recognisable constellations as the night intensified.

Still, neither of them spoke. In more ways than one, it was a time for reflection. Time to absorb and appreciate a nightscape existing for millennia and here for many more, irrespective of what one species was up to in the here and now.

It's all so… futile, she thought. *In the grand scheme of things, what's the point?*

"This is lovely, isn't it?" asked Andy. "It was worth coming just for this."

"Was it worth coming for anything else?"

Blackwell thought for a moment. "Four charities have fifty grand each. I know I'm not the only one barely in control of their own destiny. Six global leaders feel the same. They're intrigued by the idea of a more open, honest, collaborative world. And they're considering doing something about it."

"They're planning to make money from it."

"Well, of course they are," Blackwell smiled. "Whether they succeed is another matter. But we won't get people interested in this crazy notion unless they think there's a benefit for them. They need to hold on to that expectation until they're further down the path and realise the reward isn't what they envisioned."

He picked up a pebble and threw it into the small waves sneaking ashore.

"And what's in it for you?" she asked.

"That's easy," he answered. "You."

She linked to his arm and rested her head on his shoulder.

"That makes both of us winners, and we've barely started," she said.

"Then the world's our oyster! Cheers."

Mindy clinked her mug against her fiancé's.

"Cheers."

The Icarus Round

Three rounds later, the quizmaster announced the current scores with just ten questions to go. As predicted by Angus Grace, the Fishing Flops had a lead of several points over the chasing teams.

"If one of them offers you a bet on the result, take it," whispered Jimmy.

Morris turned to look at his friends, all of whom looked pretty pleased with themselves.

"And now, the final set of questions for the evening," announced the quizmaster. "The ICARUS round."

Cheers and table thumping exploded throughout the room.

Sinead walked from behind the bar with an A4 envelope and handed it ceremoniously to the quizmaster.

The Fishing Flops looked confused, thought Morris, who felt something similar. Simon Pope looked stunned.

Morris turned towards Jimmy and raised an eyebrow. Jimmy just winked and mouthed, "Tell you later."

"Question one," announced the quizmaster, after removing the question sheet. "What did Padraig Monahan put on his marrows six weeks before last month's horticultural show - the reason for his disqualification from the competition?"

"I don't believe this!"

All eyes turned towards Coldfront Davies, who had a nasty feeling that his expected victory was going to elude his grasp at the death. Angus Grace kept pushing his false teeth out with his tongue, then sucking them back in, as if he was desperate to hit somebody, but couldn't find anybody to hit.

"I don't think any of us could," remarked Margaret Doyle, breaking the uneasy tension. "Paddy's marrow may have been the biggest, but it smelt disgusting."

Laughter erupted, followed by a burst of applause as a small man in a tweed suit with a red polo-neck sweater underneath stood up from a table in the centre of the room and took a bow, his face the same colour as his jumper.

"Question two," shouted the quizmaster over the noise, "Why did Mary Kennedy leave her home for three consecutive nights last week?"

Coldfront shook his head, dropped the pen onto the answer sheet and closed his eyes, desperately seeking his happy place. Stuart Morris watched Margaret Doyle write the answer, before turning with a huge grin and winking at the Flops. Dave Westlake didn't notice. He was busy trying to catch Sinead's eye while she went about her business behind the bar, trying not to smirk.

Ten minutes and eight similar questions later, the final set of answer papers made their way to the quizmaster for marking and the queue for the toilets grew. Connor headed to the bar to pick up the drinks already purchased by his minder on his behalf.

"ICARUS?" Morris asked Jimmy Doyle.

"It's a secure page on the town's website," explained Jimmy, so quietly that Morris struggled to hear. "Exclusive to residents. We use it if we see anything unusual in the town. Over time, it's expanded to include gossip, general comments and so on, but it's there for the notifications mainly. Put one on there, click a button and everyone knows straightaway."

"Never heard of that before."

"Not every community needs it," admitted Jimmy, "But we do."

He fell silent, as if he wasn't sure what to say next.

Morris had been in the police long enough to know when to push and when to leave well alone. *It was a bit like fishing*, he mused. *Knowing when to give the line and when to reel in the catch.*

"Does it work?" he settled for. Jimmy nodded.

"Everyone knew about the drama at breakfast five minutes after it occurred," he said. "And we're also aware some of you guys have been in Ireland before; further north."

Try as he might, Morris failed miserably to keep the surprise and then the concern off his face. Jimmy looked amused.

"Don't worry," he said. "You're amongst friends here, but Coldfront needs to stop looking under the table after a local walks past. It's getting annoying. And nobody will put a bomb under your van, so you can park with other vehicles and stop starting it with your doors open. You will not get blown out, or up, for that matter."

Morris still looked slightly perturbed as Connor placed the tray of drinks on the table.

"Are you okay, Stuart?" he asked.

Morris smiled and nodded. "Still trying to get my head around the ICARUS answers," he said.

Connor laughed, but whatever he was going to say stopped as the quizmaster announced the results. To the crowd's delight, Team Landlady pipped Mag's Magicians by a single point to win the quiz, with the Fishing Flops floundering in fifth place.

To Coldfront's credit and to the surprise of his teammates, he swallowed his bitter disappointment and even started the applause for the winners.

It was a small move that imperceptibly changed the attitude of the locals to the group, not just for the evening, but for the rest of their stay.

Morris joined in the applause, but noticed his new friend didn't and was close to tears. He placed his hand on Connor's arm and gave it a squeeze.

"It's okay mate. We did well. Can't win them all."

"You can, Stuart." The answer was matter-of-fact and assertive.

"Well… maybe… but not this time. It was fun though, wasn't it? It was good to spend some time with you, Connor. You're good craic - if that's the right word."

The positive note cheered the younger man up and he clapped along.

"It was fun, Stuart," he said, "And it was good to spend some time with you."

Connor shook hands, then made his way over to congratulate Team Landlady.

Morris turned slightly to pick up his drink and caught the eye of the big fella at the bar, who had been watching the proceedings with interest and now raised his drink in salute. Morris responded in kind, then re-joined his friends.

The Fallen Hero

Jimmy and Margaret Doyle made their excuses and left, but only after Margaret gave Morris and Westlake strict guidance on what was and was not acceptable behaviour on a first date in Ireland.

Orla Brennan was still holding court after her team's win, but kept throwing a glance Stuart Morris's way. He was deep in conversation with the Flops, recounting Jimmy's revelations and discussing whether now was the time to come clean on the group's proper occupations.

"Personally, I don't know what may happen on this trip, but I don't want to start something with a lie," he said; a point that also hit home with Dave Westlake. "Jimmy says we're good here and I believe him. It's not like we're in Belfast or Armagh. Plus, they *know* we have a military background. We don't have to say anything unless we're asked, and I don't think that'll happen. Just don't maintain the warehouse thing... apart from you Simmo, obviously."

"There are a couple of other things to consider," said Angus Grace, who had just returned from having a cigarette outside with the talkative, inebriated butcher. "ICARUS isn't just a name. It means something. Independent Clonbrinny Against Republican Unionist Symbiosis."

"Catchy."

"We all know the Troubles were a great way for gangs on both sides to make a ton of money. Having a pop at each other and us justified the need for funds and the methods of securing them. Here in the south, Clonbrinny decided it wouldn't be part of it. The whole town agreed it would look after its own. Everyone a defender. Everybody a soldier. The entire town a fortress without walls."

"Did it work?"

"No. Not at first. In fact…" Angus Grace looked at Morris and Westlake. "A gang walked in here and tried to shake down Bobby Brennan for a contribution to the cause. He told them to get lost. Nicely. They left, then came back in the early hours."

Morris looked to where Orla sat, glass in hand, laughing at a joke. He felt his heart race as Angus continued.

"Sinead found her dad in the morning. She was just a kid. He must have disturbed them. They hit him and ran. He died from a blow to the head, causing a bleed on the brain."

"The Fallen Hero," mused Coldfront, looking at the picture behind the bar. "Did they come back?"

"Six weeks later. Four showed up on a quiz night. Martin Kelly and a couple of others were looking after things while Orla and Sinead were recovering. Martin asked the gang to come back after closing. The gang decided they'd stay. Most people left early." Grace took a drink from his glass.

"The following morning, the police found a car down in the valley. It had swerved off the road, smashed through a wall and tumbled into the river at the bottom. Three men were dead; one badly injured. The butcher called him the messenger. *Leave us alone*. The town prepared for reprisals. Eventually they came, but not here. The butcher didn't say where."

Stuart Morris thought back to his conversation with Jimmy.

"I know where," he said. "And I know what happened."

He recounted the story of the car bomb by the lough, then glanced towards the big man at the bar.

"He's the Kellys' muscle, but credit where it's due. He saved two lives when he was a kid and he's looked after those two lads ever since."

If there were two attributes this group recognised, they were bravery and loyalty. Pope broke the respectful silence.

"Any idea who designed or who manages the website?"

Morris shook his head.

"Maybe the council? Jimmy might know. Anyway, excuse me, boys. I have to congratulate the winning team captain."

He picked up his drink and wandered over to Orla's table. She smiled as he approached and sat down beside her. The Fishing Flops looked on approvingly. Westlake caught Sinead's eye, cleared his throat, and stood up.

"I'm off as well," he announced. "Don't wait up for me."

Pope muttered, "I don't think we'll need to," to the delight of the remnants of the group.

The Heart To Heart

Declan stood at the front window of his mother's unlit cottage and looked over the dark waters. An imposing black mass silhouetted against a cloudless sky confirmed the looming hills beyond, still and silent witnesses to his vigil.

He could hear his mother's laboured breathing as she slept in the medical bed in the far corner of the lounge. Clodagh had settled down for the night, having declined any food other than one half-round of buttered toast. For a couple of hours, mother and son had talked quietly and openly, holding each other, laughing hysterically and crying bitter tears.

It had been an interesting chat. He smiled to himself. They had both learned a lot, and were relieved that some of their fears were unfounded.

He felt... calmer. More accepting of what was to come. Clear about his future role and responsibilities. It was time to improve things - for himself, his brother and Brendan; to cement his parents' legacy; and to reconcile with Aidan. It was an exciting time, but care would be needed. Great care.

He picked up his mobile and called Brendan.

"Get Connor home, then grab some rest," he said. "It's going to be a tough weekend. And call the priest. Tell him we might need him. Ask him to stay sober."

"Ask?"

"Ask."

He rang off, his eyes drawn to faint beams of torchlight moving down a slope on the far side of the lough, to the left of the cottages.

A car passed by with no headlights showing. It stopped near the torch lights, brake lights flashing for a moment, and the interior illuminated briefly as doors opened and figures climbed in. He slipped his phone into his pocket and moved to his left, peeking from behind a curtain as the car drove along the far road, then headed away from the lough towards Clonbrinny.

Declan watched for two minutes, barely breathing as he waited for a light or movement that would reveal others in the darkness around the house.

Satisfied there was no immediate threat, he crept over to the cupboard and removed the handgun and ammunition from the hidden compartment. *Better safe than sorry.*

Entering the kitchen, he placed the gun on the table, switched on the kettle, and made coffee. It promised to be a long night.

Isaac Delemos

Saturday morning at Peace Castle was anything but peaceful. Fraught, tense and dramatic maybe, but not peaceful.

The knock at Andrew and Mindy's door came as a surprise, especially at six in the morning. What was even more surprising was they were both up, showered and dressed, with their bags already packed.

"I think we'll go tomorrow," Andy had said on their way back from the beach the night before. "We've achieved as much as we're likely to get. We'll talk to them over breakfast. Leave as quickly as we can."

Mindy had said nothing in response; just squeezed his hand. Both had struggled to sleep, and the alarm had come as a welcome relief.

Andy set down his coffee cup on the table by the picture window, walked to the door, and looked through the spyhole. Isaac Delemos stood outside, anxiously shifting from foot to foot and looking from side to side.

The owner of the largest manufacturing business in the world jumped slightly as the door opened and quickly put a finger to his lips.

Blackwell swallowed the booming welcome he was about to utter and ushered his visitor inside.

Delemos needed no second invitation.

He rushed into the room, switched on the television, the radio and the coffeemaker, then beckoned them into the bathroom, where he turned on the shower and sat down on the toilet seat.

Mindy perched on the side of the bath while Andy closed the door behind him and leaned against it, arms folded.

"Quite an entrance, Isaac," he observed quietly. "You couldn't sleep either?"

Delemos smiled and shook his head, the strain disappearing from his face for a second before returning.

"The main room's bugged. This room isn't."

"How do you know?"

"Irrelevant. I wanted to apologise for yesterday. Embarrassing and nothing to do with me. I objected to the way they treated you, but Aston... well, you know Aston..."

"I'm getting to know him," Blackwell grimaced. "Don't apologise Isaac. We knew we were entering the lions' den when we accepted the invitation."

"You're not upset? Angry?"

"The Conclave is looking at a path it wasn't on before. It aligns more closely to mine. It shows I may be on the right track."

"He wants to steal your idea; take ownership of the way forward."

"I don't have copyright on viewing openness and honesty as the way forward; on acknowledging our own weaknesses and recognising the need to address them. And I don't see him as competition. I'm not in a race."

Delemos ran his hand through his dark hair, processing what he was hearing.

"I've fought and battled my whole life to get where I am today," he mused. "All's fair in love and war, right? But this... this isn't right. This is bigger than money and power and ego."

Mindy leaned forward and put a reassuring hand on the manufacturing giant's knee.

"Isaac. Andy's right. It'll be what it'll be. Even if Aston gives people a nudge down the path before he tires of it and moves onto something else, then good luck to him."

"*Path Finder* gives you credibility…"

Blackwell smiled. "Well, I could certainly do with some."

"Everything *they* do will increase interest in what *you* have to say. People will look to see how you judge the Conclave's actions before making up their own mind."

Blackwell shrugged. "Maybe. I guess time will tell."

Delemos sat upright and stared at Blackwell, as if seeing him for the first time.

"They're dreaming up a brand, but you are the brand."

"But I won't look as good on a T-shirt or a coffee mug."

Delemos wondered what the man before him actually was and what he wanted, before realising Blackwell was probably struggling with the same questions.

Action time.

He stood up, removed an envelope from his back pocket, and gave it to Blackwell.

"I have business elsewhere, so I'm leaving this morning," he announced. "When you're ready, let's talk some more. My direct number is in there, along with a number, username and password for a bank account in Switzerland. The money in that account is untraceable. Use it as you wish."

Blackwell held the envelope in both hands and turned it around, as if he had never seen an envelope before.

"I know money isn't everything," Delemos continued, "So my entire operation stands ready to help as well. Moving manufacturing bases; increasing wages; changing production methods; developing new products - whatever it takes. If there's anything we can do to move *Path Finder* forward, then we'll play our part."

Blackwell shook the proffered hand.

"Thank you Isaac. We'll speak soon."

Delemos smiled and shook Mindy's hand.

"Just one more thing," she said. "Where's the bug?"

Having turned off the shower and flushed the toilet for good measure, the three of them emerged from the bathroom. Delemos stopped briefly to observe the two packed cases on the readymade bed and noted the lack of early morning chaos in the room. His eyes scanned the walls, then he walked over and pointed silently at an innocuous thermostat before winking at them both and heading out of the door. As it closed behind him, Mindy examined the Delemos Industries-branded thermostat.

A tiny, hyper-sensitive microphone nestled in its circuitry, Isaac had explained. Tones of human speech activated it, and it could capture voices anywhere in the room. Recordings filtered out the hum of air conditioning, the sounds of the ocean outside and even voices on television or radio, before being converted into data packets, which were slipped through the meter's network to a monitoring station.

Delemos and Hail dreamt up the design after a Conclave dinner and installed the prototype system in the castle mansion with the permission of the owners.

"It works very well," Isaac had boasted quietly. "Intelligence services love it."

"Ready for breakfast?" asked Blackwell.

Mindy wasn't sure what to say. Now she knew every word was being listened to elsewhere. She felt there was added weight to every utterance she made.

"Yes," she replied, confident she had revealed nothing to any listener, besides the state of her appetite.

The First Date

Stuart Morris woke to the faint mosquito-like whine of a small motorcycle, which grew into a loud, irritated moan as it traversed the road outside the pub before fading into the distance.

So far, so normal, he thought, a second before opening his eyes and realising that normality had ended.

Flinging off the crocheted blanket, he lifted himself into a sitting position on the settee in the living room, where he had spent the night, and set about getting his bearings.

"Good morning, handsome. Thought you could do with a coffee."

He turned to see Orla stood at the doorway, already showered and wearing a bright smile, jeans and a checked shirt, holding a mug in each hand.

She really is a good-looking woman, he thought. *But looks can't hide the sadness and the worry.*

Memories of the night before came flooding back. All of them good.

They had stayed up to the early hours, drinking tea of all things, and sharing their lives.

He must have fallen asleep, but he'd heard enough before then to know she was a fighter, a worrier, and had a wicked sense of humour.

"Good morning, gorgeous," he smiled as she walked over, set the drinks on the coffee table and gave him a kiss on the cheek. "Please don't tell me I nodded off when you were telling me something."

She laughed. Her eyes sparkled mischievously.

"You're grand. I took the cups out and you were asleep when I came back in."

She took a sip of her coffee and gazed at him over the rim of the mug.

"I could've kicked you out, but figured you'd be useful to me this morning, if you've nothing else on."

Morris resisted the urge to explain how he could be very useful to her if he had nothing on.

"I guess I told you this break is all about me," he said.

She nodded.

"Then I guess I can do what I like."

She smiled.

"Thank you Stuart," she said. "I think we'll have some fun."

"Oh, I'm sure we will," he grinned. "What's on the agenda?"

"Preparing and delivering food parcels."

The grin didn't drop one millimetre.

"I'll see if I can round up a couple more volunteers," he said.

The Fallout

Breakfast at the mansion could be summed up in one word. Awkward.

The one large table was now three smaller tables, each of which could seat four diners. A buffet bar laden with drinks, fruit, pastries and cereals stood at one end of the room, supervised by a waiter who would load the guest's plate if that felt like too much trouble for them. A chef stood nearby, ready to take the hot food orders and create dishes from scratch.

Andy and Mindy were the first in and ten minutes into their meal when media mogul Evie Marsh wandered in and sat down at their table without so much as a by-your-leave.

Nobody mentioned the day before. Conversation centred on the present UK political crisis and the trials and tribulations of the current prime minister. Conscious of the political leanings of the key publications, broadcasting channels and websites in the Marsh Media Group, the UK's former prime minister and his former deputy chief of staff remained noncommittal when asked for their opinions on the matter. Frustrated with the lack of response, Evie switched to a broader range of events, but found her companions equally unforthcoming when asked about sex scandals, ballroom dancing and the future of applied intelligence.

The one-sided conversation stalled when Evie's hot course arrived and had to be sent back to be cut up for her, then was further delayed when the four remaining members of the Conclave arrived *en masse* and settled themselves down at the furthest table from the group without so much as a greeting.

"No Isaac this morning?" asked Mindy, hoping to thaw the frosty silence.

"He's flying to Spain." Tee Takahashi didn't even look up from her menu as she spoke. "He won't be back."

The room fell silent once more. Even the waiter and chef shifted uncomfortably from side to side until Aston Hail dismissed them.

Watching them leave the room, Blackwell knew one thing: that wouldn't happen to him.

"Aston," he said, "Our work here is done. Thanks for the invitation. It's been fun. Can you arrange a flight back to the UK for us sometime today?"

Hail pushed his plate back and stared at the space it had occupied.

"You asking me if you can go, Andy?"

"No. I'm telling you we are going. I'd like you to arrange the travel."

Mindy watched as Evie's complexion paled. Across at the other table, everyone became very interested in their plates. Nobody looked up. Nobody looked at Aston, whose tanned good looks - Mindy noted - were turning a disconcerting puce.

Eventually Hail found the words.

"I'm sorry Andy. I'm afraid I can't do that."

Whatever the response every other person expected from Blackwell, it wasn't the one they got.

"What's the problem?" he smirked.

"I think you know the problem just as well as I do." Now Aston was smiling at the references to his favourite film.

"You're a control freak, are used to getting your own way and didn't decide for us to go, so you're being petulant?" asked Andy.

Aston stopped grinning. His bottom lip trembled slightly. "That wasn't in *Odyssey*," he said. "Isaac has the plane."

The silence was deafening. Even the unobtrusive mood music seeping out of the speaker system held its breath.

"Aaah," said Blackwell. "That was going to be my second guess."

This Is How It Ends

The position of the cottages meant that morning sunlight streaming through the windows was a rarity, reserved for the middle of summer. The shadows of the hills made guessing the time difficult, especially after a fitful night's sleep.

Declan raised his head from his crossed arms resting on the kitchen table and sat up slowly. His back ached. It would be a while before normal movement resumed.

He stretched gingerly, winced as a couple of vertebrae clicked into place, then checked his watch. Eight o'clock. Later than he'd expected. The birds outside were in full voice, the boiler in the corner hummed contentedly and the clock on the wall faithfully recorded the passage of time, as it had done for decades.

Today, or maybe tomorrow, this place would never feel the same again, he thought. In fact…

He stood and crept to the hallway, holding his breath and hoping he could hear his mother. There it was, a steady, rhythmic breath, although it sounded different from yesterday, as if she'd contracted a heavy cold overnight.

He peeked into the lounge and watched her sleep for a while. She looked comfortable, lying as he'd left her in a half-raised position on four pillows, well tucked into a soft, warm duvet.

He made himself some breakfast, checked his messages and emails, then returned to her side with a warm coffee and a small tumbler of whiskey. *She was still well away, bless her.* Her open mouth amplifying the wet… crackle… in her throat.

"Mammy?" he murmured. "Mammy, it's breakfast time. I've brought you a coffee and something stronger."

Clodagh opened her eyes, but they didn't seem to focus and the breathing remained the same.

Declan set the drinks on the table and sat next to her, reaching under the duvet to hold her hand and barely stopping himself from flinching when he felt how cold she was.

No! This can't be right!

He rubbed her hand in both of his and moved so he was facing her directly, staring into her blank eyes, willing her to show a gram of recognition.

"Mammy?" he repeated. "It's Declan. I've brought you some breakfast."

Again, not a glimmer, but a movement of her mouth, as if she was trying to speak. Declan leaned closer, fighting back tears. Here he was, supposedly one of the most powerful men in the country, completely powerless. Then, a faint whisper, followed by a rasping cough as the effort disturbed her breathing. Declan jolted back, but kept tight hold of her hand, desperate to put some warmth back into his mother's frail body.

"This," she had whispered. "This is how it ends."

A memory smashed into his mind. The night of his father's death. He'd seen his mother stroking his father's head; whispering those same words as the man took his last few breaths. *This is how it ends.* After last night, he now understood. The sacrifice she'd made to protect her family, even if it meant the death of the man she loved. *This is how it ends.*

He leaned forward once more, kissed her head and then stroked her hair, forcing himself to focus on the coming hours and what needed to happen next.

Ten minutes later, Clodagh had settled down again, the death rattle sounding even more pronounced now he understood what it was.

He took the drinks back into the kitchen, then called the man he trusted more than anyone else.

"It's time," he said. "Get Connor, but go to the office first. He knows what to do and what he needs to bring. Pick up the priest on your way here."

Brendan Dunne ended the call without a word.

Declan understood. It was vital to appear strong at a time you were at your weakest. This morning, he, his brother and his best friend were very vulnerable indeed, as were the people of Clonbrinny - although they didn't know it yet.

The Media Wake Up

Pope woke to the same motorcycle alarm call as Morris and surveyed the other beds in the room. Dave Westlake was snoring under his duvet, but Stu's bed was unoccupied. Maybe this trip would work out after all.

He grabbed his smartphone and sent Pippa a *Good morning!* message to prove he wasn't too hungover, and received one back straightaway.

Seen the news?

He tapped his news app and groaned.

Fears Grow For Former Prime Minister
Andrew Blackwell And Fiancée Reported Missing
Abducted Or Eloped? Vanishing PM Does It Again!

There were photographs or artist's impressions of Andy, Mindy, Andy and Mindy in several disguises, Andy's house, Andy's house with a police officer outside and Andy's house with an alien sat on the front wall.

There were demands for a House of Commons emergency statement; a denial from the current prime minister's office that the former PM was returning; and prayers from several groups of widely differing persuasions for the safe return of one of the missing, but not the other.

You vanish just the once, Pope thought, *and it sticks with you forever.*

He replied with a shrugging shoulders emoji and a couple of kisses. Blackwell had a job to do, and so did he.

Now that Stuart was venturing down a fresh path and, hopefully, cheering up, he could focus on appearing vaguely competent at intelligence gathering. The question was, how?

He lay down and stared at the ceiling, reviewing the known knowns and the known unknowns but not going any further down that wormhole.

One hour later, having fallen asleep again and then waking when a smiling Morris walked in for a shower and a change of clothes, he discovered his brain had used the nap to formulate a plan for the day. And it wasn't half bad, although whether it would survive the day was a different question entirely.

Abandoned

The beach at the foot of Peace Castle really was stunning, thought Mindy, but visiting three times in under 24 hours was a bit much.

At least today the tide was out and they could walk along the sandy shoreline rather than stumbling over the pebbles and rocks, closer to the cliff face.

They had said little since breakfast time.

She was busy playing out what might happen from here and working out how to best minimise the potential fallout. Not sure what to say, he said nothing. For the moment, at least.

Once Aston had stopped his histrionics and the rest of the Enclave had ceased flashing evil stares at them both, there wasn't much to do except make themselves scarce.

Andy helped himself to pastries and a large coffee while the drama played out at the other table. He'd even asked if others wanted something, but there'd been no response. On his return, he'd dropped some serviettes onto their table, to help with the eye drying.

Mindy had spent the time checking commercial flights from the country's major airports, although both knew that flying would be a non-starter, revealing as it would their presence in the country.

Once he'd pulled himself together and stopped acting like a spoilt child, Hail had said he would see what he could do, but might need a couple of hours.

"You'll find us on the beach," Andy had said. "We've already packed."

Neither he nor Mindy knew how things would develop, but nobody seemed in the mood for fond farewells, so they had strolled out of the room and just kept walking.

The sound of a crashing wave brought Mindy back to the present.

The sun threatened to break out from behind a surly cloud front, but the clouds resisted strongly. Despite the sea breeze, the temperature was warm enough not to require a coat, but cool enough to regret not bringing one.

Andy had meandered slightly ahead, lost in his own thoughts. Mindy watched as an errant wave covered the footprints between them, then retreated, taking with it any proof he had actually been there.

That's what we need, she thought. *A way to remove any proof we've been here.* Not that she thought it was possible. The recordings of their presence at the venue, she was sure, could present them in a poor light. The guarantee of their visit remaining secret was effectively worthless.

Even if Evie Marsh could resist providing her own media empire with a worldwide exclusive of the visit, the existence of proof would remain a threat to Andy's credibility and could gag his response to the Enclave's future activities.

"I'm sorry, Mindy. Not one of my best moments."

Blackwell had stopped and was gazing out to sea with his hands in his pockets, although she knew he wasn't taking in the view. She caught up with him and linked her arm through his.

"We've been through worse," she said.

"I'm not sure we have. This feels more important."

Mindy watched a single shaft of sunlight burst through the grey sky and settle on the water, dancing over the ocean swells a mile or so off-shore and proving to the other sun rays that it could be done.

"Answer me this," she said. "Does having six of the world's most powerful people buying into your *Path Finder* philosophy validate your ideas?"

"Yes."

"But only if the public knows that you've talked with them."

"Fair point, but soon it'll be pretty obvious that I'm not involved in their plans."

"So? As the creator of a concept that encourages people to consider their own paths not yet taken, how would your lack of involvement damage your credibility?"

Blackwell looked out to sea, but Mindy saw a glimmer in his eyes.

"You're wasted on me, you know," he said, wrapping her in his arms and kissing her forehead.

"That's funny," she smirked. "That's what Evie told me this morning, and Aston and Alexander mentioned to me separately yesterday."

Before he could respond, the unnatural rumble of jet engines disturbed the natural sounds around them. Both turned as the noise increased and, over the next few minutes, watched three planes emerge above the trees on the clifftop and roar off in different directions into the clouds.

Plans For The Day

The day unravelled unreasonably early in Pope's head. The first down for breakfast, he wondered if he was actually awake when Stuart Morris took his order, wearing a shamrock-patterned apron around his midriff.

"I'm giving Orla a hand, while Sinead is having a bit of a lie-in," Morris explained. "Once we've finished in here, we're preparing food parcels and taking them out to people who need them. It happens every weekend. We could do with some help, if you're at a loose end."

Pope declined, grateful his brain had done the heavy lifting while he was unconscious.

"I need some exercise after yesterday's debacle, Stu, so I'm doing the walk that Dave did. Might chat with that priest if he's around. Could do me some good."

Morris nodded, knowing all about Pope's army experience. "Qualified counsellors and psychologists did nothing for you, mate. Only a miracle can save you. Worth a try."

Pope swallowed and nodded. He hadn't really considered using the traumatic events of Afghanistan as part of today's subterfuge, but Stu had a point. The nightmares persisted; easier to cope with, but still there. If ICARUS was as good as the RSM feared, the priest probably knew about him already - which reminded him…

"Stu. If you get the chance, could you find out more about the website? That ICARUS stuff Angus mentioned sounds intriguing…"

Morris was trying to spell 'sausage' on his order pad and nodded vaguely.

"Website. ICARUS. I'll see what I can do."

And with that, he was off. More tables to visit; guests to serve; old people to feed and a landlady to woo. Pope watched him set about his work with something approaching envy, then headed to the cold buffet for some orange juice and cereal. He didn't know that he'd look back at this quiet moment with fondness by the day's end.

Mr Widdock

Emerging from the woods, Mindy stopped for a moment to take in Caisleán Síocháin for the last time. The grand edifice still oozed history and tradition, but had, she felt, lost some of its allure.

An older, smartly dressed man, leaning against the side of an executive van and talking animatedly into his phone, was the only sign of life. He turned as he heard their footsteps on the courtyard gravel and finished his call quickly.

"Mr and Mrs Smith?" he mumbled quickly, appearing to take a breath after every other word. "My name's Widdock. I am to take you wherever you want to go. Within reason."

Blackwell halted and looked concerned.

"Is everything alright, Widdock?" he asked. "Are you ill?"

"No, sir. I'm from Limerick."

"Ah," Mindy interrupted, as if that explained everything and before Andy asked their driver to recite poems in the style associated with the city. "Quick questions. Who arranged this? When was this organised? And how far is within reason?"

Their chauffeur appeared ready to speak, but changed his mind. He pointed his right forefinger towards the sky for a moment, then reached into his jacket pocket and withdrew an envelope.

"Hopefully this will explain," he said. He handed the envelope to Mindy, then turned and walked into the lobby. "I'll get your bags."

The typed letter was from Aston, apologising for the suddenness of the Conclave's departure but offering no explanation. He regretted the lack of private transport, but had engaged Widdock to take them wherever they wanted to go. He assured them of the driver's discretion.

Widdock had done many tasks for the Conclave but had stopped talking about them because whenever he tried to, nobody had ever believed him.

The Conclave thanked them for their time and hoped that its future actions would prove that their visit had been worthwhile.

Finally, Hail reminded them they had to keep the details of the last couple of days confidential.

"How do we manage that, traipsing anonymously across two countries?" Mindy asked nobody in particular.

Widdock emerged with the two bags and stowed them in the back of the van, then looked at them both expectantly.

"I have an idea," said Blackwell, looking uncertain that it was a good one. "But first, Mr Widdock will do a bit of shopping, then I need to make a phone call."

Good Craic

Pope left Westlake, Coldfront and Angus Grace working out over breakfast how they could evade a morning of food deliveries. He gratefully accepted a flask of coffee and some foil-wrapped sandwiches from a radiant Orla Brennan, whose eyes told him she knew more about him this morning than she had done last night.

He set off down the high street, along the terraced houses on the right and past the same couple, talking to the butcher yet again, just outside his shop on the left. Unlike yesterday, their greeting felt more genuine, although just as harsh.

"Off for a nap at St Patrick's?" grinned the butcher. The couple smiled and Pope laughed.

"I'm never going to live yesterday down, am I?"

"You're good craic, my friend. I'll give you that."

"Not sure I can better that today."

The old woman cackled. "Oh, but I think you'll give it a go."

"Oh, I hope not," smiled Pope. He gave them a wave and marched on, hoping his ears weren't burning too much and that their conversation had already moved on to other things. The three watched him go.

"Have you seen ICARUS this morning?" murmured the butcher. The couple nodded.

"He's the church fella from the army that Orla was on about. Saved them lives."

They looked on as the unsuspecting Pope headed away from them.

"Truly a miracle," said the woman. "I wouldn't bet on him being able to hold a gun, never mind shoot in the right direction."

Her husband nodded sagely.

"Truly a fecking miracle," he agreed.

New Neighbours

The house felt very empty, Pippa thought, despite the two greyhounds who rarely ventured more than six feet from her with Simon away. The former army medic settled on the sofa with a coffee and her laptop, Fred and Ginger lying at her feet and waiting patiently for a biscuit. Her position in the lounge wasn't the most comfortable, but she could keep watch for any visitors to the empty house next door.

Three years of privacy would end soon. A 'Sold' sign had recently replaced the intermittent 'For Sale' sign at the bottom of next door's garden. Pope never allowed the latter to remain standing for long before concealing it at the bottom of the hedgerow, always blaming local youths when the estate agent arrived to restore it.

This time, the new sign had only been up for three days and tradespeople had been working hard on the house and its garden ever since… ironically, ever since Pope had left for Ireland. Knowing the nerves Pope felt even before setting off on his mission, Pippa couldn't bring herself to give him news of the development - even in text form. Instead, she gathered as much information as she could from the trades and by peeking through the windows when all was quiet.

When she finally let Simmo know, she'd be prepared for the barrage of questions that would follow.

Despite the arrival of the weekend, two vans already stood outside the property.

Neither were local firms. In fact, none of the vans had any promotional graphics anywhere on their bodywork; not even a business name or a phone number.

Her anonymous enquiry, from a 'prospective buyer' to the estate agent, had revealed nothing; certainly no hint of the new owner's identity.

There was no sense it worrying about it, she reasoned. The other residents in the row of houses never socialised and rarely bumped into each other. The newcomers could well be the same.

She handed half a biscuit to each dog, sipped her coffee and then set to work revising the service budgets for the charity she helped to run, just as a chainsaw fired up in the neighbouring back garden.

With admirable self-control, she resisted the urge to take Pope's gun from the bedroom and 'pop a cap' into the machine or its handler.

Instead, she picked up the ear defenders she had retrieved from the garage the day before and popped them on her head, muffling the noise and reducing her desire to shoot something. Simmo would be back soon enough. If the trades were still there, he could shoot them himself.

On the sofa, her mobile phone lit up and rang, but the ear defenders were too good and she was focusing on how to spend the recent £50,000 donation, which had now cleared into the charity's account.

A few seconds later, the ringing stopped and a voicemail notification appeared before fading as the screen dimmed.

Sat in a rear seat of the executive van, his identity protected from the busy shoppers at the Limerick retail park by the vehicle's tinted windows, Blackwell stared at his phone and willed Pippa to return his call.

"It won't work," said Mindy without looking up from her own smartphone. "Staring at it never works."

"I could call Simmo."

Mindy hesitated.

"You could, but we don't know what he's up to," she said. "It could be dangerous for him. Maybe for us. It'll certainly be a shock."

Blackwell peered out of the window and spotted their chauffeur emerging from an outdoor pursuits store with three large bags.

"Widdock's on his way back," he reported, a hint of alarm in his voice. "What do we do?"

A Grave Problem

Finding the church closed raised mixed emotions in Pope; regret that he couldn't talk to the priest, combined with relief that he couldn't talk to the priest.

Father Aidan's address was on the door sign, in case of emergencies. Pope memorised it, but decided a home visit would raise suspicions. He'd try his luck again on the return from his walk.

He pulled Westlake's sketch map from his back pocket and went over the directions once more, then set off towards the lough.

Today was warmer and drier than yesterday, but the forecast suggested that could change later on.

Wanting to see the ruined church and to avoid the predicted rain, he picked up the pace and soon found himself with a view down the road towards a serene and shimmering body of water. He perched himself on a dry stone wall close by and took out his smartphone to photograph the scene.

A light breeze did little to distort the green and grey reflections of the undulating hills surrounding the lake and the clouds above it. The wind murmured, distant lapwings called and the grazing sheep bleated on slopes. Otherwise, quiet reigned.

Perfect, he thought, and took a couple of shots.

A thin white rippling band towards the far edge of the water caught his attention. He looked up from his screen towards the row of white cottages on the far bank.

Imagine living there with this timeless view on your doorstep. A quiet sanctuary, where the only measures of time were the drifting clouds and the sunlight dancing across the hills. He sat, entranced by the surrounding peace, then shook himself out of his reverie and looked around for any sign of the ruined church.

There it was. Behind the crest of the hill to his right, Pope could make out the remains of a dark tower or steeple. Spotting a hint of a footpath a few yards in front of him, he stepped onto it and made his way up the slope. On the crest of the hill, he stopped to catch his breath and turned to get a better view of the lough. After taking several photographs, he moved to the other side of the summit and looked for the old farm track Westlake had stumbled across a couple of hundred feet from the top. Once on the track, he headed downwards and found a narrow, pitiful lane, which led him to the derelict church.

Pope stopped at its boundary wall, took a breath and absorbed the age and the... the sadness... of the scene. There was a quietness here, but no peace. There was a restlessness. Unhappiness. Unfinished business. Dave had been right. This was not a soulless place; quite the opposite.

He located the famine memorial and entered the graveyard, reaching the mass grave. Then, he did something he hadn't done for a long time. He knelt down and prayed. He prayed for the dead and for those who laid them to rest before they left permanently. And then he sat awhile. He may have sat there a lot longer if the noise of a vehicle struggling up the track hadn't disturbed his thoughts.

Pope leapt to his feet and ran to the far corner of the graveyard, furthest away from the church.

He dived behind a couple of larger, angled gravestones, and peered between them just in time to see a car stop by the ruins.

Two figures in camouflage gear emerged, surveyed their surroundings, then moved towards the vehicle's rear. *The woman looked familiar*, thought Pope, but he couldn't place her. The couple struggled to remove two large bags, and carried them into the ruin.

Pope settled with his back to one gravestone and waited. He wasn't doing anything wrong, but he had no idea what was going on and had no intention of finding out. At least, not until the recent arrivals had gone. He felt his phone vibrate in his pocket, took it out, and read the message.

Andy in Ireland and in trouble, it read. *Needs help.*

Pope threw his head back in frustration, clunking it against the hard stone as he did so and immediately regretting his action. Why was it that every time the former prime minister disappeared, he reappeared in front of Pope? At least this time, he was giving notice and asking permission. Not turning up in a locked garage. And he had Mindy with him. Pope knew he owed Mindy big time.

A flurry of brief messages with Pippa gave him a rough idea of what had happened on the west coast. He sighed. No doubt he'd find out more that evening.

He sent one last message, neglecting to mention he was hiding in the graveyard of a ruined church on a remote hillside, waiting for strangers to leave.

No sense in alarming his fiancée. Especially as he had yet to propose. That event could provide plenty of alarm by itself.

He rubbed the back of his head and felt something wet on his fingers. He knew what it was before he brought his hand back into view. Blood. *Great.* He rummaged in his rucksack, found a small first aid pack jammed into a side pocket and dabbed an antiseptic wipe on the injured area.

Unable to see the wound, he placed a gauze pad where his head was most sore, and applied pressure with his hand. Realising he could use the gravestone to hold the dressing in place, he leaned his head against it once more.

His hiding place was the highest point of the church grounds on the hillside. The weather and local wildlife had damaged the boundary wall over time, leaving gaps where he could see the sun's rays breaking through the clouds and reflecting off the lough. Once the strangers had gone, he'd be able to have a proper look. The view promised to be spectacular.

He didn't have too long to wait, although that hadn't stopped him from falling asleep in the meantime. The sound of doors closing and an engine starting woke him up, but by the time he'd worked out who he was, where he was and why his head was banging so much, the vehicle had gone.

He peered between the stones and waited for ten minutes in case the car's occupants had forgotten something, then stood, stretched and picked up his stuff, including the bloodied gauze, which he had to peel off his hair.

He walked to the boundary wall and photographed the scene below him, then turned and headed through the cemetery, taking more pictures as he did so.

Rather than exploring the dilapidated building, he walked around it. The remains of the walls and the roof could collapse at any moment, and Pope had no desire to add his own corpse to those resting around him.

He navigated his way along the side of the church between wild undergrowth, overgrown mounds and angled graves, back to the lower boundary wall and the least-interrupted views of the lough. Below, to his left, the road he had walked from Clonbrinny reached the lough and split around it.

On his right-hand side were the terraced cottages, with one car parked by the end cottage.

A buzzard drifted into view from the right, soaring on the air currents warmed by the sun and encouraged on its way by a couple of crows, eager to defend their young. The entire scene nestled in the surrounding landscape of protective hills and woodlands.

"Stunning," he said to himself.

"I couldn't agree more," replied the calm female voice behind him.

Shocked, Pope jumped and swung around, his eyes focusing with alarm on the gun barrel pointed at him. He held up his hands, then relaxed when he saw the person holding the weapon.

"Hello Simon," said Kara Walsh.

"Hello," replied Pope, his brain working overtime to process events and decide on a course of action.

Kara was still holding the gun, so running away, leaping over the wall and tumbling down the slope didn't seem a viable option. Neither did overpowering her, even though the safety catch was still in place on the gun.

"You… er… still have the safety catch on," he offered, before mentally kicking himself so hard, his rear end hurt. *Change the subject. Fast. And play dumb. That should not be difficult.* "Have we met?"

Kara's eyes moved from examining the safety catch and focused on the confused, bloodied face in front of her. Her arms fell to her side, but she still gripped the gun in her right hand.

"Yesterday lunchtime. In the Hero. You had an annoying leg twitch. Are you okay? There's blood…"

Pope felt the back of his head and then examined his bloodied hand.

"Banged my head," he explained. "I fell and hit a gravestone." He looked down for a couple of seconds, then looked up. "You're Kara, right? You were writing a report…"

"An update." She placed the gun by a laptop on the small camping table, then pulled the chair out and set it in front of her. "Sit here."

Pope swayed over, sat down and proffered his rucksack. "I have a small first aid kit," he said. His captor - if that's what she was - retrieved it from the top of the bag.

"Might need stitches, but I'll see what I can do," she said. "Meantime, tell me how you stumbled into a police surveillance operation hidden in a deserted ruin on a remote Irish hillside."

"That's easy," said Pope, his brain having regained control of his senses. "I have no idea."

Hide And Seek

The road trip from Limerick to Dublin takes just over two hours, but the first half-hour can seem much longer if the vehicle's driver fumes in silence for every one of those thirty minutes.

Anticipating a quick dash to Limerick airport, the chauffeur-cum-undertaker-cum-estate-agent had agreed to the Conclave job despite a full and lucrative itinerary for the day, but the long haul to Dublin airport had put paid to that.

Widdock's reorganisation of tasks entailed calling in favours and negotiating financial transactions.

It delayed departure from the retail park by twenty minutes.

Mindy had spent the time researching plane flights, ferry crossings and car hire options, factoring in the associated risks of public recognition and media exposure.

When Andy returned from purchasing food and drink for the three of them, having successfully used his new beanie hat and quilted outdoor jacket to disguise his appearance, she passed over her phone with the web browser opened on a news page.

"Great," was his only comment on the media speculation regarding their disappearance from London. "What's the plan?"

"A plane is out. The arrivals area will be full of press when we get back. They'll know where we've been. I suggest we board as foot passengers on a ferry - maybe the hydrofoil - then hire a car at the other end. By the time the media knows, we'll be well away. No need to head straight back home. We could stay with Pippa for a couple of days."

"If we can get hold of her…"

The conversation stopped as Widdock climbed in and drove out of the car park without a word.

Blackwell ploughed through more news sites to pass the time.

Mindy stared out of the window, reflecting on the past 48 hours and wondering where and how this day would end.

Mercifully, a ping from Blackwell's phone broke the awkward silence. He read the message from Pippa, then showed it to his fiancée, who dialled the number provided.

Two minutes later, the frosty atmosphere in the van thawed after the chauffeur's round trip reduced in time and distance, and the UK's most-wanted couple had somewhere to stay for the night, plus a potential lift home.

Reluctant Recruits

The brains trust back at the hotel had failed to agree on a strategy to avoid the food parcels project.

Westlake concluded that getting involved would give him more time with Sinead, and would enhance relations both with her and her mother.

Coldfront and Grace couldn't argue with Stuart Morris's assertion that they were there to support him in his time of need. Besides which, they had all felt part of the community the night before and - hardened uniformed personnel that they were, or had been - wanted that to continue.

Fortunately for the good townsfolk of Clonbrinny, the guests handled packing, logistics and cleaning up. They were kept well away from food preparation.

Morris was impressed with the quality and the amount of the food involved. Each recipient would end up with a week's worth of meals plus a boxful of other useful bits and pieces.

"This must cost an arm and a leg," he observed. "How can you afford it, Orla?"

"Donations," was the simple reply, as his new friend reviewed the product list. "We use the money to buy locally when we can, then a few of us handle the prep and delivery."

"People can be very generous."

The landlady smiled and nodded, then checked on the stockpot of chicken curry.

Manoeuvring a loaded two-wheeled dolly out of the busy kitchen, Westlake halted for a moment to watch his best friend gaze after the possible new love in his life. Morris turned, looking thoughtful, then realised he was under observation and winked at his former colleague.

Westlake mouthed 'You okay?' and received a nod in reply, before Morris walked around the table and straightened two plastic tote boxes on the dolly while whispering.

"You know how we spent years recognising when somebody was hiding something?"

"Yeah?"

Morris raised his eyebrows, then patted the top box before talking slightly louder.

"You were losing one there, mate. Have fun." Then he walked back to his workstation.

Westlake pushed the supplies along the path to the back of the van, where Coldfront and Grace were loading up.

"This is the last lot," he announced. "Once it's on, we go."

Half an hour later, the hotel's own small van was in the same parking space, fully loaded, with Morris in the passenger seat. The aromas of Asia seeped through from the back, causing the former sergeant's stomach to rumble. Sat behind the steering wheel, Orla laughed at the sound.

"Patience, Stuart. We'll be back soon enough and there's plenty left."

"Have you seen my friends eat?"

"We'll be back before them. Don't worry yourself."

Morris looked down at the delivery sheet on his lap.

"You know our third call is Jimmy and Margaret?"

"Which is why your boys have twice as many stops as us!" She put her hand on his leg and gave it a squeeze. "Stop worrying. I'll look after you."

In that moment, Stuart Morris knew they'd look after each other, eventually. After he'd discovered what or who Orla was protecting. And why.

Sinead watched the van pull away, wondering if this would be the spark to ignite her future, or whether it was just another damp squib. Either way, there was excitement in her life, and she was determined to enjoy it while it lasted. The remaining volunteers were washing up and cleaning the work surfaces, so she took their coffee orders and then set about making the drinks.

Two hours until opening time, she thought. *Maybe three before Dave and the lads are back.*

Dave and the lads wondered if they'd return to the Hero ever again, never mind in time for lunch.

"We've been out forty minutes and managed two deliveries," grumbled David 'Coldfront' Davies, racing along a thin tarmac strip wedged between open fields.

"And listened to two life stories," said Angus Grace, still wondering if the old, infirm couple at the last house did actually subsidise their pension by appearing in porn movies.

"And repaired one leaking tap, fixed a gate, weeded a footpath and cleaned several windows," added Dave Westlake.

"You forgot the toilet."

"I didn't forget the toilet," Westlake shuddered. "I'll never forget the toilet."

The Shiny Man

Pope had to admit, the camouflaged tent blended in really well with the backdrop of the church's crumbling walls. From the cottages and road around the lough, it would be invisible. The technology inside was impressive.

In the corner, a high-gain directional antenna, mounted on a tripod, pointed at the far left cottage. Tuned to a specific frequency, it received radio and wi-fi signals broadcast from the property.

Through a secure link, a data processing unit received, filtered and decrypted transmissions in real time. Two tripods alongside held a video camera and a digital camera with a long telephoto lens.

"The system picks up recorded and live audio and streams it directly to the high-resolution speaker on the table, or to these headphones," explained Kara. "We convert the signals into text and relay it by satellite to our base just over the hill. We download and store all the data, then analyse it for keywords or patterns of interest."

"Just over the hill?"

"A temporary base for a detachment of the Army Rangers. You don't think I'm here by myself, do you?"

Pope absorbed the revelation that Ireland's special counterterrorism service was a mere stone's throw away.

His secret mission was truly up the creek without a paddle, and would definitely remain secret. He surveyed the kit in front of him, thinking of a similar setup he'd seen in Afghanistan.

"Sounds serious," he observed.

Kara nodded towards the row of cottages below them. "There are people of interest to us who have a strong link to that house. We believe they are involved in serious criminal activities, here and overseas."

Pope looked down at the cottage through a spy hole in the canvas. It was a small building anyway, but looked tiny from his vantage point, dwarfed by the water to its front and the surrounding hills.

"It doesn't look like the stronghold of a criminal mastermind," he said.

Kara hesitated a moment, then handed over a slim folder from the table. Opening it, Pope came scarred face to scarred face with a frowning Declan Kelly, photographed as he was leaving a police station several months earlier.

"This is the target. Runs several legitimate businesses, all of which are very successful and incredibly clean."

"So?"

"Too successful. Too clean. We think they're money laundering operations, but it's tough to prove. He has a reputation on both sides of the border. There are strong rumours linking him to murders, turf wars, bribery, blackmail, money laundering and all kinds of racketeering, but nobody will talk. We've never come up against such a wall of silence. Everybody's scared, or he's paid them off. Hence Operation Shiny."

"Shiny?"

"Nothing sticks to him."

Pope looked at the photograph again and decided he wanted nothing to do with that face, or the current situation.

He had plenty to report to the RSM and several questions he wanted answering, although the answers could wait until he was safely back in his own anonymous terraced house in the UK, drinking a cold beer and fussing his dogs. He touched the back of his head and was disappointed to note the cut had stopped bleeding, but winced anyway, as if he was in great pain.

"I think I need to be on my way," he said, handing back the folder. "I'm sorry I stumbled across your operation. Obviously, I won't say anything to anybody."

She looked at him and narrowed her eyes, as if deciding whether to let him go or put a bullet in his head.

"I read about you on ICARUS this morning. One of your friends revealed more about you than perhaps you'd have liked after last night's pub quiz."

"Oh?" he asked, as casually as possible, but failing to hide the shock on his face or the surprise in his voice. Kara didn't reply straightaway. Something about his response unsettled her for a moment, but she couldn't work out why.

"Given your actions overseas, I think I can trust you not to divulge what's going on here to anyone." *Her words were part reassurance; part threat*, Pope thought, but nodded gratefully and picked up his rucksack.

"Thank you, Kara. Hopefully, you'll get what you need sooner rather than later."

"Oh. I think we're approaching the endgame," she smiled. "Head back the way you came up, then get yourself checked out in Clonbrinny. I think you'll live."

Pope smiled, walked past her onto the lane, and then turned onto the track. Kara watched him go, then sent a message to the ARW. One lad would trail him for a while, just to make sure he didn't fall again, or head towards the cottages. If he did the latter, his head injury would be the least of his worries.

Revelations

Mindy stared out of the van window and took another bite of her ham and cheese ciabatta.

Widdock had tuned the radio to a local music station, whose team of presenters sounded worse than the awkward silence they'd replaced. The occasional song interrupted their scripted and predictable banter, but did little to break the mood either on-air or in the van. Neither did the half-hourly news headlines, which gave the missing ex-prime minister a curiously sizeable amount of airtime on a station serving the Republic of Ireland.

Mindy googled the station name and found, to her complete non-surprise, it was part of an international radio conglomerate owned by the Marsh Media Group.

"Looks like Evie's been busy," she handed her phone over to Blackwell, who looked at the screen for a moment, grunted, then handed it back and returned to his own thoughts.

"Mr Widdock," she said to their driver. "What do you make of this missing prime minister story?"

Widdock remained silent for longer than considered socially acceptable elsewhere, but Mindy thought him to be a man careful with his words and resolved to remain silent herself until he finally replied.

Even so, his reluctance to answer sorely tested her patience, and she was just about to repeat herself when Widdock finally spoke, his eyes never wavering off the road ahead.

"Nothing," he said, then popped a green grape into his mouth, hoping that would be the end of the conversation.

Mindy waited patiently until he'd finished the grape before trying again. "Nothing? Care to elaborate?"

Widdock stifled an exasperated sigh and contemplated eating another grape.

"He's not my prime minister. He's irrelevant. Just because the press can't find him doesn't mean he's vanished. He's just gone off somewhere with his fiancée."

Blackwell cocked his head to one side and nodded thoughtfully. *A fair summary*, he thought.

Mindy bridled. "Irrelevant?"

"He's a nobody now, so yes, irrelevant." Widdock popped two grapes in his mouth to prevent further discussion. Mindy took the hint.

The radio presenters were speculating where the missing couple could be, then the primary host announced reports of three sightings from south-west Ireland.

"This could be interesting folks," she laughed. "Is the most-wanted couple in Britain actually here in Ireland? Let's find them and stop our neighbours fretting. We've popped the most recent pictures of former prime minister Andrew Blackwell and Amanda Abbott on the website. Have a look and call us if you see them. We'll get our nearest reporter on the case and maybe get them on air for a chat."

The discussion switched to excited speculation on how the missing couple could use disguises. This alarmed Mindy and intrigued Blackwell. Widdock was totally uninterested. Without a word, he leaned over, fiddled with the radio and changed station.

Blackwell leaned back and closed his eyes. Widdock grabbed another couple of grapes. Mindy opened a new document on her phone and started typing furiously.

If the radio coverage was a warning shot from the Conclave, then it was time to devise a defensive strategy and, in Mindy's experience, attack was always the best form of defence.

Andrew Blackwell half-opened his eyes, saw the love of his life typing furiously, and smiled to himself. He didn't know who was behind the latest developments or what they hoped to gain, but he knew they were going to regret it.

He cast his mind back over the last couple of days. *How to make the most out of them, without risking a lawsuit?* The public knew he was in favour of more openness in politics, so he should let them know what he'd been up to.

Maybe a news release confirming the safety of them both, explaining they had been with a group of key influencers who were interested in *Path Finder*.

Let the media work out the Conclave's involvement. Difficult for Aston and company to deny it without some loss of face.

Encourage the involvement of everyone in the debate. Emphasise no individual or organisation has the rights to the idea - not even him - and that's how it should be. Nobody has a solution, but everyone can work towards what works for them and we review and refine those developments until we have something that works for all of us.

He opened his eyes again and saw Widdock looking at him in the rear-view mirror.

"Mister Widdock," he smiled, "How long have you worked for Caisleán Síocháin?"

Widdock's eyes shifted forward, much to the relief of the former prime minister, who didn't want to end up in a road accident.

"Eight and a half years," came the reply. Neither Widdock nor his passengers knew who was most surprised by the answer. Blackwell had expected prevarication. Mindy had expected silence. For the last five years, Widdock had known nobody to show any interest in what he did and welcomed the chance to talk, although felt shocked by his own willingness to do so.

"It was certainly very impressive. We had a great time," said Mindy. "I guess with picking up guests and then dropping them off at the end of their stay, you've been an important part of the whole Caisleán Síocháin experience."

Widdock said nothing, but sat up straighter in his seat, to Mindy's satisfaction. Neither passenger continued the conversation, hoping the driver would fill the silence. Widdock didn't disappoint.

"The house has certainly seen its fair share of the great and the good," he said. "I've chauffeured many of them around."

"And the not so good, I bet," laughed Blackwell. "That wine cellar's very impressive."

Mindy pinched his leg, keen to keep Widdock talking. Sat directly behind the driver, she activated the dictation app on her phone, keen to collect the potential goldmine of information. *You never know what might come in useful*, she told herself.

"What have been the best events you've been involved in?" she asked.

Widdock gave the answer almost before the question finished. The stories he'd wanted to tell had increased over the years, with no chance of being heard or believed, thanks to sceptical friends and his bored family.

Now, he had a captive audience, and they were genuinely interested in what he had to say. So interested, in fact, that he slowed down his Limerick rate of delivery to make sure they got every word.

As if he were talking to a child, or an old relative with a dodgy hearing aid.

He defined 'best events' as the highest profile or most secret, cross-referenced with his most famous passengers or involving the most outrageous behaviour or sensational gossip. Even for the former public servants in the back of the van, who had operated at the highest levels of government with access to intelligence briefings and newspaper editors alike, the revelations were eye-opening and occasionally gob-smacking. Both had their own favourite memories and best anecdotes from their time in office, but this wasn't a competition and it was more useful to keep Widdock talking, encouraging him with the occasional laugh or exclamation.

The man from Limerick was in his element, finally feeling valued for what he did and respected for the status he had achieved. The trick now was to guide the driver gently towards revealing any information he may have on their recent hosts at Caisleán Síocháin, none of whom had appeared in the highlights reel.

"It's amazing how your perception of people can change the longer you're with them," said Blackwell, as Widdock paused for breath and to negotiate a set of road works. "For example, I've been with Aston Hail at conferences two or three times over the years and he's always been polite, knowledgeable, and charming. And yet, just this morning, he had a hissy fit when I told him we were leaving. Never seen him like that before."

"Ah, you don't want to upset Mister Hail. The man's a real control freak."

Mindy breathed a sigh of relief that her fiancé's gamble had paid off.

"Do you remember twelve months ago, when he acquired Claskett Micro Distribution in a hostile takeover, then kicked out the entire board just a day later?"

Blackwell nodded.

"Aston and Wade Claskett had been playing pool here for a bottle of wine they had found in the cellar, worth about 220,000 euros," explained Widdock, shaking his head at the price.

"Aston won the game. Claskett claimed he'd cheated, opened the bottle and drank the wine himself. He offered a glass to the others, but nobody dared to touch it. There was a big argument. Hail was in tears. Next morning, Claskett was gone, and the Conclave broke up. By the time Claskett landed in Texas, Aston had bought his business and Claskett was out of a job. One month later, CMD ceased to exist. Hail kept the good stuff, closed down the business and wrote off the acquisition, claiming Claskett had exaggerated its value."

Widdock shook his head again. "Claskett's never worked since and the court case will ruin him, even if he wins. Not my words."

"Wow," offered Blackwell. "Who'd have thought it?"

"But the others in the Conclave, they're okay, though. Right?" asked Mindy.

Widdock smiled, just as the van approached the end of the road works and the motorway beckoned. "Strap in folks," he warned as he pressed down on the accelerator.

Questions And Answers

Pope stood at the gate to catch his breath and decide on his next move. The church loomed in front of him, looking as unwelcome as ever. He glanced back down the lane and imagined a leisurely lunch in the hotels bar, followed by a catch up with Pippa. *Pippa*. He'd forgotten about her message regarding the former prime minister, stranded in Ireland. They could discuss that as well.

The walk from the lough had done little to help him process the morning's events, but the head pain had subsided. At least the Gardaí intelligence unit and the Army Ranger Wing were literally on top of the situation, and seemed confident they'd have their man soon. Pope just had to make sure the priest was safe and in no danger, then he could report to the RSM that the situation was okay and needed no Garden Club intervention. Then he could enjoy the rest of his break.

The gate creaked as he pushed it open and one of the resident crows cawed a grim welcome as he walked between the gravestones, pushed at the heavy, half-open door and stepped into the quiet darkness beyond. The church was empty apart from an elderly lady, Marie, near the pulpit, who took his entrance as her cue to sigh heavily, put down her newspaper, and shuffle through a door beyond the altar.

Moments later, she reappeared and switched on an ancient vacuum cleaner, which groaned in protest before being put to work. Pope wandered towards the confessional on the other side of the church. Out of the corner of his eye, he spotted the priest emerging by the altar and walking down the aisle towards him, adjusting his robes as he walked.

"Hello, Simon Pope. I'm glad you're back."

"Hello again, Father. Any reason?"

The priest smiled.

"I felt you had unfinished business here."

Pope reflected for a moment, then nodded.

"I guess there's only one way to find out."

Father Aidan headed for the confessional, opened both doors, and turned to his visitor.

"Off the record?" asked Pope.

"If it gets you in there."

The priest stepped in and closed his door. Pope settled into his seat and closed the door, muffling the noise of the angry vacuum outside. "Bless me, Father, for I have sinned," he started.

"Oh, I'm sure you have," replied the priest, "But let's just have a chat."

Pope took a breath. He had worked out what to say after last leaving the church, but now the opportunity was here…

"I once had genuine faith," he started. "In fact, I was a priest. Church of England. One of the youngest ever, apparently."

He listened, expecting a reply, but only heard the vacuum cleaner increase in volume as it approached.

"I worked in a small parish for a couple of years, then my boss suggested I apply for a commission in the British army. Apparently it's easier to get applicants for the role when we're not at war, but we were. I applied, scraped through and ended up with a regiment."

"And how did that go?"

"Not great. I was there for several weeks, then we deployed… abroad. I'd been there for several months, avoided most engagements, then got caught in a bad one." Pope gathered his thoughts and fought off the terrible memories. "Long story short. People died. I picked up a gun… I lost friends; lost my commission; my position in the church; my faith… Now, I work in a warehouse, play golf, and walk my dogs."

Father Aidan rarely experienced emergency confessions, but he was prepared for any eventuality. He leaned forward, opened a small cupboard, and removed two tumblers and a bottle of whiskey. Pope heard the clink of the glasses and the glug of liquor being poured. Then a drink appeared by the side of the lattice and he accepted it gratefully.

"Just so you know," said Father Aidan, "This isn't a penance."

"Might it end up on ICARUS?"

"I never post on ICARUS."

The two of them lapsed into a comfortable silence, reflecting on the conversation so far and savouring the spirit in the glass. The vacuum cleaner reached a crescendo as Marie pushed it past the confessional and off towards the entrance door. Pope took the plunge.

"Who is the programmer behind the Clonbrinny website, Father? That ICARUS section seems to be very popular, but I've never seen it anywhere else."

"Have you actually seen it, then?" The priest sounded surprised.

"Heard about it. People were talking after the quiz."

Father Aidan took a sip of his only alcohol since the call from Brendan Dunne the night before. ICARUS helped the community in so many ways, but it wasn't standard on other sites? That came as a surprise.

"The local council launched the website several years ago. They'll know the designers. I'd have thought ICARUS would have been a goldmine for them." He paused and waited for Marie to move further down the far aisle and turn off the cleaner. "There was a time when we all felt in danger. There had been some incidents. ICARUS tells us what's happening in real time, so everybody knows and can react if needed. It protects us. Makes us feel safer. And it's brought us closer together as a community."

Pope heard a vehicle crunch to a halt in the church car park and, seconds later, the church door creaking in protest as it opened again. *Time to go for broke*.

"And what about you, Father? You lived through those times. Do you feel safe now, or still in danger?"

Before the priest could answer, the door to his side of the confessional swung open, with Brendan Dunne's enormous silhouette blocking the light that would have normally flooded in.

"Father…" the big man's tremulous voice had lost its usual threatening timbre, "It's time." He leaned into the confessional, took the priest by the arm, then the gentle smoky aroma dragged his attention to the glass on the small shelf. "Bejaysus, man!" The voice had recovered its standard level of threat, with a layer of fury draped over the top. "You promised!"

Pope watched as the priest behind the lattice was yanked out of the confessional.

Just two more minutes, he thought. Two minutes for the priest to confirm he felt safe. Then Pope could make his excuses and leave, send the report to the Garden Club and get on with his life. Now, there was no time to call for reinforcements, and he was about to be discovered.

"Er… excuse me. We're not done yet," he exclaimed, holding his glass and squinting as his door was flung open.

He recognised the man holding the priest. He'd been sitting at the bar the previous night. The Kellys' minder.

"Then you'd better come with us." Connor Kelly was holding Pope's confessional door. He looked pale, even in the dim light of the church, and his eyes were red.

"Simon. It's alright. Come with us." The priest was calmer than Pope felt and the others looked. No weapons were visible, but Pope was fairly sure they'd be somewhere. He wondered what might happen if he declined the invitation, but decided he didn't want to find out. "Simon. One of my congregation is dying. I have to give the last rites."

Pope nodded. He felt an obligation to the priest. Plus, it felt the right thing to do, and he could give a full report to the RSM afterwards, assuming he was still alive to do so.

The four men walked out of the church, climbed into the car, and drove away.

Marie emerged from the shadows, followed them into the daylight, then took out her mobile phone.

Food For Thought

Reviewing the scribbled notes she'd jotted down surreptitiously over the past thirty miles, Mindy reflected on the last two days she'd spent with a raging and vengeful control freak, a software guru with close links to three major, government-sponsored hacking groups and a cloning genius fixated on creating the Fourth Reich.

Why do I never get to mix with nice people, she wondered, before remembering her career had been politics from the start, so she only had herself to blame.

Andrew Blackwell puzzled over who invested in Alexander Alcock's portfolio of sovereign nations when the man had done nothing for two decades.

His bet was China. Evie Marsh's financial links to American hi-tech bros bent on world domination were hardly a surprise, although the lack of information on Isaac Delemos had been curious.

"He'll say hello when he gets in the car, thank you and goodbye when he gets out and not a word in between - even if he's tipsy," confirmed Widdock. "He works on his phone - rarely looks up from it actually - but he never makes or takes a call."

Hardly a surprise, given the global manufacturer's bug warning that very morning.

Blackwell watched as the driver drove serenely through the late morning traffic, a contented, vindicated smile on the man's face, satisfied at last that his experience and observations over the years had value, after all.

"Mr Widdock," began Mindy, "Does the Conclave invite many outside guests to its gatherings?"

The driver furrowed his brow for a moment.

"I'm not sure what they do when they meet elsewhere, but you're the first that I know of here."

He drove on in silence, leaving his passengers to think about their conversation. *Not that they'd had much to say*, he thought, *but it felt good to be listened to, rather than talked at.*

"Did you drive any of the Conclave to the airfield this morning?"

"I did. Miss Marsh and Mister Alcock."

"Did they talk about us at all?"

Widdock grinned.

"There was a certain amount of… annoyance and amazement at your man's behaviour over breakfast."

"Good!" exclaimed Blackwell. "And anything about our discussions with them?"

"Only that you hadn't exceeded their expectations," the driver reported faithfully and with slight regret. "We're thirty minutes from Clonbrinny."

Visiting The Doyles

Politely declining all requests for additional help from food recipients, Stuart and Orla arrived at Jimmy and Margaret's with plenty of time for a drink and a chat before heading back to the Hero and the lunchtime crowd.

The couple's home, a whitewashed thatched cottage from the 1800s, sat at the edge of the town on a sizeable piece of land, flanked by a couple of small outbuildings and a small barn at the back. The quarter mile of winding track from the main road, Morris noted, was tricky to navigate, even for someone who knew it as well as Orla.

While Margaret made the drinks with the landlady's help, Jimmy took Stuart on a brief tour of the property. Having spent his career in the construction industry, Jimmy was proud of the renovations and improvements he had made to the family home.

The single storey cottage had an extension to one side and across the back, creating additional space for a spacious, easily accessible bedroom and an en-suite, plus a dining area and a larger kitchen. Custom-made, double-glazed windows in steel-reinforced frames replaced the original timber windows and a sturdy steel-reinforced oak door mounted on iron hinges improved the building's insulation and security without affecting the cottage's rustic charm.

"It's my design, and I did most of the work myself," said Jimmy.

He had insulated and plaster boarded the thick external walls, while the thatched roof now had a layer beneath the thatch to offer protection from fire hazards. Underfloor heating and flat ceramic tiles had replaced the original flagstone floor to help with Margaret's movement, but the central hearth remained as the focal point of the living space, even though it now housed a high efficiency wood burner.

"You've done a cracking job, Jimmy," mused Morris admiringly. "How about coming to the Midlands and sorting out my house?"

Jimmy smiled. "Maybe I'll have a look when we visit you and Orla."

Not quite knowing how to respond, Morris peered out of a window towards the road, a view partially obscured by a thick stone wall about waist high, which marked the boundaries of the garden or the limit of the surrounding field, depending on your point of view.

Fortunately, or otherwise, a shout from the kitchen interrupted the conversation, and the men joined the women at the dining table, where mugs of tea, a plate of biscuits and Bella, the biscuit-loving brindle greyhound, welcomed them.

"Do you like my love nest then, Stuart?" Margaret asked with sparkling eyes.

"It's excellent, Margaret. Your man's done a fine job."

Margaret smiled and put her hand on her husband's arm.

"It wasn't his first and I'm sure it won't be his last."

Before Jimmy could respond, either with wit, gratitude or affection, three mobile phones suddenly buzzed or lit up. Morris watched as Orla and their hosts each studied their own phone intently. He could just make out 'ICARUS' on Orla's screen, and watched the faces around the table drop as quickly as the atmosphere in the room.

"Oh, poor Clodagh," said Margaret, her hand trembling a little.

"We must go." Orla shut off her phone and stood up. "Jimmy…?"

"I'm on it." Margaret watched as her husband walked out of the kitchen door and headed towards the nearest outbuilding.

Orla looked at her new boyfriend, uncertain what would happen next.

"Stuart, we have to go," she said. "I'll explain on the way. Then you have a decision to make."

Morris stumbled to his feet and followed her towards the front door. He turned to thank Margaret for her hospitality, but she was staring out of the back window, tears running down her cheeks with her devoted dog leaning against her but still staring at the biscuits.

Orla was already in the van, starting up the engine before he closed the front door behind him. Trying to calm his racing heart, he settled in beside her as she reversed onto the track and then headed towards the road. Once they were safely on tarmac and heading towards Clonbrinny, he spoke.

"I don't have a decision to make. I'm going with you. Wherever. Whatever. Now, take a few breaths, then tell me what I need to know without crashing the van."

If she hadn't been careering down the road well above the speed limit, Orla might have leaned over and hugged him. Fortunately, common sense prevailed. As they hurtled through Clonbrinny, she summarised all she needed to say in a few short sentences. It was the final one that sent chills through Stuart Morris, despite all his years in the police force.

"At least one person will die today, Stuart, but it could be more. We might be among them."

Fortress

Margaret's eyes never wavered from the outbuilding door until it opened again and Jimmy emerged, pulling a trolley loaded with three bags. He dragged it over to the car and heaved the two largest bags into the boot, then carried the third bag into the kitchen and set it on the dining table.

Neither of them said a word as he put on a ballistic vest, groaning slightly as his body reacted to the weight of the metal plates.

"I've put on some weight since I last wore this," he commented, "And that was only twelve years ago."

He wrapped a holster belt around his waist and held his stomach in tight as he struggled to fasten the buckle. Margaret fought back tears as her husband pulled a pistol from the bag, checked its mechanism and put it on the table.

"I'm far too old for this," he grumbled, loading two full magazines onto the left side of his belt and one into the gun. He rooted through the bag, removing several grenades and then a black balaclava, with the letter 'I' printed in white across the forehead. While Bella sniffed the grenades, he pulled on the balaclava so it lay around his neck, then coaxed the dog away and stowed the grenades back in the bag.

He knelt down by the side of his wife's wheelchair and let her put her arms around him and rest her head on his.

"Come back safe," she said. "Promise me you'll come back safe."

He held onto her arms and looked her into her eyes, ignoring the dog's nose in his armpit.

"I promise I'll do my very best," he smiled, "And I've a 100 percent record so far on that score. I just wish the horses I picked were as reliable."

Margaret smiled back and kissed him on the forehead.

"Make sure you keep that record," she said, letting him go. "I love you."

Jimmy struggled to a standing position and patted Bella's head. "I love you too," he smiled. "You know what to do. I'll call you."

He grabbed the bag and sauntered as casually as possible out of the back door, waited for the only love of his life to lock it, and prayed he'd hear that sound again soon. Margaret listened until she heard the car drive off, then wheeled herself into the front room and watched her husband weave down the drive and onto the road.

She turned on the television and switched from the local news to a dedicated channel, which showed the view from four external CCTV cameras concealed around the outside of the house. Removing an electronic tablet from the side of her wheelchair, she swiped to a control panel and touched a virtual button, then watched the television screen as the gate at the end of the drive closed.

Another swipe took her to a screen which showed the location of the eight anti-personnel landmines planted with great precision on the property. Touching each location illuminated the small image of the mine, signifying its status was now active.

A final screen helped her to deadbolt the front and back doors and to lower the discreetly hidden metal shutters on the cottage windows.

Defences in place, she slotted the tablet back into the wheelchair, then picked up her phone and dialled a number, which was answered in two rings.

"Fortress has started," she said. "This is not a drill. You take care."

Then she rang off, made herself another coffee, settled in front of the television and burst into tears, while Bella waited expectantly by her side.

Action Stations

Kara looked at her phone as if she had never seen one before, processing the call from her former maths professor, worrying about her uncle's safety and trying to work out her next move.

Fortress. After all this time.

She called Sergeant Daley at the camp over the hill.

"Looks like something's kicking off. This is not a drill."

"You said that last time," came the reply. "And it was."

Kara closed her eyes and counted to five. Time was too short to reach ten.

"The target's bodyguard and brother have taken the local priest from the church, possibly with a third party," she said. "If they turn up here, we can assume the mother's on her way out."

The phone went silent for a while before Mick Daley spoke again.

"There's nothing in the transcripts that suggests a problem," he reported.

"The abduction says there is… hang on…"

The sound of vehicles driving around the lough carried over the water and bounced up the slopes. This one was no different. Kara looked through the camera viewfinder.

"Hang on," she said again. "They have visitors."

She snapped away as the four men emerged from the car and disappeared into the cottage. Dunne stood out a mile, as did Connor and, of course, her uncle, but the fourth man was a mystery. She flipped through the shots on the display screen, catching the stranger rub the back of his head and turn to look at the ruined church before being pushed inside the house.

Was Pope an innocent bystander or was he involved with Declan? If the latter, it compromised the mission.

"We have Connor and Dunne, together with the priest and this morning's visitor to our site, Simon Pope. What's the transcript saying?"

"Nothing. Television's on, and there's chatter between Kelly and his mother. Are we screwed?"

"Probably. Plus, Clonbrinny has started Fortress."

"Shit. Something's going down."

"The town has a shared history with the Kellys. If word's out about Clodagh, someone might have a crack at either target."

"Or both."

"Get your team down here, locked and loaded. Whatever we're facing, we need to be ready for it."

"Roger that."

Kara rang off and then called the superintendent in charge of the operation to update her on the situation.

"Get a couple of lads to bring the GP here, now," she told her boss. "I don't want any delays."

The Kellys' Story

The confusion and concern at the cottage matched that near the derelict church. Pope was greeted with a scowl and a "Who the hell is this?" from the head Kelly, while Connor sobbed uncontrollably as he stroked the hair of his dying mother. As Brendan explained, Pope walked quietly to the bed in the corner and placed his hand on Connor's shoulder.

"Talk to her, Connor," he suggested. "Your mother's going, but they say hearing is the last sense to go. Try to think of the good times; the happy times. Give her some wonderful memories to take with her."

The youngest Kelly stifled his sobs, nodded and sat down, holding his mother's hand as he did so. Between the sniffs, he talked quietly close to her ear. Pope kept hold of Connor's shoulder for another couple of minutes, until he was much more settled, then patted his back and walked towards the others, who were deep in conversation.

He was sure that Declan Kelly had frowned all the time he'd been with Connor, but the man with a face to match his fearsome reputation nodded his thanks as Pope approached.

"She doesn't have too much time, I'm afraid," murmured Pope. "Maybe another hour or two. I'm very sorry."

Father Aidan cleared his throat.

"Declan…"

The senior Kelly nodded and stepped to the side, allowing the priest to pass by, then followed him to Clodagh's bedside for the last rites. Brendan Dunne turned and walked into the hallway, ducking as he encountered the doorframe. Pope gave him a minute and then followed, finding the minder in the kitchen, staring at the back garden.

"We had so much fun in that garden," Dunne smiled. "And rolling down the hill behind it."

Pope said nothing. He found the kettle, filled it with water and put it on to boil. He searched the cupboards and found the coffee mugs as Brendan continued.

"I always felt *at home* here. Part of the family. Martin and Clodagh were so good to me; to all of us, the priest and his brother included. And then the Troubles came to town…"

Pope put coffee into the mugs and added hot water, before hunting down the sugar and the milk.

"He was a really nice man, Martin. Loved Clonbrinny. Big part of the community. Had time for everyone." Dunne moved from the door and sat down at the table, pulling a mug towards him and adding the milk and sugar.

"He was so upset when Bobby died at the pub. Actually… not upset… outraged. He helped Orla to run the pub while she got herself sorted out. Others did as well. Then, one night…"

"I heard the story," interrupted Pope. "Back in a minute."

He removed his mug from the tray and carried the rest into the lounge, placing them on a table quietly, so as not to disturb the last rites, before retreating to the kitchen. Dunne looked deep in thought.

"They'd sent a message. Don't mess with us. Martin wanted everybody to be there for everyone else. All for one and one for all; that kind of thing. But we weren't quick enough. You heard about the car bomb just outside here?"

Pope nodded.

"That's when everything changed. Martin became a monster. We'd hear about stuff happening on both sides of the border - assassinations, bombs, reprisal killings. Paramilitaries fought others on the same side. None of them knew who to trust." Brendan shook his head, partly in admiration, partly in disbelief. "Most were Martin's work. He'd light the blue touch paper and move on. We'd hear bits and pieces. Clo would argue with him, but he'd argue back. *If they're looking at themselves, they're not looking at us*, he'd say. *I'm keeping our kids safe; our people safe.*"

"I was up at the church yesterday," mused Pope. "There was a large grave for three Kelly children and one further away for Martin Kelly."

Dunne fell silent and looked at his coffee; not sure what to say next.

"My brother and sister died in the bombing." Both of them swung round and saw Declan Kelly in the hallway. He walked into the kitchen, coffee in his hand, and pointed the mug towards Dunne. "This man - only a kid himself - saved me and my brother. We owe him. We'll always owe him."

Dunne sat, head bowed.

"And we owe my father a great deal, too. He kept us safe, the best way he knew how." Declan dragged out a chair and slumped onto it. "But he crossed the line with Sean."

"Sean?"

"My eldest brother. He was eighteen. Wanted to help Pappy in his *mission*, he called it, so Pappy took him along to see what it was all about. It was a disaster. Pappy got hurt; a car hit Sean as he ran away terrified. He died two days later."

"I'm sorry to hear that."

"Pappy couldn't do much after that. He had pain in his leg all the time. Drove him to drink. My mother was worried he'd get Connor and myself involved as we got older, but it never came to that."

Declan looked down at the flagstones beneath their feet. "He died here. Heart attack. I was fourteen. The only thing he left us was this house and ICARUS."

"The website?"

"No. That came later."

A contemplative silence settled over the kitchen, disturbed by the same wall clock from all those years ago and the murmur of voices at prayer in the front room. Then an urgent, loud banging on the front door broke the fragile peace.

Great Timing

"This is weird," muttered Coldfront as the Fishing Flops' van pulled into the empty car park at the back of the hotel. "Have we missed something?"

"Maybe the locals walk here at the weekend, so the traffic police don't spend their entire budget on breathalysers," offered Angus Grace, hungry and dying for his first pint of the day. "Dear God, these people can drink."

Being a creature of habit and liking to park his van as far as possible from other vehicles, the empty area presented Coldfront with a problem. Eventually, after a couple of false parks and suffering a barrage of insults from his passengers, he opted to park as far away as possible from the hotel, in a corner near to the bushes and the river beyond.

"Look at it this way," he tried to explain as he locked the vehicle behind him, "We've shown ourselves to be the perfect visitors, allowing all the locals closer, unimpeded access from their vehicles to the bar."

"I can see them queueing up to thank us," said Dave Westlake, already halfway to the hotel and keen to put as many beers as possible between him and the toilet blockage. Just at that moment, the rear entrance to the building banged open. A relieved Sinead Brennan ran across the ground and into his arms.

"You took your time," she said, giving him a quick kiss. "Inside, quickly."

Two minutes later, the three of them sat at the bar while Sinead poured their drinks.

"Clonbrinny has had no gang-related problems for some years because of the link to Declan Kelly. Everyone has… let's say… a great deal of respect for Declan," she started. "He's probably the most powerful and successful criminal you've never heard of."

"Pablo Escobar? Al Capone?" suggested Coldfront.

"Idiot," responded Angus Grace. "If you know their names, then you've heard of them."

"You met his brother Connor last night. The big fella was Brendan Dunne, a friend of the Kellys since school and the brothers' minder," Sinead rushed on. "Long story short, we're left alone and feel pretty safe. Any potential trouble and we have the Fortress system. Basically, everyone gets involved to protect everyone else. Martin Kelly - the father - set that up after the attacks here and at his house near the lough."

"So, you have your own civil defence force," laughed Coldfront. Sinead flashed him the look practised by bar staff everywhere; when they want to convey their opinion without actually giving it. Restaurant staff don't need the look. They just spit in the food.

"Martin lost two of his children in the car bomb. He set up Fortress; lost his mind and another child by going after the gangs himself; then had a heart attack and died. Declan follows in his footsteps, but is much smarter. He has massive influence; has fingers in so many pies; and has plenty of illegal stuff linked to him, but nothing's ever proven."

Sinead spotted some movement on the CCTV screen and watched an executive van pull into the car park, closely followed by a car. Two individuals, one male, one female, exited the van; each held a coat and bag.

They both shook hands with the driver, who insisted on giving them his business card before reversing his van and setting off to Limerick.

"Great timing. New guests." Sinead picked up her keys and headed for the back door.

"Do my eyes deceive me?" asked Westlake. "Oh God, I hope so."

The men's attention switched to Jimmy Doyle, who struggled out of his car, wearing what looked like an armoured vest, and called over to the couple. The man handed his holdall to his companion, walked to the back of the car and lifted out a large bag, which was instantly recognisable to the drinkers.

Westlake turned and stared at Coldfront.

"David. Do not even remotely hint that you recognise the couple who walk through that door. To anyone. Understand? If you talk to either of them, or talk about them with someone else, I swear I will knock you out, then keep knocking you out whenever you come round until it's time for us to go home."

Davies was nonplussed.

"Who is it?" he asked. Westlake took a deep breath.

"It's our former prime minister and his former assistant chief of staff; walking into an Irish hotel preparing for an attack by unknown assailants; carrying a rifle bag for a pensioner wearing a blast plate on his chest and a pistol at his side."

"Ah!" nodded Coldfront. "Of course it is. My former golfing partner. This day's becoming more surreal by the hour."

The group fell silent, watched the CCTV until they saw Sinead invite the couple into the hotel, then turned their attention to the reception desk. They heard a familiar Welsh accent before they saw anybody.

"I have to say, your West coast? Absolutely stunning. Don't get me wrong, we have a beautiful coastline ourselves, but here? Stunning!"

Westlake grimaced. "He's gone for the Welsh accent again," he said. Coldfront's eyes widened.

"He's faking it?"

"Well, of course he is! He's probably adopted the name Paul Morgan, just like last time."

Sinead emerged from the hallway and stepped behind the bar.

"I'm pleased your holiday's going so well, Mister Morgan. Now, if you could just fill out this form… I'll get your key and will show you both to your room."

Andy Blackwell stepped into the room wearing his quilted jacket and beanie hat. He took the proffered pen and read the form. Mindy emerged from behind him, but stopped when she noticed the group at the bar. Recognising Dave Westlake, she gently shook her head.

"That's settled then," murmured Westlake, "We don't know them."

The group returned to their drinks and made small talk about the morning's deliveries. Angus kept his eye on the CCTV images and watched Jimmy Doyle move his car to the far corner of the car park, where he manoeuvred it behind an old skip.

"Look at Jimmy," he whispered. "The old boy's done this before."

The old boy certainly had. He put on a pair of gloves and hauled an iron frame and two sheets of steel out of the skip. The frame went next to the skip, and the steel rested against it. Both sheets had viewing and firing holes cut into them.

"He can cover the entire car park from there," commented Coldfront, "But he's left any targets an escape route via the entry point. What the…"

The screen went black. Eyes turned towards Sinead, demanding to know if this marked the start of an attack. The girl simply winked at them, set the remote control back on the top of the bar and turned towards her new guests.

"Right, let's get you people to your room."

Blackwell picked up the two holdalls and followed Sinead and Mindy as they walked past the group and out of the bar.

"Alright boys?" he said, winking as he sailed past.

The group waited for the door to close, then Westlake pulled out his mobile.

"Simmo's never going to believe this. He's going to get the shock of his life," he said, writing a brief text message.

New Arrivals

Simon Pope had plenty on his plate when the text message came through. So much so that he didn't realise he had one. Within a second of the door knock, Brendan was in the hallway with a gun in his hand.

"Bren!"

Dunne turned and looked at his boss.

"No killer's going to knock first," said Declan. "Lose the hardware."

"Not today, boss."

Dunne walked to the door, peered through the spyhole and put the gun away.

"It's Orla," he announced, "With the fella she was with last night."

Pope's heart missed a beat. "That'll be my mate, Stuart," he said. "He's helping her with a food run this morning."

Declan nodded, Dunne opened the door, and Orla stepped inside.

"Where is she?"

Dunne pointed to the front room and moved aside as the landlady brushed past. Morris stood holding a box of food, only entering when Dunne gave him the nod and making straight for the kitchen, where he stopped in surprise when he saw Pope sat down with the biggest mobster in Ireland.

"Stuart, this is Declan. Declan, this is Stuart Morris."

Morris set the box down on the worktop and shook Declan's hand.

"You looked after Connor last night?"

"Let's say we looked after each other."

In the front room, Connor recognised the voice, rushed to the kitchen and into Morris's arms. Thanks to years of policing, Morris knew when to taser somebody and when to hug them. Here, wisely, he chose the latter.

"Stuart. My mammy…" The man's voice crumbled as he tried to say the unsayable.

"I know, mate. I know." Morris grabbed him even tighter and held on, even when the sobs became uncontrollable. Declan looked on, touched but taken aback by his brother's trust in the stranger - something he could never imagine for himself.

Time stood still while Connor cried himself out and made a mess of his new friend's shirt. Orla looked down the hallway into the brightly lit kitchen and saw a man full of compassion winning the hearts of others, as well as her own.

The Set-Up

Sinead returned to the bar, switched the CCTV on, poured herself a small whiskey and sipped it while she collected her thoughts.

"Where was I?" she asked.

"Declan Kelly."

"Right. No gang in Ireland would raise their hand against him, as much as they'd like to. They fear him." She wondered how much she could say without incurring the man's wrath. "Today is different."

"And that's because…?"

"Declan's mother's been very ill for ages. The priest disappeared from the church late this morning. Word gets around quickly. Clodagh's dying, and the Kellys are all together, with no support, in a small cottage by the lough. If you want rid of them and to send a message to other towns by hitting Clonbrinny, today's the day."

Angus Grace searched the television screen for movement around the skip.

"I don't see any sign of Jimmy," he said.

"That's because I'm here," gasped a voice around the corner. "I have to pee and could really use a hand."

Coldfront looked revolted, but Grace and Westlake rushed to the hallway. Each grabbed a rifle bag from the pensioner.

Westlake heaved a bag onto the pool table, unzipped it and pulled out three handguns and two self-loading rifles. Grace whistled quietly as he looked into his bag. "Ammo, stun grenades, tasers, body armour and commando knives," he reported, "A veritable selection box. What do you have out there, Jimmy?"

"AK-47, ammo and grenades. It's not the most modern kit, but it works. Everything is clean, charged and tested."

Sinead glanced at Westlake, who looked serious as he checked out a pistol.

"What kind of assault are you expecting?" asked Coldfront. "I can't see this lot being much use against rocket-propelled grenades or car bombs or a vehicle mounted machine gun."

"Look out of any front window," suggested Jimmy. "Tell me if you see the road."

A line of neatly parked farm vehicles and delivery vans extending beyond the boundaries of the hotel provided the answer.

"We funnel them to the car park or along the front pavement, then take things from there," explained Jimmy. "If it's an attack, we defend from inside the building and surprise them from the flanks. If they show no weapons but enter the building…"

He looked at the group in front of him and smiled.

Angus Grace smiled back.

"This is turning into the best short break *ever*," he grinned.

Nearing The End

Father Aidan moved away from Clodagh's bedside to let the boys say their goodbyes. Her breathing had become more intense; the rasping turned into more of a rattle.

"Oh, the poor woman. Shouldn't we call the doctor? The ambulance maybe?" asked Orla. "They could give her something to calm her down. Take her somewhere to…"

"No," said Declan, eyes fixed on his mother's face; his hand stroking her hair. "She's not going anywhere."

"But Declan…" Connor's face flushed. "Why not?"

The new head of the family swallowed hard as he gazed through tear-filled eyes at his mother's strained features.

"Because this is how it ends." Heads turned in surprise towards the priest, who stood holding a crucifix in his left hand, silently blessing the gathering with his right.

Declan nodded and flashed a smile at Aidan despite the circumstances, feeling a wave of relief surge through him and lift the weight from his shoulders.

"This is how it ends," he echoed. The priest would divulge nothing from Clodagh's last confession, but the comment told Declan all he needed to know.

Connor sat close by, face pale and drawn, struggling to cope with events. Declan motioned to Dunne, who was standing by the door, to come over.

"You were as much a son to Mammy as we were," he told him. "You belong here, just as we do. Sit yourself down, Bren. Say your goodbyes." He walked past Morris, whose arm held Orla tight, and into the kitchen, where Simon Pope sat at the kitchen table, holding his phone and looking worried.

"I've just seen a message sent to me a while ago," he started. "My friends are back at the Hero after delivering food parcels. Something about Fortress…"

Declan pulled out a chair and slumped onto it. "Has anything happened?"

Pope shook his head. "The lads are setting up a few things. Just in case."

Declan nodded in appreciation. *His mother hadn't even passed away, and the wolves were at the door. Some could be on their way to the cottage.*

Pope hesitated. What had Kara said to him? *I can trust you not to divulge what's going on here to anyone?* Well, he was about to blow that trust to bits.

"There's something else," he whispered. "There's a police surveillance operation based at the church ruin, supported by the Army Ranger Wing."

"I know."

Anxious at the volume of the reply, Pope tried again and whispered, "They're listening to your every word - real hi-tech stuff."

"No. They think they are, but…" Declan paused. "Do me a favour? Ask Connor to come and see me? Tell him to bring his laptop."

Pope rose, then paused as the gangland boss's hand grabbed his arm. For the second time that day, scarred face stared at scarred face, but this time neither was an image.

"I appreciate what you and your friends are doing for me and for my community. I owe you for this and I always pay my debts."

"Let's just hope we're all alive for that to happen."

Kelly stifled a laugh and removed his hand. "Go get my brother."

Pope walked into the front room, made his way to Connor's side, and whispered his message. The younger Kelly didn't hesitate. He stood and kissed his mother on her forehead, stroking her cheek as he did so, then picked up a laptop on the sideboard and disappeared out of the door.

Pope looked around to see if Orla wanted to sit at Clodagh's side, but saw the landlady lost in her own nightmares, her head buried in Stuart's chest, adding more tears to those shed earlier by a heartbroken Connor.

Brendan Dunne didn't move. He had a duty to the brothers - his brothers - but he also owed a final debt to the woman who regarded him as a son; to be with her at the end.

Pope sat next to him. Aidan stood at the top of the bed, eyes closed, mouthing his own prayers of intercession on Clodagh's behalf. Having been out of the room for a while, Pope sensed the woman's laboured breathing was getting slower and softer. In his mind, Clo had already gone. Her life support system was shutting down with no soul to protect anymore. The end wasn't far away, and Pope knew his role.

Game On

At the Hero, Jimmy settled back behind his defences with a quarter bottle of brandy and a bowl of curry and rice. Coldfront's van backed onto the same hedgerow, but in the corner directly facing the car park's entrance, with a view down the side of the pub to the main road.

Both positions provided flanking crossfire across the entire car park, with Coldfront also able to cover movement down the side of the hotel.

With Angus Grace's help, he had rolled several beer barrels into place in the parking space next to the van.

To a casual observer, they looked ready for the brewery to pick up, but they also provided protection and firing locations for the man working at the back door of the vehicle, checking and positioning his own weapons arsenal.

Depending on how things panned out, the flankers could escape their position onto the bank of the river and use the hedgerow as cover to reach the other, or to retreat away from the hotel.

On the second floor of the hotel, behind the net curtain covering their blast-resistant bedroom window, Blackwell and Mindy watched on with interest. The holdalls sat on the bed, unpacked. "What on earth are they up to? And why are they facing the hotel?" mused Blackwell.

"Guards usually point their guns away from whatever they're protecting, surely? Is this to do with us?"

Mindy watched Angus Grace walk along the back edge of the car park and talk to someone concealed behind a skip in the far right corner, before trotting back towards the hotel and disappearing out of sight. *No cars in sight*, she thought, *and no locals in the bar area - just Simmo's friends, but no Simmo.*

"The lads downstairs weren't expecting us," she said. "Did you see their faces? I thought Dave Westlake was going to fall off his bar stool."

A sharp knock at the door disturbed the discussion. Blackwell walked over and peered through the spy hole. "Talk of the devil," he exclaimed, opening the door.

Dave Westlake walked in, carrying a package, which he placed on one holdall before turning and shaking Blackwell's hand, then hugging Mindy.

"I'd say it's nice to see you both and what a pleasant surprise," he started, "But it's not and it isn't."

"Simmo's known we were coming since this morning," Blackwell responded, slightly defensively.

"I've not heard from Simmo since just after breakfast, and he's not responding to text messages. Why are you here?"

Mindy intervened, as time was of the essence.

"We need to get back home without causing too much fuss," she said. "Pippa gave us the details of this place and we booked a room, hoping you could help. Is this a bad time?"

"You could say that," Westlake grimaced. He spent the next ten minutes focusing on the elements key to the current situation and omitting any reference to the burgeoning romances.

"So," he summarised, "If anyone's brave enough to move against the Kellys, today's the day. Something may happen; it might not. It's a waiting game."

"And a former British prime minister is in the middle of it all," reflected Blackwell ruefully. "Talk about bad timing."

"You can only be part of a story if there's a story to...," Westlake stopped as the sound of a vehicle turning into the car park disturbed the conversation. He looked down onto a large four-wheel drive with tinted windows as it swung around the car park and came to a halt side-on to the hotel, facing towards the exit. *Game on.* "I have to go. Stay here and lock the door." He pointed at the package on the holdall and looked at Mindy. "That's for you."

The door closed quietly behind him and the new arrivals heard him run down the corridor and through the fire door at its end. Blackwell moved cautiously towards the window.

"The engine's still running," he reported, "And the doors are all closed."

"They're ready to bolt in case there's a reception committee." Mindy unwrapped the package and picked up the handgun, checked the safety catch was on, then waved the weapon around, getting used to its weight and balance.

Blackwell watched her release and check the magazine before snapping it back into position.

"Nobody even thinks about handing me a weapon," he observed.

"There's a reason for that," she replied as she checked the two spare magazines Westlake had thoughtfully included. "You're dangerous enough without one; an accident waiting to happen. In fact, there's more than one reason..."

"No need to go into that now," interrupted her loving, if slightly irritated, fiancé. "We have defences to prepare."

Calling In Support

Orla Brennan read the message twice, then handed her phone to Stuart Morris for his opinion.

"Talk to Declan," he urged, trying to sound calm. The Hero's landlady walked out of the front room into the kitchen, where the Kelly brothers sat at the table, Connor focusing on his laptop.

"A car's just arrived at the Hero," she said. "In the car park, but nobody's come out and the engine's still running."

"Can they not even give us a day?" Declan said, his tone a mix of alarm and despair; his body language something else entirely.

Morris and Pope appeared in the hallway, worried about their friends and disturbed by the turn of events. Declan stared at Orla with a finger to his lips, even as he continued to sound upset and worried. "They'll be after the records. If the police got their hands on them…"

Connor's eyes never left the screen as he interjected. "They'll never find them, Dec, in which case they may come here as well…"

"Then we need to be ready. I'll grab the papers, but I'll need Brendan." Declan rose, walked to the back door, opened it and watched as Connor pressed 'return' and closed his laptop.

"They'll be two minutes; maybe three max," the younger brother smiled.

Declan closed the door and addressed Orla, Pope, and Morris.

"My brother is a technical genius," he announced.

Military Response

Kara and Sergeant Mick Daley listened in on the kitchen discussion, while reading the real-time transcription on the laptop, just in case their ears were deceiving them. They heard Brendan Dunne walk through the kitchen and help Declan in the back garden, while two or three others sounded as if they were rearranging the furniture.

"We need a team at the Hero asap to repel any attack," she said. "On no account must anybody access or remove any records being held there. I'll get a police search unit there, but we can't wait for them."

Daley spoke to his second-in-command, who ran to one vehicle already loaded with soldiers armed to the teeth. Moments later, it was on its way towards the lough before turning left and speeding towards Clonbrinny.

"We'll establish a defensive perimeter around the cottages," Daley continued. "Three-man checkpoint at each end of the road and a mobile patrol across the lough, in case anyone fancies their chances over the water. We'll leave a drone crew here to provide aerial reconnaissance and cover the hills at the back."

Kara nodded her agreement and watched Daley walk away to organise his men. Then she sent a long text message to her uncle.

Final Preparations

Aidan Walsh left his position at the head of Clodagh's bed and walked to the front window of the cottage, just in time to watch the ARW response team drive off towards the town. After looking at the message once more, he took a deep breath and made his way to the kitchen. There, he handed his phone to Declan Kelly before going back to Clodagh.

"It looks like reinforcements are on their way to the Hero," Kelly announced, looking at Stuart Morris. "Should be there in six minutes."

Morris nodded and walked into the hallway to call Westlake. Orla followed, so she could talk to, or leave a message for, Sinead.

"Orla." The landlady looked at Declan. "Tell Sinead to access ICARUS from their phones. Then ask her to call me so I can talk to them."

Kelly looked around the room.

"In a minute or two, we'll have our own protection unit outside, but they won't come into the house unless we let them," he said. "Our focus is Clo." He turned back to his brother, whose short-lived but welcome escape into his hi-tech world had ended, leaving him with a reality he did not want to face.

"Come on, bro," he said. "It's time."

The two of them walked with Brendan into the front room. Pope stayed at the table, half-listening to the call Morris was making to Westlake, but trying hard to make sense of the situation rapidly evolving around him.

This wasn't the vicious criminal monster he'd been expecting. And the priest wasn't frightened for his life. In fact, he was more focused on the poor woman in the front room. Even Kara had priorities other than her own safety. And if this man was the head of a major crime gang, where was his own protection? Brendan was away with Connor most of the time. Pope shook his head. There was something to resolve here, but he wasn't sure what it was.

Stuart Morris walked into the room, his face looking flushed. "I gave Dave the good news and Orla had a quick chat with Sinead, but the phone went dead," he said. "It's about to kick off."

Mayhem

It was the rear entrance door opening and then slamming shut that ended the telephone conversation.

Sinead tossed the phone back to Westlake. He grabbed a cue, rejoined Angus Grace at the pool table, and bent down to get a better look at the four remaining balls. Three men wearing bomber jackets walked into the bar just as he was about to take a shot. He stood up and chalked the cue tip, waiting for them to move out of his line of sight, then knocked a blue ball into the far right pocket.

"Shot," approved Angus Grace, studiously ignoring the newcomers.

Westlake sized up his next effort, realised a pot wasn't on, and played a snooker on his opponent. Moving around the table, he saw two of the men sitting on bar stools watching the game.

The third waited for Sinead to finish washing some glasses. "Is the landlady about?" he asked.

"I'm in charge at the moment." Sinead dried her hands and walked over to the group, smiling sweetly. "What can I get you, lads?"

"We're doing a collection for the cause," smiled the leader of the three. "Money's tight at the moment and we'd like a contribution."

Grace sized up an improbable pot via three cushes but eventually settled for a double, which he missed completely.

"I thought you were good at this," laughed Westlake. Grace grunted, watching the white ball run through to make the potting of the final blue a formality.

"Oh, we only support local causes with our fundraising," smiled Sinead, pointing at a board summarising the Hero's achievements to date. "Meals, days out, that kind of thing."

"Perhaps I wasn't making myself clear." The man sounded annoyed. His associates stood up, one heading towards the main entrance to the bar and locking it; the other towards the two pool players. "We're collecting. Not asking for donations."

The clunk of the final blue ball dropping into a middle pocket was followed swiftly by the black ball into a corner.

"My round," said Grace, turning towards the bar, pool cue in one hand, pint glass in the other. "Oops." The pint glass dropped to the ground and smashed. Three heads couldn't help themselves and glanced towards the floor, even as they reached for the shoulder holsters inside their bomber jackets.

The handle of Grace's pool cue crashed into the leader's wrist, followed by a toothless head butt into the man's face. Westlake slung the white ball at the head of the man closest to him, then grabbed him in a bear hug as he dodged, pinning his arms to his side and ramming his back into the bar with a sickening crunch. The third man saw little of the mayhem. Sinead tasered him, twice for good measure, and left him twitching on the floor in a pool of his own urine.

"Phones," Sinead demanded, handing Westlake a handgun to cover the three on the floor. Grace searched each man, pulling out guns and phones, persuading each owner to open access despite their own pain and then handing them over. Sinead found the community website on each phone, clicked on ICARUS and left them on top of the bar.

The rear entrance door crashed open again, but the immediate shout of "Coldfront! Coldfront!" calmed any adrenaline-fuelled desire to shoot at whoever came around the corner. Sure enough, David Davies appeared, preceded by a fourth would-be robber with his arms strapped behind his back, just in case anyone was still trigger happy.

"You haven't hurt him," observed Angus Grace, disappointed, as a fourth phone followed the other three onto the bar.

"There was no need," explained Coldfront. "Our friend walked up to the passenger side, knocked on the window, showed a grenade, pulled the pin, then dropped it and ran away. This one flew out of the driver's door, saw me and fell to the ground."

"I didn't hear a bang."

"The grenade was a dummy."

Grace and Westlake both knew the account would change dramatically before the end of the night.

"And where is our friend?" asked Westlake.

"Ready to roll. I'll wave him off."

Moments later, the group heard a vehicle leave the car park with a triumphant honk.

"It's over," said Sinead into her phone. "They're all alive."

She switched to speakerphone.

"Hello Jamie. Sean. Finn. Oscar. I was going to ask my friends to drop you all in the river with a bullet in your heads, but time is against us. Here's the deal, boys. You have about ninety seconds to leave the Hero once I've finished talking. That's when the police and the army arrive. I have frozen your bank accounts, although your bank will swear blind everything's fine. To unfreeze them, just tell people the truth about your welcome to Clonbrinny. It's not worth trying anything, at any time - even when the Kellys are supporting their mother in her final hours."

The brief silence that followed was terrifying.

"Do that and you'll get access to your accounts in one week's time. If you don't spread that message - and I will know - you'll still have access to your money, but there will be extra funds in there for you. A significant amount, made from the accounts of your organisation. Your bosses will find out around the same time that you do. Then those funds will vanish; never to be seen again. Am I making myself clear?"

"You are," confirmed Sinead, looking at the petrified faces.

"Because of your action, I now control almost every aspect of your lives and I will never let go. Never cross me, my family or my friends ever again. If you do, I will destroy everything you hold dear. Once you've witnessed it and felt that pain, then I will destroy you. Understand?"

Even Grace and Westlake felt the chill.

"They do," confirmed Sinead, wondering if all four would start crying or just the two who'd already started.

"Right boys. Ninety seconds. Off you go."

Coldfront and Grace gave them an armed escort, while Westlake and Sinead shared a hug.

"No time for that," said Declan Kelly. "Listen to what I say while you're clearing up. You'll have other visitors shortly."

Westlake spun around, searching for the hidden camera.

"Oh, don't bother, my friend," laughed Declan Kelly. "You'll never find it."

Farewell

Declan put his phone on the kitchen table and looked at the worried faces of Stuart, Simon and Orla, standing in the hallway.

"It's okay," he smiled. "Everyone is safe… What…?"

Despite the good news and the relief each of them must be feeling, their expressions stayed the same. Tears rolling down Orla's face reflected the kitchen lights and Clodagh Kelly's eldest surviving son suddenly realised the weight of the moment. He rushed past them into the living room.

The rattling breaths were no more, replaced by gentle gasps that grew softer by the second. Father Aidan prayed feverishly, holding his cross in one hand and making the sign of the cross over Clodagh's body with the other. Held tightly by his loyal, tearful protector, Connor grasped his mother's hand, staring at her face and whispering, "Go to God, ma. Go to God."

Declan moved to the other side of the bed, so he could stroke his mother's hair, just as she had done for his father, all those years ago.

"This," he whispered, "This is how it ends."

Then all was silence.

The Late Arrivals

Blackwell watched as four men in the car park staggered to the vehicle and climbed in, supervised by two men he couldn't identify from behind, but whose pointed guns put them in charge.

Moments later, the car pulled away and disappeared down the side of the hotel.

"It's over," he said. "We should get down there."

Mindy engaged the safety switch on the gun and laid it back on the holdall. She helped to push the bed back to the wall and drag the chest of drawers away from the door, then repacked the weapon.

Blackwell slowly opened the door, checked the empty corridor, and nodded. Both hurried down the stairs, but the locked bar entrance stopped them.

Westlake heard the knock and rushed to open it.

"The gun," he demanded, then handed the weapon to Coldfront, who packed it into the holdall, then headed out to the high street and threw it into the last farm vehicle to drive away.

"Are you all okay?" asked Mindy, as Sinead set some half-empty glasses on the bar, conscious of the growing roar of a powerful 4x4 driving towards their location.

"We're fine," said Westlake. "Listen carefully…"

Coldfront waited outside the front door of the hotel, pacing anxiously and then waving as the men of the Army Ranger Wing pulled to a halt twenty yards away, split into two groups and advanced cautiously towards him.

"I'm glad to see you, lads," he called.

"Hands on your head! Turn around! Kneel!" screamed one rescuer, pointing his weapon.

Coldfront did as ordered, much to the amusement of the people in the bar who watched him toppling forward and almost face planting the pavement without his hands for support.

"Don't laugh," Angus Grace warned, sat at the bar with a beer, "We'll get the same treatment in a minute."

Sinead rushed from the kitchen with two half-plates of chicken curry, which she placed in front of Blackwell and Mindy, who were sitting at a table in the guests' dining area.

"Enjoy," she winked, before running into the bar and stacking some clean glasses into the dishwasher, so she could remove them just moments later. The front door opened just as the back door crashed open yet again. Within seconds, the ARW were in the bar and all the hotel defenders were kneeling on the floor with their hands behind their heads.

"This is outrageous," grumbled Blackwell in his best Welsh accent, "We only checked in less than an hour ago, and this is how we're treated. I feel a one-star review coming up."

"You'll be lucky to write anything ever again if you don't shut up," remarked the soldier left to guard them while the others swept the property.

Certification

Connor reconfigured the wi-fi address to the police monitoring hardware, so it picked up live sound from the cottage again, rather than the AI feed. It solved the bugging problem, especially as the bug itself was impossible to alter without it self-destructing.

To the man with the adolescent mind, being unable to beat the bug was a major failure. He detested failure. Fortunately, finding the transmission device and altering the data source had been straightforward.

A direct line to the police gave the Kellys a useful security system, as long as the police only heard what the family wanted them to hear.

Connor backed up all the data and systems on the laptop to four remote media, then secured those files on the hard drive through a mix of encryption and hidden folders. He opened some personal files and games, then closed the machine.

"I can't reach the doctor, but the undertaker's coming." Declan walked into the kitchen, looking haggard. "If you want to see Mammy…"

"The doctor's walking up the path," Brendan reported from the front room, before heading to the front door, then stopping in surprise. "With a police escort."

Declan walked down the hallway to greet the GP, who held his medical bag in a white-knuckled grip and tried hard not to look nervous.

"Hello, David. My mother's in here." Declan walked into the front room and the GP followed, hesitating when Brendan closed the front door on the two police officers outside. The doctor surveyed the room, then swallowed hard, seeing Clodagh.

"Oh, poor Clo," he said, before crossing himself and pulling a pad out of his bag and placing it on the sideboard. Taking a pen out of his inside jacket pocket, he started to fill the top form, writing with care to stop his hand shaking.

"Aren't you going to check Clodagh's condition?" asked an incredulous Pope.

"Is she alive?"

"No."

"Grand. That's good enough for me."

"But not for me." Declan's scarred face blocked the doctor's view of Pope. If anybody in the room doubted the senior Kelly's ability to create abject terror with just a frown, they doubted no more. He handed a tumbler of whiskey to the frightened GP, who took it and downed it in one even though he didn't care for the drink.

"David," said Declan, accepting the empty glass and handing it to Connor to refill. "You've done your best for my mother and we all appreciate that. Now, I want this done properly."

The GP gulped, finished the second whiskey, and walked to the body. He observed the lifeless stare; pupils dilated and unresponsive - much like his own were feeling. He spent two minutes looking and listening for signs of breathing and a similar amount of time checking for a central pulse and heart activity. Then he stood back and drank the third glass to be offered to him.

"What time did she die, Declan?"

"Fifteen minutes ago."

The GP nodded, stumbled back to the pad on the sideboard and completed and signed the certificate before tearing it off and handing it to Connor.

"Cardiovascular disease," he announced to nobody in particular, putting the pad and pen back in his bag, then shaking hands with anybody within reach. "I'm very sorry for your loss."

He spun into the hallway, straight into the front door that Stuart Morris had just opened for him.

"Oh dear," he giggled, pulling out a handkerchief and holding it to the bleeding split in his forehead. "I think I might need a doctor."

Eager to remove himself from the scene, he fell down the step and into the arms of the two police officers, who shoved him into their car and drove off.

Departure

"Declan. I need to get back to the Hero." Orla Brennan stood at the kitchen sink washing the doctor's glass, Stuart Morris alongside her.

Declan walked over to the landlady and gave her a hug.

"I'm so very sorry Dec. And after everything you've done." Tears flowed again. "Let me know if you need anything."

Morris made his way round the table and put his hand on Connor's shoulder.

"The same goes for you, son," he said. "Whatever you need, just give me a shout."

Connor looked at the mobile number scribbled onto a scrap of paper as if it was a gold bar, and nodded. Orla turned to Pope, standing by the back door.

"Need a lift?" she smiled.

"Thanks, but I'll leave with Aidan. I'll see you soon."

The couple turned and walked out to their car, where Kara, a soldier and a policewoman, waited for them.

"Is it over, Orla?"

"It's over."

"I'm afraid we need to…"

Orla nodded and allowed herself to be frisked by the police officer, while Morris received similar treatment from the soldier.

Embarrassed for her friend, Kara looked to fill the silence.

"Our people are at the Hero. Everyone is fine. Nothing's happened and I doubt it will now we're there."

Orla smiled her thanks, then the couple climbed into the car, completed a three-point turn and headed off towards Clonbrinny.

"Nothing's happened, my arse," she said quietly to Stuart Morris. "Everything has changed today."

Back Again

Jimmy watched the gate open as he turned off the road and onto the winding track to his home. He drove straight past the cottage to the outbuilding beyond and reversed up to its door. As soon as he emerged, Margaret used her tablet to unbolt the windows and doors and to raise the shutters on the cottage windows.

She put the kettle on while her husband loaded the gun bags onto the trolley and decanted their contents into their hiding places, locked the outbuilding and parked the car in its usual space, just outside the back door. He walked in, stroked Bella, then knelt down and kissed his wife.

"Promised you I'd come back safe," he grinned.

"You said you'd try," she corrected him, "But I'm glad you maintained your 100% record."

Five minutes later, they were sitting in the living room, Jimmy talking through the events of the afternoon and trying to make them as boring as possible while his wife held his hand.

"Let me get this straight," she said. Jimmy tried not to swallow hard, but failed miserably. He knew what was coming next.

"The driver stepped out of the vehicle and looked at Coldfront's gun?"

"Correct."

"But why did he step out?"

"Because I had walked across the car park - carefully mind, keeping in his blind spot - and knocked at the passenger window. I made him jump."

"How?"

Jimmy barely knew his new friends at the Hero, but he knew Coldfront liked to talk. He had no choice but to tell his beloved wife the truth before she had to sift through all kinds of embellishments.

"I waved a dummy grenade," he admitted. "Then rolled it under the car and ran off."

"You ran?"

"Stumbled really. That ballistics vest is heavy."

Margaret closed her eyes, imagining the scene.

"Then Coldfront took him into the Hero. A minute later, he came out and gave me the thumbs up."

"And I'm so happy you're back," she smiled, opting not to roast her husband for walking across a car park, grenade in hand, with four armed, hostile men nearby. She'd keep that powder dry. "We should go out later to celebrate."

The Search

Two minutes after the undertaker had left, there was a firm rap on the front door of the cottage. The priest answered it. The others had stripped the bed in the front room and were manoeuvring it back upstairs, Simon Pope seriously wondering how they would be managing if it hadn't been for the brute strength of Brendan Dunne.

"Good afternoon, Father," said a police officer, feeling brave as ten other police personnel, plus the military stood in support. "We have a warrant to search these premises for materials which may relate to serious criminal activities. Is Mister Declan Kelly here?"

"You know he is," said the priest. "You've just seen him carry out his dead mother and place her in the back of a hearse."

"A simple 'yes' would have done, Father."

"It's alright Aidan." Declan walked down the stairs and examined the search warrant. "That's fine, officer. Please try to leave things tidy, though. It's been a tough day."

The search team piled into the small cottage and split up. The Kellys, Brendan, Pope and the priest sat at the kitchen table with a coffee each and a plate of biscuits between them.

"I thought we might have seen Kara," said Connor, sounding disappointed.

"She's just left for the Hero," said a passing police officer. "We have a team there as well."

Pope caught the two brothers exchanging a smile at the news - a smile which, unusually, started at the eyes but didn't reach the mouth.

The presence of so many people in the cottage killed the opportunity for serious conversation.

However, the following couple of hours passed reasonably well, with the elder Kelly happy to share memories of Clo and to discuss current, innocuous local topics to stave off boredom.

By the end, Pope understood the long-term relationship between the four men. The more he knew, the less he grasped the reason for his mission.

"And you, Simon." The comment and the eyes on him brought Pope back to the present with a jolt. "I understand all is not as it seems." Pope blushed and remained silent. "I understand we're in the presence of a genuine hero."

Thanks a bunch, Stuart.

"It's not something I like to talk about," he said.

Declan nodded. "I get that," he said. "Sometimes we're thrown into unprecedented situations. Events happen over which we have no control. We just respond as best we can and hope we're making the right choices. Often, we don't even know what choices we're making. How they might affect the rest of our lives. Sometimes it benefits us. Sometimes…" He shrugged, then raised his mug. "To you, my friend."

The others raised their mugs in salute. Pope raised his own in reply, thinking how that speech would sit with someone else he knew.

"Mister Kelly?" Declan turned to face the police superintendent stood at the door. "Might I have a chat, sir?"

Declan stood and pushed his chair under the table.

"Superintendent, these people have supported my brother and myself all day. Could you take them back to Clonbrinny or would it be okay for my friend to take them? You're welcome to assign an officer to accompany them."

The police officer nodded. "I'll just need their contact details. Sergeant Malone here will go with them."

"Thank you," Declan looked at Pope. "We'll meet again, under better circumstances."

Pope nodded. "I look forward to it."

To understand things, he had no choice.

The Church Of St. Dominic

The return journey to Clonbrinny was quiet, with Sergeant Malone in the car. In fact, nobody spoke until Brendan dropped Pope and the priest near the hotel, then headed back to the cottages. Father Aidan looked at the police vehicles outside the Hero.

"I've a bottle at home," offered the priest.

"Let's do that," agreed Pope. "I've had enough drama."

The priest led him back along the road past the butchers, towards the church, then stopped outside the third from last terraced house and pulled a key from his pocket. Once inside, the men walked down the dark hallway, into the small kitchen, where the priest offered a chair to his guest before taking a bottle from the work surface and two tumblers from a cupboard. He poured a finger of whiskey for each of them.

"Thank you, Simon," he said. "You didn't have to come this morning. I'm grateful that you did."

Both men drank, then fell silent once more, feeling the liquor burning at the back of their throats. *The next sip will taste better*, thought Pope. Each man tried to process the day's events and to work out the implications. Both failed.

"How are you feeling, Father? I understand your relationship with the Kellys has been... difficult... these last few years?"

"It has." The priest took another sip of his drink. "I think it'll improve, though." He tipped his glass from side to side, watching the amber liquid swirl around. "Time will tell."

"Are the Kellys in trouble?"

"The Kellys have always *been* trouble. Whether they're *in* trouble... I'm not so sure."

"And what about you, Father? When we talked in the church, I asked if you felt safe, or whether you were in danger."

"I remember. Personally, I've never felt in danger... I've worried for my wider family, but not for myself..."

"For Kara? I met her at the bar yesterday. She told me she's your niece. Then I met her again this morning, up at the church ruin..."

Father Aidan looked surprised, started to say something, then stopped.

He looked at the battered postcard on the floor and picked it up, examining the image on its front. He handed it over to Pope.

"The Church of St Dominic in Lisbon," he said. "Igreja de São Domingos in Portuguese."

Pope examined the photograph of the church's interior - a dramatic, imposing space.

There was an impressive grandeur implied in the picture, but... Pope looked more closely... the visible wear and devastating damage to the building's fabric suggested a more sombre ambience.

"The church has what you might call a chequered past," explained the priest.

"Once, the largest church in Lisbon. The venue for many royal weddings before the republic. Beautiful, stunning, evocative."

"I can see why," said Pope, deciding he would add the church to his 'to be visited' list.

"That's the good side. In 1506, there were Jews in the congregation who had converted to Christianity. The people attacked and killed them. The violence spread across the city. They massacred up to 4,000 'new Christians' - many just outside the church. In 1531, the Lisbon earthquake damaged the building. It was the home of the Portuguese Inquisition in the 1700s. In 1755, another earthquake almost destroyed it. In 1959, a fire broke out in the building. Accounts say it was hotter than hell inside; so hot, the marble melted. In 1994, the church was reopened, but they kept much of the damage."

The priest stopped and took another drink.

"Some people see it as a symbol of Lisbon's resilience. Others see it as a reminder of the Church's guilt and God's response. Go there. See how you feel when you're in that space. The Lord knows, I've given absolution on some appalling confessions over the last few years. Many priests have. I struggle to believe I did the right thing. I feel guilty."

"But not in danger?"

The priest raised his glass. "Maybe from alcoholic poisoning."

"And your family?"

Father Aidan took his glass to the kitchen sink and emptied the contents down the plughole and switched on the kettle, then returned to the table.

"Their lives aren't in danger, but their standing in their community is under threat. That can have serious consequences."

Pope sensed the detail behind the statement would remain confidential.

"Is that still the case?" he asked.

"After today? I don't think it is." The priest surprised himself with his newfound optimism.

Pope raised his glass.

"Amen to that," he said.

The Return To The Hero

Stuart Morris and Orla Brennan sat and fumed in the van, while the search of the Hero and the questioning of the staff and guests continued.

Besides Coldfront's van still parked by the barrels in the corner, the car park also contained four police cars, a forensics van, a communications van and two military vehicles. The soldiers stood guard outside the property, while the police took the tasks inside.

Morris eyed the soldier assigned to protect them... or to keep them in the vehicle but prevent them driving off, depending on your point of view. Orla was definitely in the latter camp. "Two hours. This is ridiculous," she muttered. "I can't believe he'll do anything if I get out of my vehicle and enter my hotel, or drive off to Margaret's until this is all finished."

"Oh, I think he'd shoot you," said Morris. "These guys are on edge. Remember, they're expecting an attack. They don't know it's already happened."

Orla sighed and checked her wing mirror.

"And why are those beer barrels down by your van?"

Morris shrugged. "Maybe somebody was thirsty."

A blur of movement at the rear entrance to the bar caught their attention.

Moments later, a police sergeant knocked on the driver's window and waited patiently for Orla to wind it down. Slowly. *I've had to wait. So can he*, she thought. The officer didn't speak until the window was all the way down.

"The coast is clear, Mrs Brennan," he said, an amused look on his face. "We've been through every room. There's a search team in your office and one in the cellar, but they'll be done in half an hour and shouldn't leave any mess."

"What are they looking for?"

The police officer shrugged. "No idea," he said, "But whatever it is, they haven't found it."

"Thank you, sergeant," interjected Morris, before Orla said anything else. "Are you leaving now?"

"Not all of us," came the reply. "We'll have an increased presence around the town for the next 24 hours at least. The army will be here overnight. We'll review in the morning."

Orla nodded her thanks, wound up the window, and got out. Morris followed her into the hotel, where the group at the bar rushed to greet them.

Westlake was the first to them.

"We'll tell you what happened later," he muttered, followed by a louder, "The prodigals return! Where've you been? Get lost?"

Sinead hugged her mother as if she'd never let her go. The feeling was mutual. Morris fist-bumped Grace and Coldfront, then Westlake led him firmly by the arm to meet the latest arrivals, who had remained seated at a table with their backs to the reunion.

"Stu, this is Paul and Amanda Morgan. They're Welsh people, on holiday here from Wales. They'll have quite a story to tell when they get back to Wales."

He looked meaningfully into his former colleague's eyes, then stepped to the side. Morris smiled at the couple, realised who they were and almost fell into a chair at the table.

"Alright boy?" beamed Andrew Blackwell, clearly enjoying every moment. Mindy looked wary, hoping Morris's brain wasn't so scrambled by events that he was going to give them away. She needn't have worried. Morris was too shocked to do anything.

Could this day get any stranger? he wondered.

A Change In Tactics

Kara Walsh returned to the cottage and looked across the lough. The light was fading, dragging a thick, velvety silence across the waters. It was a peaceful end to a tumultuous day. A stressful, exciting and - she suspected - ultimately frustrating day. At least things were moving on. There'd be no more tedium on top of the hill, trying to ignore the dead who surrounded her. There was no point. Someone had tampered with the data and compromised the mission.

Footsteps on the road told her the moment of solitude was ending.

"Anything?" she asked.

The search leader stopped beside her and produced a cigarette. "Nothing," he answered. "Are you surprised?"

"It's called Operation Shiny for a reason. Are you done in there?"

"Just tidying up."

The man decided against a smoke and turned to retrace his steps.

"You know," he said, "If I didn't know better…"

Kara didn't respond; just listened to the footsteps heading away. The Kellys had lost their mother; probably felt emotional; possibly vulnerable, especially with Fortress being implemented in the town. People were on edge.

Maybe it was time to change tactics. Hoping Declan Kelly was fallible was getting them nowhere because the man plainly wasn't. Perhaps it was time for some straight talking.

She strolled along the path by the water away from the cottages, towards one of the army checkpoints. The question was what to say; how to push Declan's buttons; maybe prise something from Connor, or even Brendan Dunne.

Hearing the vehicles starting up behind her, she turned and headed back towards the cottages, waving to her team as they drove past.

The Kellys' reputation didn't scare her. There were special forces surrounding the place; and she had a secret weapon.

The lights were glowing from the cottage as she approached, especially from the open doorway, silhouetting the figure leaning against the frame.

Taking a deep breath, she crossed the road and walked up the short path to the door.

"Hello, Uncle Declan," she smiled.

Reporting In

Pope left the priest's house, nodding at the two soldiers protected by a hastily constructed sangar as he walked by them.

Hesitating at the hotel entrance, he opted to walk past the building and down the lane to the car park. Once there, he headed for the cover of the van in the corner. He called the RSM, reporting on the day's events and seeking guidance on what to do next.

"We asked you to report on the priest's situation, Simmo. From what you're saying, we can leave well alone."

Pope whispered a silent prayer of thanks.

"However," continued the RSM, making Pope reflect on the Lord's sense of humour, "It sounds like the situation is volatile. Monitor things for a couple of days. See how it all pans out. Maintain that low profile and keep out of trouble."

"Sounds straightforward," said Pope, having failed so far.

"But get more information on ICARUS. Our friends at GCHQ want as much as possible about that Pandora's box."

"I'll try, but no promises. One more thing. The stories about Andrew Blackwell and Mindy Abbott being missing? They're in the hotel."

The silence - as brief as it was - was deafening.

"Not my problem," said the RSM, and rang off.

Pope looked down at his phone, realising that he was up the creek without a paddle regarding the former prime minister, and he'd missed four calls from Pippa during the day.

He called her. After today's events, he needed to hear her voice, to share his thoughts, receive some calm advice, to talk about things at home and enjoy some semblance of normality.

"Where have you been?" she screamed down the phone to make herself heard over the war zone in the background. "It sounds like they're destroying the house next door brick by brick. They're working into the night because they're on a tight deadline. I have floodlights blasting through the front windows. You've had a visit from special branch. They've left you a form to fill in. And tell Andy the net is closing in. Someone is dropping big hints, and the speculation isn't positive."

"Pip? Pip? Are you there? The signal's awful here today. I'll try to…"

He rang off, feeling no guilt and relishing a few moments of peace before walking into the chaos that was the Fallen Hero.

Maeve's Marauders

As soon as Pope entered the bar, he wished he'd stayed outside, listening to the chaos at home. A disgruntled police contingent was wrapping up the wild goose chase of the search Declan and Connor had sent them on.

Because of the police presence, the Fishing Flops concealed the adrenaline rush of foiling an armed raid by swapping unfunny and uninteresting food delivery stories with Sinead and Orla. Stuart Morris appeared spooked, forced to engage in trivial chatter while wanting to scream "What are you doing here?!" at the two new guests.

Pope might have received a better welcome if he was just returning from a visit to the gents' toilet. Nobody acknowledged his appearance.

He took an empty seat at the bar and listened to Angus Grace recount the life story of the pensioner porn stars he had met that morning.

Sinead made him an Irish coffee he hadn't requested, then served it to him with wide eyes and an overly-bright, manic smile.

The UK's former prime minister stared at Stuart Morris, and garbled away, focusing on a plausible Welsh accent. Meanwhile, Mindy Abbott was struggling to grasp what was happening around her; very much like everybody else.

The last police officer traipsed through the bar and out to her vehicle, with not so much as a sheet of paper as confiscated potential evidence. The senior officer had a quiet word with Orla, then followed his team through the exit. An uneasy silence fell over the group in the bar and remained until all six police vehicles had gone.

"Well, hello all," said Pope, breaking the silence. Before anyone could reply, the front door of the hotel crashed open, followed by the door into the bar. Four men and two women stumbled in, each hampered by the instrument cases they carried. They stopped, surprised by the lack of atmosphere and customers, as well as the aggressive and apprehensive stares directed at them.

"Sorry we're late," said Maeve, the lead singer and flautist of Maeve's Marauders, "Had trouble persuading the soldiers outside we hadn't come to kill you all." She waited for some form of amused response, then realised it wasn't coming. "Anyway, we're here now, so that's grand. Where shall we set up?"

Sinead was the first to realise what was happening, as she'd been the one to book the evening's entertainment. "Mammy, it's the folk band."

"Irish folk music!" chuckled a delighted Blackwell. "Brilliant!"

"I'm not sure it's worth them setting up," Orla whispered to her daughter. "We won't be busy tonight, given the events of the day."

"But we've posted nothing on ICARUS," smiled Sinead. "People will be dying to know what's happened. Give it a minute."

She guided the band to the far corner of the room and the small stage used by the quizmaster the night before, asking Maeve for instrumental versions of the set list.

"There's been a death in the town today," she explained.

"There'll be folk mourning and others gossiping. Not sure of the mood."

As she returned to the bar, the first of the night's customers entered, trying to look nonchalant, as if a Fortress success, armed guards all over the place and the death of a gangland boss's mother down the road were everyday occurrences in Clonbrinny.

"Get your glad rags on," Stuart told Orla and Sinead. "We'll help at the bar. You'll have a lot of talking to do."

The Kitchen Summit

Sitting next to the target of Operation Shiny in the kitchen of his family home, sipping a mug of coffee and helping herself to the occasional biscuit, should have filled Kara with trepidation and fear, but it didn't. If anyone experienced those feelings, it was Declan Kelly and Brendan Dunne. She was fuming and didn't even bother to hide it.

The only one to look happy and excited by the unexpected visit was Connor.

He had always struggled to recognise or correctly respond to the feelings of others, and his bomb injuries had not helped that issue.

"I'm very sorry about Clodagh, Declan," Kara said. "I know how close you were."

The elder Kelly looked down at his drink, unwilling to talk to the girl he'd known forever until he knew more about the visit. His brother, however, had no such concerns.

"Is that because you've been monitoring us, Kara?"

Kara smiled. She had always had a soft spot for Connor. Her dad and Aidan had been good friends with the Kellys since school, and remained close until rumours of Declan's activities created a distance between them. Uncle Declan's birthday and Christmas gifts continued for a time after the split, but Connor always acted as the courier.

Five years younger than the others, and 'special in his own way', as her mother described him, Connor had always been in her life. With no siblings, Kara regarded him as the nearest thing to an older brother - a relationship maintained until she joined the police. It had been sad, she reflected, losing the two men in her life over a couple of years. But it was good to see him again.

"I've always known how close you all are, Connor… how protective your brother is of the family. I know that without monitoring you."

"But you did, though."

Kara nodded. "Fat lot of good it did us," she smiled. "That operation's probably being shut down as I speak but…" she looked directly at Declan, "The checkpoints on the road will remain until tomorrow; maybe the day after."

"I appreciate that, Kara, but it really isn't necessary anymore." The elder Kelly absent-mindedly stroked the scar on his right cheek. "Now mother's gone…" He choked up. Uttering those words had brought the sad reality to the fore, hitting him straight in his emotional solar plexus. Connor placed his hand on his brother's shoulder - a rare display of well-timed and well-judged empathy. Brendan looked at the ceiling, working hard to keep the tears at bay.

The scene took Kara by surprise. She knew what it was like to lose someone close, but to suppress the feelings of loss and desolation until the grief became overwhelming. She knew what she had to do. Make the most of the situation.

"Then I'll remove them," she said. "I just thought you might need some extra protection."

Declan shook his head. "Thanks, but we're good."

"That wasn't the case at the Hero earlier. I know something started and ended before we arrived."

"It was just some idiots trying to make a name for themselves."

So, there had been an incident.

"How do you know there won't be something else?"

"I know."

Kara took a sip from her mug and grabbed another biscuit. One thing her time in the police had taught her was the power of silence.

Connor disappeared into the front room and returned with his laptop. Brendan wandered to the back door and peered through the window into the back garden. Declan looked at his mug, a slight frown making his scar appear more vivid and his face even more threatening than normal.

Celebration

The band was excellent, thought Pope, listening to the accomplished set of musicians play a series of Irish airs and laments; a fitting backdrop to the earnest, sombre conversations he could hear across the bar.

Orla moved from group to group, table to table, greeting everybody and answering questions they might have about the events of the day. It had been a long while since the last Fortress. Although everything had gone well this time, the fact another had been needed had a sobering effect on the crowd.

Sinead sat at a small corner table in animated conversation with Maeve of Maeve's Marauders, making notes on sheets of paper. Morris and Westlake collected glasses and served food while monitoring their respective love interests. Grace and Coldfront helped behind the bar, spending most of their time shaking hands with strangers who wanted to say hello or thank you.

Pope made his way outside carrying a tray loaded with hot foil-wrapped sandwiches and half a dozen mugs of coffee, which he distributed to the members of the Army Ranger Wing standing guard around the hotel. As he chatted with the soldiers watching the rear car park, a familiar car rolled in and parked in the only disabled bay.

Emerging from the driver's door, Jimmy Doyle stopped for a moment and surveyed the scene of his recent action, before hurrying to help his beloved and happy wife into her wheelchair. Pope held the outside and then the inside doors open for them, determined not to miss what he hoped would be a memorable entrance.

The couple emerged from the dim hallway into the bar. The crowd broke into loud applause and the band segued from an anonymous dirge into *Hail To The Chief*.

Showing admirable self-control and stopping only to greet the landlady and her daughter, Jimmy guided Margaret to a reserved table before advancing to the bar and being enveloped by well-wishers. Margaret didn't care. She was explaining to her own audience that her husband could be a hero and an idiot at the same time, just as long as he came home safe and sound.

Pope stooped to kiss her on the cheek and whispered, "It's almost as if you're proud of him, Margaret."

"That I am, Simmo," she beamed, "But if you ever tell him that, I'll kill you."

Pope backed off with his hands up in mock surrender, then walked over to the resident's dining area, where a couple were struggling to eat their meal while monitoring the action in the bar next to them.

He sat down on a spare chair and helped himself to a chip off the man's plate. "Fancy seeing you here," he smiled, then shook hands with the couple.

"No hug?" asked Mindy. "Nobody's looking."

"Don't bet on it," said Pope. "Assume everyone knows everything about you at all times in Clonbrinny."

"Why?"

"Because they do."

Andrew Blackwell was enthused by what he'd seen and heard.

"Think about it," he urged. "This community understands and accepts it's not in total control, but has a process in place to deal with any eventuality. People live their own lives, help each other out and come together as one powerful entity when circumstances require it. It's a microcosm of what needs to happen if *Path Finder* is to work. Amazing!"

"As is the fact that you're here to witness it, when you should be on the west coast, or hiding from the media in suburbia," pointed out Mindy.

Britain's former prime minister looked gobsmacked.

"Truly serendipitous!" he exclaimed, proud that he'd remembered to use his Welsh accent at the last moment.

The Kitchen Confession

The wall clock kept a formal record of how long the silence lasted. Kara counted 300 ticks; the last 150 or so feeling twice as long as the first.

"Are you wired, Kara?"

"No, but there are bugs in the cottage. We've been monitoring what you say in here for a good while, so our system may pick this up."

Declan looked neither surprised nor bothered.

"Then tell me. Why are you here?"

"To find out the truth."

"The truth." Declan took his cup to the sink and rinsed it, then filled the kettle and put it on to boil. "And if I tell you the truth, what do you expect to hear?"

Kara stood and brought her cup over to the sink, rinsed it, then set it next to Declan's.

"You wanted to support and protect your family after your father died. Times were tough. Credit to you. You worked hard, even in your teens. Helped to create what Fortress is today. Finished what your dad started, but differently. You started a business, then built others. Most are legal; some aren't, but you cover your tracks well."

She watched his face, impassive as he prepared fresh drinks; a real poker face.

"You're linked to so many criminal activities, here and occasionally abroad. Serious crimes, but you leave the drugs and the prostitution well alone. We think that's your mother's influence, as well as her being behind your regular confessions to Uncle Aidan as well."

Again, the poker face, even when bringing Clodagh into the spotlight.

"The links are all there. People talk. Gangs are fearful; treat you with respect. But there is never enough hard evidence to take you to court, never mind gain a conviction. You are always one step ahead. You probably have connections in the police force, local and national politics, finance, who knows?"

Declan went back to his chair while Brendan walked through the kitchen, down the hallway, and into the front room. Connor continued to mess about on his laptop, oblivious to the conversation.

"The truth," Declan murmured, "Where to begin?"

Kara sat down, trying to look casual but failing miserably.

"Long story short," suggested Connor, without looking up from his screen.

"Fine. You are talking about the perception of me; not the reality."

"Slightly longer story," suggested Connor.

Declan raised his eyes to the ceiling and sighed.

"I worked hard and built businesses. Construction, property management, estate agency, insurance, finance, debt recovery, computer services - all successful; all totally legit. Check the published accounts. Send in an audit team if you like. My people are good people - well-treated, well rewarded and loyal. All I ask is they do a great job for the customer. That brings repeat business and referrals. Everybody's happy. That's how I provide for my family - and that includes my mother, Connor, Brendan, my local community and my team."

"That doesn't explain the links to the criminal activities."

"There aren't any. Not real ones. They're designed to create a perception. You don't cross me and you don't cross my family. Leave me alone and I'll leave you alone. That's how I protect everyone."

"Designed?"

"I have a system that monitors police radio traffic. The algorithm cross-references any details it picks up with material in our database. If it has potential value to me, it creates a tenuous link between me and the ongoing incident. That's pushed into the public domain well before the reporting of the actual event. When that happens, people draw their own conclusions."

"If that's the case, the real criminals would know you weren't involved."

"I'm harmless to them. If the police investigate me, it takes some of the heat off the people who actually committed the crime. Plus, I don't take up many of the algorithm's suggestions. Just enough to maintain my reputation."

"How about an example?"

Declan thought carefully. He rarely remembered individual stories.

"The death in the Liffey. Paddy O'Brien. You'll have reports I was looking for him a couple of days prior to his death."

"But that was a road accident. Hit by a police car when he stumbled out of a pub after a hard day's drinking."

"And now, people believe I have hitmen in the Gardaí."

Declan didn't even smile as he said it, thought Kara. *It's not funny to him; it's a statement of fact. All just part of the protection strategy.*

"But there must be criminal organisations who've called you out on this," she said.

Declan shook his head.

"There's some ego there, but it's all about the money. Take that away, or threaten to take it away…"

Kara's heart quickened.

"You can do that?"

"Yes."

"How?"

"A secret weapon."

"Which is…?"

"Ah. If he tells you that, I won't be a secret anymore," beamed Connor.

Catch-Up

The emotions experienced and expressed in the bar and the residents' dining area were pretty similar. Outrage, disbelief, admiration and sober reflection topped the list - the latter despite the amount of alcohol being put away.

Pope, Blackwell and Mindy swapped their news from the last few days, confident that everyone else had far too much on their minds to bother eavesdropping on their comparatively mundane conversation.

Pope listened to the entire account of the Peace Castle summit and the subsequent retreat from the West coast without comment, then considered it all carefully before offering an opinion.

"They stitched you up," he said. "They talked money and got you out of your shell by feeding your ego; flying you to an exclusive, secret meeting of the great and the good who were there just for you. In return, you've given credibility to whatever some of the wealthiest, most powerful people in the world choose to do or say about your ideas. And you have no involvement in their plans. You've lost your… what's it called… intellectual property, and have no control over what is done with it. Plus, they're using the media manhunt to keep you otherwise occupied while they complete their plans and get things moving."

Blackwell looked at his plate and used his fork to move several garden peas into a straight line. There was no point responding when all he could do was agree with his friend's summary. Much better to focus on the peas and wait for the ground to swallow him up.

Mindy listened to the conversation without comment, eager to see how Andy's favourable account of his trip would be received by someone unfamiliar with it, but who felt some goodwill towards her fiancé - much like the public.

They stitched you up wasn't necessarily a criticism, more a sad observation. The money issue was straightforward, as they had donated the fee to various charities before the meeting took place.

Regaining ownership of *Path Finder* was key, but would be easier if they could show they had never lost it. The challenge was to get that message out at the right time and in the right format - and that meant using the media, even the media owned by the Conclave.

Simmo had mentioned credibility. Widdock's revelations suggested the Conclave's members might have credibility issues of their own. Maybe there were opportunities to cut the legs from underneath them before they could launch whatever they planned to launch. *So much to do*, she reflected, *but so little time*.

Conscious his summary may have hurt Blackwell's feelings and eager to change the subject, Pope brought his friends up-to-date with edited details of Stuart Morris and Dave Westlake's new love interests, meeting the priest, and events at the cottage by the lough.

"So, mission accomplished?" asked Mindy, relieved that any threats to Simmo had been limited to being a virtual captive of Ireland's rumoured *capo dei capi*, having a gun pointed at him at a derelict church and almost having his ribs cracked by Dave Westlake after drinking a cup of air.

"Almost," Pope replied. "Just need to finish a couple of things, then I think we'll be done and on our way."

"Excellent!" said Blackwell, with what he hoped was a persuasive smile. "Any room for a couple of stowaways on your return home?"

The Genius

Martin Kelly and others formed ICARUS a few weeks before the death of hotel and bar owner Bobby Brennan. It started life as a flag and a small newsletter, designed to encourage the town's community to resist the outside threat of criminal gangs, who used their claimed religious or political affiliations to justify their illegal activities.

A couple of months after the bombing at the lough, the campaign to discourage gang action in the town became more organised, more visceral and more violent in its response to any threat.

The flag now flew above a Fortress, but that implied defence. As successful as that deterrence became, Martin Kelly waged war on those who made war. He implemented a low-profile 'skirmishing' campaign, designed to disrupt, destabilise and destroy those his decaying mind decided were a threat to his family and community.

It was years after his death and that of his eldest son, Seán, that Clonbrinny launched a community website to bring its residents even closer together. A couple of years later, it added the ICARUS function to ensure locals were aware of any current threats in real time.

That was as much as Kara knew. Until now.

"The bomb seriously damaged Connor's chances of a normal life," explained Declan. "Brendan and I do our best to protect him day-to-day. But over time, the brain's miraculous capacity for self-repair helped him create a world where he is successful, content and can largely cope with what life throws at him."

"Throws at all of us," added Connor, then, seeing the frown flit across Kara's face, "I think differently to everyone else, Kara. And I enjoy working with computers. They don't get angry or upset. They don't laugh at me when I don't understand."

"You mean you mend them? Or you like computer programmes?"

Declan stood and walked behind Connor, placing his hands on his brother's shoulders.

"Connor created and maintains ICARUS," he explained. "He's a genius."

"It's true," smiled Connor.

"Because?"

Declan fell silent, feeling as if he was about to cross the point of no return. Brendan Dunne crossed it for him.

"ICARUS is as threatening in its own way as Martin Kelly was in his. On the surface, it's a benign programme that keeps the town aware of threats and helps coordinate responses. But if you try to access ICARUS without permission, or if you're refused access, it could become your worst nightmare."

Kara tried to maintain her composure.

"How so?"

"It disables security systems, accesses and copies data, and takes full control of the visiting machine and the network behind it." Connor genuinely looked and sounded as if it was no big deal.

"And it works?"

"Every time."

"And every bad actor in the country has had a go?"

"For a while, we were a target, but not anymore," confirmed Declan. "Now, we're a sword of Damocles hanging over the operations of every major player out there. They're smart. They leave us well alone and we do the same with them."

"But you could finish them. Freeze their assets. Hand over their records."

"Not going to happen. Others would take their place. We'd have to start again. Our job is to protect those closest to us. Full stop. Besides, if we wiped out the bad actors, your intelligence network would vanish overnight. You'd be operating blind."

Kara looked at the three men in front of her, searching for any suggestion that the revelations were a crude ploy to throw her off track.

A slight smirk, maybe, or a breaking of eye contact. *Nothing*.

"But you're an ongoing threat. They could kill you. Kidnap you."

"ICARUS operates with a contingency for that. We can't override it, no matter what. We accept that. The people who could threaten us won't do, because they know that. It would be mutually assured destruction. In fact, it's in their interests to keep us healthy."

The detective stood and walked to the end of the kitchen, looking at the illuminated reflection of herself and the men behind her in the window.

"So you're telling me every report we've received over the last decade linking you to…"

"None are true."

"But you blackmailed my uncle. You drove him to drink. Made his life miserable."

She watched the reflection as Declan flinched while Brendan and Connor shifted uncomfortably.

"You'd need Aidan to testify to make that stick, and that's never going to happen. He took my confession, that's all. I made his life difficult, but that's going to change now. I told him earlier. And I would never say anything about your father's death. You have my word."

"Then why confess to crimes you didn't commit?"

Connor cleared his throat.

"My idea," he said. "Confession made the rumours seem more real."

"And I did the penances," interrupted Declan. "All of them."

Kara gave a slight snort of derision and turned around, fire in her eyes.

"And why would you do that?"

"To intercede on someone else's behalf." Brendan pushed his chair away from the kitchen table, his eyes not shifting from Kara's face. "Clodagh never forgave herself for pretending to call an ambulance the night Martin passed away. He couldn't live, you see, without risking all their lives. God knows, they'd already lost enough. She felt her action - or lack of it - killed him. She was ashamed and kept it secret."

"Until yesterday, when she told me she'd confessed to Aidan," added Declan. "But I'd always known, you see. The argument woke me up. All those years ago. I heard everything, sitting in the shadows on the landing. As the years went by and she got older and sicker, I worried for her. I didn't want her going with that around her neck." He paused, trying to make sure his explanation was clear.

"Intercession's all about putting in a good word for someone or something, but it's done with prayer and I've never been much good with that. Prayer's an abdication of responsibility - 'I've prayed, so it's up to God now; I've done my bit'. That's not the case. You must invest. That might be time, work, or even cash. Here it was penance. I carried them all out - everything Aidan told me to do to atone for things I hadn't done - and I carried them out thinking of Mammy, doing everything on her behalf. Sometimes I doubled the penances, so there was a surplus on the balance sheet, but never for myself."

Kara sat down again, her face in her hands; an emotional mess. They all were. So much had happened in such a short space of time. So much had changed. Finally, she looked at them again, surprised she saw them in a different light - unsure of themselves, upset and vulnerable. Looking very much like she felt.

"You've sacrificed your lives to protect others."

Declan sat up straight. "It's what my father did. It's what my mother did when she let my father die. Circumstances led us to this place, but we're not victims. We decided what to do and were prepared to live with the outcome."

Connor nodded. "Circumstances have changed again now. We will mourn. Then we can be ourselves. Let perceptions fade."

"Jaysus," Brendan was stunned. "That's profound. What do you mean?"

"No idea," admitted Connor, "But it sounded great, didn't it?"

The smiles around the table turned into grins; then chuckles into belly laughs that helped release the stress and tension all were feeling, albeit for different reasons.

By the time the laughter subsided, Kara had decided.

"Uncle Declan," she said, "Tell me what we need to do."

The Big Man Returns

The loud and persistent knocking at the priest's back door woke him from his armchair doze, which was itself a surprise as Aidan struggled with sleep. Putting on his glasses, he jumped in surprise when he saw the face at his back window. Connor Kelly grinned and gave him the thumbs up.

"Open your front door, Father," he shouted, then disappeared. Worried that the day's stressful events were about to take a turn for the worst, Aidan hurried down the hallway and opened the door, to be confronted by the Kelly brothers and Brendan Dunne.

"Aidan," said Declan Kelly. "I believe there's a part-Fortress celebration and a part pre-funeral wake for my mother happening across the road. Would you like to join us?"

"Do I have a choice?"

"No," smiled Brendan Dunne. "Get your shoes on and grab a jacket."

Leaving the car parked outside the house, the four men walked past the nearest guard checkpoint and through the front door of the hotel. Declan stopped in the vestibule and listened to the music and chatter coming from the bar area.

"One day," he predicted, "I'll walk through this door and the noise level won't drop."

He put his hand on the doorknob and turned to look at them with a smile.

"But I bet everything I own that today is not that day."

Four seconds later, he was correct. Facing a sea of hushed faces, he sent Brendan to get the drinks. Flanked by Aidan and Connor, he walked through the silent crowd until he reached Orla and Sinead's table, hugged them both, and asked permission to address the gathering. At the band area, he asked to borrow the microphone, which had to be switched on. Then he faced the crowd, some frozen to the spot by fear; others by curiosity.

"I have a confession to make," he announced. "You know, like my father, I have always had a deep and lasting affection for Clonbrinny. I also have huge respect for the wonderful people who live here, including this hotel's guests and even Paddy Monahan, despite the marrow shenanigans." He waited for the chuckles to die down.

"Today has been one of many days where you have shown your courage and your charity. I'm delighted to see you all here, celebrating the latest successful defence of all we hold dear and remembering Clodagh. She was as proud of you all as I am." Again, a brief halt, this time to regain his composure after a smattering of sympathetic applause.

"With Orla's permission, the drinks are on me. But remember, Father Aidan and I want you all at St Patrick's tomorrow morning to give thanks for what we have. And no sleeping in the pews."

Ignoring the mixture of applause, laughter, random cheers and the race to get to the bar, Declan returned the microphone to Maeve of the Marauders. "Leave it switched on," he smiled. "Let's have some proper songs."

The Car Park Hero

From the other side of the bar, at the door leading into the residents' dining room, Pope watched developments alongside Blackwell and Mindy, thankful they had just had their drinks delivered by Coldfront moments before the elder Kelly's announcement. Brendan Dunne had also received notice of the tidal wave that was about to hit, with drinks grouped on a nearby table.

Coming to the aid of their beleaguered staff, Sinead and Orla appeared behind the bar.

Declan, meanwhile, sought Margaret and Jimmy Doyle for a chat, while Connor caught up with Stuart Morris.

"I know you've been keeping an eye on Aidan for Kara, Margaret. Thank you for that and I apologise for putting you in that position."

Margaret was long past the age when she considered what to say to anybody. Besides, she had known the man standing in front of her since he was in nappies.

"There have been times he's struggled, Declan," she admonished.

Declan nodded. "I'm ashamed of that," he admitted. "I'll make it up to him."

"How? With everything you're involved in, how will you..."

"Talk to Kara, Margaret. Tell her I said it's okay."

For once, the wheelchair-bound maths genius had no words. Declan used the silence to turn his attention to her husband and shook his hand.

"You, sir, are a hero. You have been for a long time, but you surpassed yourself today."

Jimmy allowed himself a rueful smile.

"Your dad would have been by my side if he were still here."

"He would," Declan agreed, "But he wouldn't have had your style."

"You wouldn't call me stylish, if you'd seen me running away from that car."

"Ah, but I did." Declan handed over his phone, displaying the car park CCTV feed at the time of the attack. Margaret leaned in, watching her husband leave the skip's side.

"Where's your ballistic vest gone?" she exclaimed.

"It was fecking heavy, plus I didn't want to arouse suspicion," Jimmy explained.

"Then why are you wearing a balaclava and tossing that grenade in your hand?"

"I was nervous."

They watched as Jimmy approached the vehicle with reckless abandon. As he knocked on the front passenger window, Coldfront emerged from his own hiding place, and moved towards the driver's side, rifle raised.

Jimmy showed the grenade to the driver, rolled it under the vehicle, then waved and trotted away, back towards the skip. Stumbling from the car, the driver fell to the ground and stared at the barrel of Coldfront's gun as he tried to stand up. Seconds later, Jimmy appeared back on the screen, tied the driver's hands behind his back, then helped him to his feet.

"I will never tire of watching that," declared Declan. "Just heroic."

"See? Heroic," smiled Jimmy, risking a glance at his annoyed other half.

"Just wait until I get you home," she said.

Neither man could decide if that was a promise or a threat. Fortunately, neither needed to say anything. Brendan walked over with Stuart Morris, then both of them and Declan headed out to the rear car park.

"Stuart, I have a favour to ask," said Declan. "I'd like you to stay awhile. There's a lot to organise. I need someone to help keep Connor company. You're the man for the job. I'll cover your costs and pay for your time. Think about it, talk to whoever, and let me know your decision by tomorrow."

He patted a nonplussed Morris on his shoulder, then turned and walked back into the bar.

"What was that all about?" Morris asked, without turning around.

"I'm the one who suggested it," replied Brendan Dunne from behind him. "You'll be grand. If you have questions, let me have them."

The Big Fan

Back in the bar, with the rush for free drinks calming down and the folk group now in full swing, Declan spotted Pope standing next to a couple of other guests, looking concerned as they studied a mobile phone.

"Not bad news, I hope?" he asked, reaching past them to pick up a drink from his table. "We've had enough of that today."

"Unfortunately, there's always more just around the corner," said Andrew Blackwell, extending his hand. "Paul Morgan. And this is my wife, Amanda. Thank you for the drink. I'm very sorry to hear about your mother."

"Thank you," Declan watched Mindy as she remained focused on the news website they'd all been reading. "Pleased to meet you, Miss Abbott."

"Likewise," she replied, distracted by the news that reports of the couple's whereabouts were flying in from all over the world, including quite a few from the Emerald Isle, although none matched where they actually were or what they were doing. A sixth sense told her something was wrong, so she looked up. The stares on the faces of Pope and Blackwell reassured the sixth sense it was correct, but it still didn't know why. The grin on the face of the newcomer to the group hit her like a bucket of cold water.

"Ah, Abbott," she said. "I see what you did there."

Without another word, Declan beckoned them to follow and led them out of the bar and into the administration office at the foot of the stairs, where he locked the door behind them.

"How did you know?" asked Blackwell, more curious than concerned.

"I'm a big fan - only recently, mind; ever since you gave your resignation speech. Hated you as a politician. I relate a lot to your *Path Finder* philosophy. Plus, you can't look anywhere without seeing your faces in the media today, and neither of you has worked hard on your disguise."

"But nobody's recognised us here," said Blackwell.

"We've all been busy," replied Pope, eager not to upset the elder Kelly when the man's help - at least his silence - might be needed.

"And you, Simon."

Pope immediately regretted speaking. In fact, he regretted ever coming to Ireland and fervently wished he was sitting at home, listening to the late-night racket being made by the tradespeople in the house next door.

"What's your group's link to Mr Blackwell and Miss Abbott?"

"Call me Andy, please," smiled Blackwell. "Mr Kelly, Simon here was good enough to help me after my disappearance. I was in a bad way, mentally and emotionally. He looked after me, got me drunk several times, and eventually helped with my safe passage back to London. Those events either involved or are known to all the group who are here with Simon. You are, in fact, one of a tiny number of people in the world to know that secret. I wouldn't like to see that number get any higher. Simon has survived two assassination attempts because of his involvement."

Declan turned and stared at Pope.

"They were both on the same day," Pope felt obliged to explain, as if that made them less of an issue.

Declan nodded absent-mindedly, as if they weren't important.

"Please, call me Declan," he told the new guests. "Your secret's safe with me." He looked at Pope. "All your secrets are safe with me."

"Then perhaps you might help us resolve our problems," smiled Mindy.

Declan returned the smile.

"Tell me what they are," he said. "I'll see what I can do."

Mush-A-Ring Dumb-A-Do

Brendan Dunne walked quietly up to the administration office and listened. Satisfied, he returned to the bar, grabbed a drink and sat where he could view the entire room, as well as the vestibule.

The Marauders had resorted to an instrumental interlude as Maeve took a break from vocals, standing just off-stage, chatting to Sinead.

Stuart Morris was also in a deep conversation with Orla, standing just inside the empty residents' dining area. Brendan could guess the topic and, given Orla's embrace, its outcome.

Morris was a decent man; a good, very capable man, he thought. He'd be a highly valuable addition to the organisation and that would benefit everyone, including Morris. He just didn't know it yet.

The band broke into the opening of *Whiskey In The Jar*. Brendan would have sung, given different circumstances; however, that was impossible tonight. He needn't have worried. A bar full of inebriated locals would not allow an instrumental version of that classic.

Mush-a ring dumb-a do dumb-a da indeed. The entire room erupted into a passionate *Whack fall the daddy-o* with nobody having a clue what it meant, but because it was what it was.

Brendan smiled to himself, took another drink, and settled back to enjoy the entertainment.

The door opened forty-five minutes later, announcing the end of the administration room meeting. The crowd, ably led by Connor, remained focused on the band, and the band responded enthusiastically to the raucous reception. Father Aidan had left fifteen minutes earlier, having spent a good while talking to Margaret and Jimmy while sipping an orange juice which hid a hefty vodka. But only the one. Tomorrow would be an important service. He'd had a quick word with Brendan and received an enormous bear hug for his trouble, then disappeared.

Sinead was the first to react. She spotted the group in the vestibule and kept Declan there while the rest walked in. Brendan watched as she handed over a piece of paper while explaining what it was. Declan read it with a smile on his face, handed it back with a nod, and received a hug and a kiss on the cheek before the girl headed for the stage. Declan followed her in.

"This could be special," he said to his friend. "Once it's finished, we go."

Brendan nodded and headed off to speak to Connor. Declan surveyed the room and caught the eye of Stuart Morris, who was talking to the Fishing Flops. Morris winked, and that was all that Declan needed. The weight on his shoulders lifted ever so slightly, yet again. What a monumental day, in many ways. He sipped his whiskey and took a deep breath. He knew what was coming next.

Clodagh's Song

Sinead made her way to the front of the stage and waved at Maeve, who waited until the end of *The Fields of Athenry* and the applause that followed before making her announcement.

"Tonight has been a night of celebration," said Maeve, "But also of remembrance. Tomorrow is the start of a new era for this town and we'll be glad to come back and be part of it as often as you'll have us, but for now, we leave you with a song from one of your own - Sinead Brennan - in memory of Clodagh Kelly."

With the crowd hushed, Sinead stepped onto the stage and behind the microphone, the only sign of her nerves being the slight tremble of the lyric sheet in her hand. As agreed, the band played an instrumental verse and chorus of a lament, before Maeve gave her a nod to start.

> *The winds blow soft upon the hill,*
> *The evening sun is low,*
> *And we gather here in sorrow, still,*
> *To bid dear Clodagh go.*
> *Her laughter spilled across the lough,*
> *Her voice was soft and kind,*
> *Now silence falls where once she'd stay,*
> *Leaving her heart behind.*

* * *

Oh, may the earth rise up to meet her,
And the stars light up her way,
For Clo's life will live forever,
In the hearts of those who stay.
Raise a glass to this fine woman,
Who bravely lived with fear,
Though gone, she's not forgotten,
For her spirit lingers here.

We knew the story of her past,
The days she had to fight,
The man she loved but could not last,
She showed us all her might.
From dawn to dusk, her heart was full,
Of kindness, warm and true,
Now in the fields, the silence calls,
As we remember you.

Oh, may the earth rise up to meet her,
And the stars light up her way,
For Clo's love will live forever,
In the hearts of those who stay.
Raise a glass to this fine woman,
Who bravely lived with fear,
Though gone, she's not forgotten,
For her spirit lingers here.

Farewell then, dear Clodagh, until we meet again,
In the ripples of the lough, in the wind or summer rain,
Your light shines in the hearts you've touched,
For evermore the same.

Sobs and sniffs disturbed the stunned silence after Sinead

finished singing.

She looked to the far end of the bar, where Declan, Connor and Brendan stood with smiles on their faces. Declan nodded to her and started the applause before the Kellys and their minder turned and walked out.

"Thank you everybody," said Maeve into the microphone. "Tonight has been one for the ages. Good night. God bless."

The Gathering

The 11 o'clock church service at St Patrick's the following morning was certainly one for the ages. Half the congregation had read about the previous day's events at the Hero on ICARUS and wanted to witness whatever happened next. Most of the other half were still hungover from the night before, although the majority would claim they were just 'emotional' after such a stressful day.

Either way, the church was packed, and many had to stand outside, listening to whatever they could hear through the open doors. Some had attended the 9a.m. holy communion service just to make sure they had a seat for the main event.

Having arrived early, the Kelly family and Brendan sat halfway down the aisle alongside the Brennans, the Doyles, and Kara Walsh and her mother. The Fishing Flops were in the porch, delayed by helping with the clean-up from the previous night and seriously underestimating the service's popularity. A hum of conversation ran through the church, hovering just above a slow, classical version of *Danny Boy* being played on the organ.

A flurry of movement by the altar signified the priest's arrival. Father Aidan looked resplendent and, more importantly, clean and sober as he climbed into the pulpit, timing his entry to coincide with the end of the organ recital.

The size of his congregation took his breath away. Nobody noticed. His presence and the silence of the organ quietened the conversations. People sat a little straighter in their pews.

Whispering a silent prayer in case the Lord had been busy when he had offered one up just sixty seconds earlier in the sacristy, the priest cleared his throat.

Show time.

Damn Satellite Phones

Five weeks into the three-years-overdue-ruby-wedding world cruise with his wife Mavis, Martin Barnwell sat on a comfortable sun bed as far away from the large, popular swimming pool as possible, gazing at the Indian Ocean, afternoon cocktail in hand, the sun on his face and savouring every moment.

Andrew Blackwell's former chief-of-staff had struggled to wind down after leaving Downing Street on the same day as his boss. He was in demand as much as Blackwell, but for high-ranking jobs and consultancy roles rather than to check on his mental state and to find out what the crazy, yet intriguing *Path Finder* notion was all about. The answer to Barnwell's issue had been surprisingly straightforward. Mavis presented him with a new mobile phone, complete with new SIM card and number, together with a list of contact details he could transfer from his old phone, which was confiscated until they returned from their global adventure.

Having also agreed to cut all web or email-related activity during the voyage, he was pleasantly surprised to avoid the expected withdrawal symptoms through a combination of alcohol, catching up on his reading list and enjoying exotic lands without worrying over whether anyone was going to upset an entire nation by saying the wrong thing.

Having handed over whom to talk to and what to wear to his wife, the biggest decisions he had to make during the cruise were which events to attend, what to eat and how long to sleep.

"Mr Barnwell?" The appearance of the ship's purser did little to disturb this newfound inner peace, although the woman's follow up threatened to demolish it. "There's a call for you on the satellite phone. It's the UK prime minister's office. A Mister Crockett wants to talk to you. They say it's urgent."

"Did you tell them I was in an important meeting and was not to be disturbed?"

"They said it's an urgent matter of national interest and - quote - 'a mutual friend is involved' - unquote. I'm sorry, sir. They also said if you still refused to talk to them, then we are to throw you in the brig pending your arrest in Mauritius and subsequent return to London."

"But I've done nothing wrong."

"They don't care."

Barnwell sighed. He felt like a drug user on the cusp of breaking the habit and getting his life back, being offered one last hit that could knock him off the rails once more. And that would incur the wrath of an adoring, immensely patient and tremendously vengeful wife, on a luxurious cruise liner for another seven weeks with no prospect of release, save drowning. He held out his hand. The purser gave him the cumbersome handset and took a few paces back, ready to prevent any interloper from getting too close, but also looking out in case Mrs Barnwell made an unexpectedly early return from her exercise class.

Just five minutes later, Mavis did, indeed, return early from her exercise class to find her husband snoozing in his chair, the cocktail glass dangling precariously by its elegant stem from the relaxed fingers of his left hand.

She removed the glass carefully and set it down on the nearby table, then gave her husband a kiss on his forehead. Barnwell stirred, looked up at her, and smiled.

"Had a good time?" he asked.

"The best!" she smiled. "The televisions were on in the gym. You'll never believe the fuss over Andy and Mindy."

Barnwell put both hands to his ears.

"Don't tell me!" he said. "Unless he's hurt or arrested, I don't want to know. This is our holiday. Don't spoil it."

"Oh, Martin, that's so sweet," she said, kneeling down by his side and giving him a hug, then biting his ear hard enough for it to hurt but not enough to draw blood.

"Look at that," she added, as he yelped in pain, "It's still warm from the satellite phone being pressed against it."

Smoke And Mirrors

The Fallen Hero's most recent arrivals sat in the residents' lounge of the hotel, nursing coffees and slight hangovers and struggling to make sense of the latest news stories concerning their whereabouts.

"So, what did we do?" muttered Blackwell, eager not to disturb his headache.

"We flew secretly from Limerick late last night on a private jet to Cranfield. A helicopter then flew us to the prime minister's country residence at Chequers. Following a good night's rest, we will attend an off-the-record meeting with the PM's key advisors. They're working on a secret strategy to get the government back on track, apparently."

Blackwell marvelled at how such a clandestine series of events could find itself as the headline for news pages, websites, and airwaves across the world, when nothing in the story was true. Even members of the Marsh Media Group had felt obliged to pick it up. Even funnier still, Limerick Airport, Cranfield Airport and the UK government had refused to confirm or deny the reports. Limerick and Cranfield, he could understand. It was good publicity for them. But the UK government? He looked across at his fiancée and shook his head admiringly.

"You truly are a tactical genius," he said.

"Not me." Mindy read through the third report again. "I don't know how our new friend did this, but there's a printout of a Limerick manifest with our names on it, plus an email approving the temporary deactivation of the plane's transponder as a security measure. A 'source' has confirmed our arrival and departure from Cranfield. In such a short timeframe, that's truly stunning."

She thought again about the government's response. Whoever was calling the shots knew there was apparent evidence behind the story, so would look foolish denying it. Andy's reluctance to behave like a politician definitely had genuine political value, especially when compared to the lack of the latter in Downing Street.

It made sense, in the short term at least, to align the government with this exciting news - and maybe Blackwell's return to the fold - without directly substantiating it.

"Look," said Blackwell, looking at his mobile phone, "Government ministers are now turning up at Chequers and are refusing to make any comment to the media at the gates. They must know we're not there, but they're turning up to meet us with smug smiles on their faces. It's crazy!"

"I wonder how the Conclave is feeling?" mused Mindy. "Aston Hail must be tearing his hair out."

"Oh, I hope so," Blackwell laughed.

After The Service

The church service over, Declan and Connor stood in the porch alongside the priest, shaking hands and having a brief word with everyone as the congregation filed out.

One uplifting, positive sermon had demolished Father Aidan's reputation for doom, gloom, hell, and damnation. It focused on the courage needed to live life in the service of others and the certainty of redemption for doing so. Several in the church felt the priest was talking directly to them. Many more knew exactly who the priest was talking about.

Declan had walked to the front to deliver a heartfelt tribute to his mother, followed by Connor reading Sinead's lyrics from the night before as a poem.

Although no one had spoken openly, every member of the congregation sensed impending change. All-in-all, a wonderful service. And everyone wanted to comment on it. Simon Pope left last, by which time hands were aching and stomachs were grumbling.

"Thank you, Aidan," he said to the priest. "Fine words, Declan. Connor, I'm sure your mother's very proud of you." He turned to walk off, but halted when Declan called.

"The Hero will be busy, Simon. Could you get Orla to do six plates from the carvery, then bring them to the cottage with your friends?"

Pope looked puzzled for a moment.

"Your two friends from last night; not the rest of your rabble," added Declan.

Pope laughed and walked away. Strolling to the pub, he called Pippa, who sounded more relaxed than the previous day.

"We've had a delivery, a thank you gift from our new neighbours," she explained, "And an apology for all the noise from the project manager. All will be quiet from now on; just the sound of paintbrushes on walls and carpets being fitted. Radios are now banned from the site."

"What about the newcomers?"

Pippa hesitated. "There are a few clues."

"Tell me."

"Well… hello… are you there? Hello?"

Pippa pressed 'End' on her phone, then switched it off completely, a broad grin on her face.

Mobile signals were as intermittent down their road as they were in Ireland, apparently. Besides, it was perhaps best if she kept her suspicions to herself for now.

Chequers

Damien Crockett loved the approach to Chequers, the former 16th century manor house, which became the official countryside retreat of the UK's prime minister in 1921. Every time his convoy turned into the 1500-acre estate, wending its way through the park, woodlands, and alongside the formal gardens to the mansion, the former policeman-turned-Home Secretary, and now the country's leader since Blackwell's resignation, felt the burden of office lift off his shoulders.

Today, however, felt different. Roaring past the television cameras and reporters assembled at the main entrance, he felt every inch a charlatan. Grand entrances were very much his thing, but this one was purely for show. For that, he had nobody to blame but himself and an inebriated former employee floating on the Indian Ocean, who made it abundantly clear he wanted nothing to do with the whole sorry episode.

"Martin. You won't have seen the news, but your former boss has gone missing again, this time with your former assistant," Crockett had opened the conversation over the satellite phone. "News is coming out this morning that they flew back to England overnight, then took a helicopter ride to Chequers, where they're meeting with members of the government this morning."

"Not interested," came the reply.

"Look, Andrew has been a hermit since his resignation, but his popularity has grown. Any link between him and the government can only have positive connotations for the party, given the wretched time we've had since he left."

"So?"

"So I'm thinking of going to meet him at Chequers along with a few colleagues, even though I'm pretty sure he's not there."

There had been a few seconds' delay in transmission, which the prime minister took for deep thought on behalf of his predecessor's chief-of-staff.

"Sounds eminently sensible," came the slightly slurred reply. "Goodbye."

The connection ended, which Crockett charitably put down to satellite movements, before calling his secretary and putting his plan into effect - not that it appeared eminently sensible now he had arrived.

Two junior cabinet ministers and the Chancellor of the Exchequer Emily Helms were already in the drawing room, standing together at one of the large windows, looking out onto the gardens.

"I don't suppose they're actually here then?" Crockett broke the silence as he marched in.

"There's been nobody here since you and the prime minister of France left two weeks ago." Emily Helms tried to keep the worry and exasperation out of her voice.

If only her brother and family still lived in Cardiff rather than just up the road in Aylesbury, she wouldn't be here and part of this ridiculous charade. "I am concerned that our appearance here… Damien, this could make us a laughing stock…"

"But what else are we to do if the media are reporting he is here? Nothing? How would that make us look?"

"We could have called the staff and asked them to confirm things. Then, when we knew he wasn't here, we could have told the media their information was wrong." Henry McInnes swallowed hard, not sure whether a junior minister should have risked his career by offering common sense when all around appeared to be madness.

Crockett rewarded him with a hard stare before making for the drinks cabinet and helping himself to a rum and coke. He settled in one of the comfortable armchairs and gestured to the others to join him.

"Look," he said once they had all settled and realised nobody was going to be bawled out; not yet, at least. "The media have credible documentary proof he arrived here last night. If we deny it, they'll say we're hiding something. I suggest their proof means we can say he is here and is talking to us either about a return to the party or a discussion about his *Path Finder* stuff. Either way, I think it would invigorate the public and hopefully provide a much-needed boost for us in the polls."

"God knows, we need it." McInnes wondered if he'd had too much to drink, but kept talking anyway. "And think about it, the media have committed to the fact he's here and we've confirmed it by saying we have held talks with him. If he says that isn't the case, then we and the media lose credibility. It's in all of our interest to maintain the pretence. Then it's his word against ours and the fiction becomes the fact even though… you know… it's fiction."

The four of them sat quietly for a couple of minutes, processing what had been said and searching for a better alternative.

"I think it's our best shot," said Emily Helms, surprising even herself at how desperate she had become. "We might even get Andrew back in the fold. If we work through some points now and announce them as a summary of our discussions with him, he might like what we say enough to return. That gives us the boost. If he denies the discussion ever took place, both ourselves and media will say it's sour grapes because we wouldn't agree to all his demands. That could turn sections of the public away from him and towards us."

Crockett looked around the members of the group and received nods of assent from each of them, then smiled.

"That's our strategy, then. We'll draft the news release over lunch," he said. "Let's get the prodigal back."

Sensor Sensibility

Brendan opened the cottage door as the van drew to a halt outside.

Mindy stepped out and took in the scenery. Blackwell surveyed the pristine white cottage and the five next to it, each of the five in a sad state of disrepair.

The checkpoints around the lough had disappeared.

Pope looked at the church on the hilltop, searching for movement.

"They went early this morning," said Brendan. "They didn't hang around. Helicoptered out."

"Ah. Right." Pope opened the side door of the van, picked up the two delivery bags, and carried them into the kitchen, where Connor had already set the table for the six of them.

Not knowing what Declan had said about the meeting the night before, Pope waited for him to make the introductions.

"Everything that's said in here remains in here," said Declan. "This is my younger brother, Connor, and my good friend Brendan. Connor, Brendan, this is Andrew Blackwell, the former prime minister of the UK and his fiancée and former assistant chief-of-staff, Amanda Abbott. You already know Simon Pope. He's a former church minister; a reluctant war hero; and he looked after Andy when he vanished for a while just over six months ago."

Connor stepped forward to shake Mindy's hand and then Blackwell's, genuinely thrilled to have somebody famous in their small house, even if he knew very little about them and certainly failed to recognise them, despite the lack of disguise.

"Declan, may I have a word?" asked Blackwell, having clocked the thermostat in the hallway. Declan opened the back door and walked outside, followed by his guest. Blackwell surveyed the garden and hillside.

"Everything said in your house may not remain private," he said, before explaining the previous morning's meeting with Isaac Delemos. "The thermostat in your hallway is a Delemos product," he said. "If it's been installed in the last twelve months, it could be a bug."

The honesty of a near stranger, aware of the information's importance, struck a chord with a man who had spent the last thirty years trusting virtually nobody.

"Thank you, Andy. We're onto it, but I'm more interested in why you've told me?"

Why indeed. The former prime minister wanted to say it was because he needed allies he could trust, rather than fair-weather friends. That *Path Finder* demanded openness and honesty - even if that meant hearing the candid opinion that he was a hated politician until he became… human, once he reappeared after his vanishing trick.

"I liked what I saw and heard from you yesterday. And Mindy and I are grateful for what you did overnight - even though we don't know how you did it. More importantly, Simon trusts you. That's good enough for me."

Declan clapped him on the back. "Let's go eat."

The Busy Bar

As predicted by Declan Kelly, the Fallen Hero was full after the church service.

Several of the congregation had persuaded the priest to attend - the more positive tone of his sermon reaping the unexpected bonus of free food and drink offers from grateful sinners.

Still dressed in their Sunday best, Orla and Sinead got to work. Without being asked or seeking permission, Westlake and Morris joined them. Coldfront and Angus Grace stood by the kitchen, ready to deliver trays of food to the carvery, and to clear tables and return used glasses to the washing up area on their way back.

"Have to say, I didn't expect this break to involve so much work," observed Angus Grace, heading out with two trays of roast potatoes and mixed vegetables. "But I'm happy with it."

Coldfront was about to disagree, but then realised he didn't. Certainly, he'd have a lot to talk about back at the golf club. The other golfers would be pleased.

Dave Westlake watched as Sinead stood at one end of the bar, managing three conversations at once while pouring pint after pint of lager, beer and, of course, the black stuff, which she lined up on the bar next to her for the other staff to hand over to customers. Her smile lit up the space around her.

"How do you do it?" he asked her as he grabbed two of the pints she'd poured. "Keep so happy when you've so much to do?"

"I have a lot to be happy about," she answered, her eyes never leaving the glasses being filled.

"Including me?"

"No." She threw a comment into one conversation on the other side of the bar, then turned to face him. "I'm thrilled about you."

Westlake grinned and turned to find himself face to face with his new girlfriend's mother, weighing him up as he had done with potential criminals hundreds of times. Her eyes narrowed, and he felt as if he'd been rumbled, even though he'd done nothing wrong. In her position, he'd have kept quiet until the suspect said something, but she didn't have his experience.

"Careful with those drinks. You're going to spill them," she said, then winked and moved on.

The phone call, when it arrived, coincided nicely with a lull at the bar. Most people had settled at tables and were enjoying their roast dinners. Father Aidan sat laughing with Margaret and Jimmy Doyle, Kara and a woman who could only be Kara's elder sister or mother. Coldfront and Grace flitted around, chatting and smiling with the customers as they cleared away the plates and cutlery, delighted to be linked to the previous day's Fortress activity and luxuriating in the warmth of the recognition.

Orla was serving the only two people currently wanting a refill of their drinks while Stuart Morris stood close by, moving clean glasses from the dishwasher onto the shelves.

"Well, that was interesting."

Westlake turned to Sinead, who had walked up behind him, looking slightly flustered as she brushed her hair away from her face.

"Are you okay?" he frowned.

"That was Maeve. From the band. They had a great time last night and loved Clo's song."

"I'm not surprised. They were great lyrics. Heartfelt. And you sang them beautifully. Even Angus had tears in his eyes and one of them's glass."

Sinead smiled a thank you, but it didn't wipe away the worry.

"Also, she asked if I'd be interested in auditioning to join the band."

Opening Up

Sunday's cottage lunch proved memorable, although the food, barely surviving its journey from the Hero, was lukewarm at best. The conversation was lively; the brief chat in the garden having thawed any lingering tension between the two key men.

At Declan's invitation, Andy explained how his last year in power had opened his eyes to the dependence of government on events outside their control to maintain a semblance of order.

He had grown disillusioned with the pretence, especially when the public and the media were onto what was happening, but without actually realising it.

For his part, Declan talked about the events outside his own control that had shaped his own life, and how - as in government - he had learned to manage perceptions of himself and his family in order to protect them all. Like governments, the elder Kelly had looked for ways to weigh the odds in his favour. Unlike governments, and with the help of his younger brother, he had succeeded.

"Highly impressive," admired Blackwell. "The rumour generator sounds amazing. ICARUS sounds fearsome, and that name is so apt - get too close to us and you'll crash and burn."

Mindy watched as Declan glanced across at Connor and Brendan and received an almost imperceptible nod. Before he could speak again, Blackwell's phone vibrated on the table, the screen illuminating the side of his plate.

Both Andy and Mindy had switched off their cellular service the previous evening, relying instead on Signal and a Virtual Private Network provided by Connor, which used Tor to route the communication and so prevent identification of their phone's location.

"Declan, sorry. It's from Aston Hail."

Nobody spoke as Blackwell read through the message, then cleared his throat.

"Well, your work on our behalf appears to have been highly successful," he announced. "According to Hail, the media and the government are reporting Mindy and I have just met with the current prime minister and others at Chequers, where we have discussed the exciting prospect of my return to the party and implementing the *Path Finder* philosophy to drive innovative policies for the duration of this Parliament."

Connor clapped his hands and high-fived Brendan, but Blackwell's expression suggested more was about to come.

"Hail says a letter is on its way from his attorneys, reminding me of our responsibility not to discuss anything regarding the Global Conclave and threatening to pursue us through every channel - 'legal and otherwise' - should we do so."

Mindy snorted. "But they're the ones who've spread the word and landed us where we are."

"I know, but we can't prove that. And the news from the UK obviously has him angry and concerned. He believes we've moved faster than he expected. That's knocked him off balance and we already know what he's like if he's not in full control."

Declan absent-mindedly stroked the scar on his face. "We touched on the Conclave last night," he said eventually. "If you have any more details, tell me everything. We might get this issue resolved before it gets too messy."

"We have some possible dirt as well," added Mindy, thinking of the revelations provided by their driver on the trip to Clonbrinny.

The elder Kelly smiled. With Clodagh now gone, and the defences in place to protect all who mattered, maybe now was the time to make a real impact.

"Let's clear the table," he ordered. "Connor, grab your laptop. Brendan, there are pads and pens in the lounge sideboard." He looked at the bemused faces of his three guests.

"Andrew, Mindy, Simon," he intoned with a deep sense of gravitas and a mischievous look, "It's time we introduced you to DEDALUS."

Dinner Disturbed

In the middle of the Indian Ocean, Martin Barnwell had redeemed himself in the eyes of his wife by arranging with the purser for them to be seated at the Captain's Table for the evening meal. Alongside them were a renowned author of historical fiction, a racehorse trainer, a documentary film producer and a science personality more famous for their television appearances than any contribution they had actually made to science. The food was excellent, the wine superb and the conversation absolutely sparkled, thanks in part to the captain's hosting expertise, but mostly due the egos of the diners, Barnwell and wife excepted.

He was more than content watching Mavis immersing herself fully in the evening, while he just sat quietly, attracting no attention. No attention, that was, until he eventually saw the purser, part hidden by a column beyond the far side of the table, trying to catch *his* attention by waving the dreaded satellite phone.

"Sorry folks, please excuse me a minute," he said, throwing an apologetic glance towards his wife, who ignored it completely while laughing at the latest anecdote from the author. He followed the purser out of the dining room onto the deck, then took the proffered phone.

"It's the leader of the opposition," she whispered.

Barnwell rolled his eyes, mouthed a 'thank you' and turned to face the myriad of stars hanging patiently above the dark, calm waters.

"Barnwell," she heard him say, "That's okay… Yes… Yes… No, haven't heard from him… Right… But he didn't appear and hasn't responded, so you'd like to… Then do it and don't bother me again… You're welcome…Bye."

Barnwell returned the phone.

"If I receive any more phone calls from any political party, please give them this message. I haven't heard from him. I have no idea where he is. Neither does anyone else, so if you want to claim you've talked with him, nobody can prove you haven't, so knock yourself out."

The purser took out a small notebook and jotted down the gist of the instruction, then nodded.

"Thank you," smiled Barnwell, then walked back into the restaurant and took his place at the captain's table.

"Everything okay, dear?" asked Mavis, her look a mixture of concern, annoyance and inebriation.

"It was a wrong number," he explained, placing his napkin back on his lap and taking a sip of the Puligny-Montrachet 2016. "Now then, where were we?"

Decisions Decisions

With the carvery section cleared away and the tables mostly empty, Coldfront and Grace looked after the bar by sitting at the front of it and nipping behind when a customer approached.

Sinead sat with her mother and their respective potential love interests in the residents' dining area, finishing their late lunch in silence. After receiving Sinead's exciting news, nobody knew quite what to say apart from offering their initial congratulations.

The chance to make a new life and the most of her talents was the fulfilment of a dream, but one which came with significant cost, should the audition be successful.

"We'll cross those bridges when we come to them," Orla had said, as the discussion about leaving home, boyfriend, widowed mother, and Clonbrinny had become too much for the two women to bear. Lunch arrived soon after, but minds remained focused on the future and what to talk about when the conversation resumed.

Morris was the last to finish his meal. No sooner had he put down his knife and fork than his best friend whisked them and the plate away from him.

"Give us a hand, Sinead," Westlake said, putting his own plate and cutlery on top and heading for the kitchen.

Sinead followed with the rest and the door closed firmly behind them, leaving only the clock and bar sounds as company for the remaining couple.

"How are you doing, Orla?" asked Morris.

"Not good," whispered the landlady, tears filling her eyes.

Morris shifted his chair closer and put his arm around her, kissing her cheek.

"A lot needs to happen before Sinead's thing becomes a thing, you know." Orla nodded, holding on to his hand resting on her shoulder. "And a lot can happen in that time, which could make things easier for everybody."

Orla sat up straighter and turned towards him.

"Stuart Morris," she said, "Are you trying to get me in bed?"

He hadn't been, but Morris still turned bright red. He had no idea what the correct answer was to that question. Orla saved him the bother.

"I'll take the colour of your face as a yes," she said, standing up. "Come on."

In the kitchen, Westlake finished the washing up, pulled the plug and wiped everything down, while Sinead dried the plates and cutlery and stored them away.

"What should I do, Dave?"

Westlake dried his hands, walked over and brushed a strand of Sinead's hair off her face.

"You know, I have never enjoyed wondering about what I might have missed," he confided. "I hate the idea of 'what if?'. I think you should do whatever feels right for you. Regret it later if you must. Go with what feels right in the moment."

Sinead pulled him closer and kissed him on the lips.

"Does that chat up line work with all the girls you've pulled?" she whispered.

"It's the first time I've ever used it."

"Well, congratulations," she smiled. "It's a cracker."

Dedalus

Everyone sat around the kitchen table, the notebooks and pens making the event look like a small university seminar in a professor's rooms.

Declan touched briefly on the development of the technology behind ICARUS and its ability to deter future attacks by retaining lifelong access to the systems and computers used by would-be hackers.

Thanks to Connor's unique set of skills, the programme was at least two generations ahead of anything similar in the world.

Just in time, Pope stopped himself from nodding in agreement. He was no programming expert - everybody in the room knew that - and he didn't want any focus on the interest of GCHQ in the system design.

Oblivious to the near-miss, Declan moved on to explain how his desire to strengthen the defences of his family's community coincided with a need to earn money for his family to actually survive.

Here, he was lucky.

He knew how to blag and had the discipline to never cross the line.

He created a business empire, focusing on anything where the gift of the gab and being honest meant success.

"I have an insurance business where we sell the right cover for the customer rather than our commission rates," he explained. "The car dealership won't sell anything that's too big for the customer, either size-wise or financially. The estate agency network and mortgage business both operate on the same lines. Everything is scrupulously clean. Our reputation is excellent - check the reviews online. Each team member operates in the same way. There's a lot of cross selling and business falls into their hands. They earn good money. We just ask them to do the right thing."

It was when business customers enquired about debt recovery services that Declan thought about using a version of ICARUS for something more than defensive action. "If we were to operate successfully in this field, we needed to close cases quickly and fairly and to make our offering financially attractive to customers," explained Declan. He pointed at Brendan. "We already had a physical threat, but we never wanted to use it."

"And we haven't," interjected the big man.

"But we wanted a range of actions that would 'encourage' debtors to behave - much like our ability to deter organised crime from attacking us. We realised that accessing and controlling the debtor's IT systems gave us what we wanted. So Connor came up with DEDALUS."

"Distributed Entry, Detection Avoidance, Lateral Undetectable System," explained Connor, answering the question each of the three newcomers was silently asking. "Basically, we find our way into a system, avoiding detection. Then, we sneak into other systems, applications and data within the network. This expands our range of control, just in case we need to use it, without raising alarms or being detected and neutralised."

The silence was deafening. Brendan Dunne was the first to understand why.

"Here's an example," he said. "A few days ago, we collected a debt from the developer who runs the Phoenix Park Tech Zone. Connor used a username and password on a reception desk to access the system. He had visibility and control of the developer's finance department. We could have paid ourselves and put it through their system as a legitimate transaction, but that's not us. We talked to their representatives, waited until the funds transferred to our bank account, and then left."

"Then we set off the fire alarms, so the building evacuated and nobody had time to pull the payment. We moved the funds into another account, just in case." Connor smiled happily at the memory.

"But are you still in their systems?" Mindy asked. "What could you do from there?"

Connor giggled. "We are, and unless they're very lucky, we're undetectable. What can we do? Empty their bank accounts. Download the details of every single employee. Access the parent company's mainframe. Send rude emails from anyone in the business. Copy commercially sensitive data. Wipe their customer details. Anything really."

"And do they know?"

"No, and why would we tell them?" said Declan. "These latent bugs sit quietly in the system. We don't monitor them. We don't activate them, unless - in Brendan's example - we run into Phoenix Park Tech Zone again or any other AA Enterprises company - their parent - further down the road."

"That's how you sorted the flight plan, the email and so on last night - and look at the impact that's had. Absolutely fascinating." All eyes turned towards Andrew Blackwell, who was doodling on his notepad. "So, how do we use DEDALUS to get *Path Finder* back on track?"

The unanswered question lingered, punctuated only by the occasional coffee slurp.

Decompression

Three hours after the DEDALUS conversation began, Andrew Blackwell, Mindy Abbott and Simon Pope walked into the Hero's bar, ordered three Irish coffees, and settled down at a table. Each checked their own mobile phone.

"Apparently I've been in discussions with the four main political parties in England," Blackwell reported. "Each of them strongly disputes the claims of the other three and equally strongly confirms the accuracy of its own statement. Unfortunately, not one of them feels able to confirm my current location because it would constitute a breach of confidentiality."

"I've had a death threat from Aston Hail," said Mindy, "But he's also sent me a second email, offering me the position of Vice President - Europe for Hail Electronics. He's asked me to decide on my own pay package and to include it in my letter of acceptance."

"Are you going to accept, or file it along with the offers from Evie and Alexander?"

"Have you actually seen the bank account Isaac Delemos set up for us?" Mindy handed over her phone. Blackwell looked at the screen and whistled.

"So you'll stay with me then?" he asked, more in expectation than hope.

"I'm not sure," she answered, her eyes sparkling with fake defiance. "After all, we're both signatories on the account..."

Pope's face looked pained as he stared at his own phone. So it was true, not a mean trick being pulled by somebody who had loved the idea of a romantic holiday in Ireland until Pope dispelled her of the notion just seconds later. Admittedly, the holiday was a great idea; just not this time around.

Now he looked at a dozen photographs proving that the solitude he had enjoyed for the last three years was ending. In fairness, the neighbouring front garden now looked a picture. The rear garden, which had resembled a jungle, was immaculate. It may be the last time he saw it, Pippa had warned, as a higher fence - at the new owner's expense - had been mentioned, if Mr Pope was amenable to enhancing the privacy of his own garden.

He could decide later. He flicked through the other photographs. The security seemed a bit much, thought Pope, although maybe he was too used to the local youths to see them as a threat. He flicked to the last picture and his heart skipped a beat. Two beautiful females and a handsome black greyhound. Admittedly, one of the beautiful females was also a greyhound. He had to admit, he was definitely punching above his weight in the partner and pet department.

"Everything okay, Simon?" Mindy had noticed the dopey look on his face. He handed her his phone, and she smiled at the photograph before handing it on to Blackwell, who looked slightly morose as he handed it back.

"I really miss those dogs, you know," he said. "When you think how involved they were... you know..."

Both Pope and Mindy nodded.

Despite meeting up three or four times since the Great Disappearance, conversation always focused on the present and the future.

They avoided the events of half a year ago, because it was easier to ignore them. Some things were best left alone, but they had also ignored the importance of the two dogs.

"We should treat them when we get back," suggested Blackwell, a suggestion of guilt in his voice. "Do something special for them, as a thank you."

Pope simply nodded and drank his Irish coffee. *The afternoon had been so interesting; possibly epoch making*, he thought, trying to get his mind onto other things. *But really, it was nothing to do with him and, actually, he wished he knew nothing about it.*

What had started as a plan to restrict the Conclave's efforts to hijack the *Path Finder* movement had transformed rapidly into a discussion about what that movement should actually be and how DEDALUS could help bring it to fruition.

DEDALUS was used in the Kellys' businesses to right wrongs, ensure good practice, create pressure to act or to check on matters of fact.

Now, events had opened up a new and exciting opportunity for two brothers who had spent the vast majority of their lives on the defensive.

Using DEDALUS for something positive on a far larger scale, as long as they managed it carefully and secretly, so it didn't lead to recriminations.

Putting it at Blackwell's service for *Path Finder*.

Pope was pretty sure that what he'd written during the afternoon would become more understandable, the drunker he became.

- Accept you can't control everything.
- Be open and honest about what you can achieve.
- Collaborate to overcome problems on a global scale for the good of humanity and the environment.
- Get governments and politicians to buy into Path Finder by creating momentum at ground level.

- Secure the commitment and investment of tech giants and billionaires who stump up the cash and the required technology and then walk away - living forever as selfless legends, with Path Finder as their legacy.
- Make all donors a founder, even small donations, so everybody feels they have a say in their future.
- Build a new online platform, with ICARUS as its guardian; a platform designed to enthral and encourage, to share a positive vision and facilitate its creation.
- Attract the great and the good in their specialised fields, with the maturity and sense to work together.
- Build a momentum that's impossible to stop. Halt current conflicts by making the prize too big to ignore, with any state or religion unwilling to work towards the goal replaced by a people or community who see the benefits and want them for themselves.

And achieve that from a position of unrecognised strength, which meant DEDALUS - a system that would perform exactly as intended on a colossal scale, but only to achieve highly specific objectives.

Pope shuddered, almost comprehended the immensity of the task for a moment, then realised with a massive wave of relief that he couldn't and it wasn't his job, anyway.

He looked at his two friends, staring at each other and clasping hands, faces pale and tightly drawn. It would be their mission; they had just realised that fact; and he didn't envy them one bit.

"Come on," he said, feeling brighter, "Let me treat you both to a proper pre-dinner drink."

Sleeping On A Plan

Declan sat in an armchair in the front room, staring blankly through the window as the sky gradually darkened The copious handwritten notes he had made throughout the afternoon were lying on the floor. He could hear Brendan snoring upstairs, and the sounds of Connor at his keyboard in the kitchen, interrupted by the occasional expletive. When Connor focused on his work, the best idea was to stay well out of his way.

Declan looked over his right shoulder, towards the corner where his mother's bed had been until yesterday afternoon. *How quickly we depart this world*, he thought. *How quickly others fill the space we leave behind, as if we were never there.*

What was left? The memories made, which would fade with time, and the things achieved - good or bad - which had relevance for others and could last much longer, theoretically at least.

He turned on the table light and flicked through the papers, stopping at the profiles of the Conclave members.

Hail was the problem. The leader in the Conclave. A bright, powerful and vindictive ego-maniac with money to burn and a very short fuse; used to getting his own way and happy to destroy anybody who prevented that. Highly influential as well.

Even the 'dirt' on Hail - destroying Wade Claskett and everything he had built - simply burnished his reputation with his adoring fans.

Tee Takahashi's links to the hacking groups - protecting her own intellectual property while damaging or destroying that of others - could be problematic for her, especially if those groups were a threat to certain governments.

The public would only view Elena Marchetti's hopes for a fourth Reich seriously if she had a clone farm somewhere with thousands of little Hitlers running around.

Revealing Alexander Alcock's financial backer would be neat, but the sovereign nations he controlled hadn't done badly over the last couple of decades and had kept their noses clean. People might shrug their shoulders, but until a huge military buildup started somewhere sensitive, nobody would care.

Exposing Evie Marsh's financial links to the tech bros looking to rule the world would barely cause a ripple, because Evie basically controlled the ripple-making machine.

That left Isaac Delemos. According to Andy and Mindy, he was an ally. The driver suggested he was squeaky clean. Declan wasn't so sure. Throwing money at a cause and warning of bugs was one thing. Making and planting the bugs in the first place and happy to go behind the backs of a group you'd been part of since its inception? That was something else.

He read through the notes he had made so they were fresh in his mind, then settled back and closed his eyes.

It had been a busy, stressful, and exhausting weekend. Time to leave things to the expert. He listened to the snoring from the bedroom above him and the tip-tapping from the kitchen, and fell into a deep sleep.

Return To The River

The group split up on the final full day of the break. Against his better judgement, Stuart Morris gave fishing another go, at the spot where his introduction to the pastime had failed so emphatically.

"You're here for at least a couple more months," Jimmy Doyle had said, "And I could do with getting out a bit more, even if it means we drag young Connor along with us." Morris couldn't really say no. He'd enjoyed the peace by the riverbank. Jimmy was good company and future trips would give the younger Kelly the chance to create more of a life for himself.

Coldfront and Angus Grace had spent time since the last trip swapping fishing stories, giving each other advice on how to improve and boring everybody else. Today was a chance for each to prove who, indeed, was the better angler.

Pope sat by his swim, with less of an idea about fishing than Morris, partly because he felt guilty about the lack of time he'd spent with the boys. He also felt he could do with a bit of a break. And he wanted to put as much distance as possible between himself and whatever was happening in the cottage by the lough. Besides, Stuart's description of the Doyle's cottage had aroused his curiosity, and this trip was likely to be the only chance he'd have to find out more.

Dave Westlake wasn't with them, having gone out with Sinead for the day to attend her audition with the Marauders in Dublin. That would happen after the band had set up for the evening's performance, and the couple then planned to watch the gig itself. Nobody expected to see either of them until the following morning.

Pope smiled to himself. Stuart Morris had discovered a new purpose in life. Although it was still early days, that part of the trip had been an unqualified success as, indeed, had his secret mission for the Garden Club.

"You've done well, Simmo," the RSM had told him the previous evening. "We can wrap this up. God knows how, but you've done well."

'God knows how' indeed, thought Pope, watching the float bob up and down in the flowing water. Apart from the plan to meet Father Aidan that second time, all he had done… all any of them had done… was to respond as best they could to events that happened around them. '*Are we actually in control of anything other than ourselves?*' he asked himself.

"Are you planning to let that line out to the Irish Sea, Simmo?" Jimmy Doyle sat down alongside Pope, winked and cracked open a couple of beers. "Tell me to mind my own business," he said quietly, "But we've a few hours to kill and I'd love to know about Afghanistan." He glanced across at Stuart Morris, who was looking suitably abashed, having been the inadvertent source of the news to the community. "I'd like to hear it from the horse's mouth, you see. Make sure our newest resident doesn't just talk a load of old blarney."

Pope hesitated, but it was only what he had planned to tell the priest. Maybe confession was good for the soul wherever it took place. *What the hell.* He took a swig of beer. Besides, if he talked, then maybe he'd get more out of Jimmy.

The Dublin Diversion

Brendan Dunne picked them both up from the Hero in the black sedan with the tinted windows. He looked even smarter than usual and felt refreshed after a decent night's sleep.

"Where are we off to, Brendan?" Mindy's bright smile didn't reflect how nervous she felt, climbing into a car in Ireland owned by a man with a high profile in criminal circles, with no idea where she was going.

"Dublin. Declan and Connor have been at the office since seven. Dec thought you might like to see our centre of operations."

"The alternatives were hiding out at the Hero, or going fishing," said Andrew Blackwell with a firm grip on his fiancée's hand. "This sounds much more interesting."

Brendan caught the worried look the couple shared in his rear-view mirror. It made a change, driving others besides the Kellys. The brothers were quite phlegmatic about the potential risks. Surviving a car bombing helped, not to mention the fact that their death would bring destruction upon the criminal fraternity of the island.

That fraternity was keen that the Kellys stayed alive. His current passengers didn't know that. He smiled to himself. *Time for a bit of fun. Bring some excitement into their lives.*

Something they could look back on when reminiscing about their visit. Something he could share with Connor and Declan later in the day.

He waited until they were out of Clonbrinny - pointed out the Doyle's cottage at the edge of the town - then accelerated along a mile-and-a-half stretch of straight road.

"There's no cover and nowhere to pull off," he explained. "It's best we're only exposed for the shortest possible time."

The couple relaxed when he slowed down driving through woodland, but tensed again when he said, "Do me a favour. If you see any movement in the trees, shout and hold on tight."

Both the heads he could see in the mirror started scanning the hundreds of blurred trees on each side of the road. Trying not to laugh, the driver muttered a quiet 'Hail Mary', which was just loud enough to be heard in the back.

"How long until we get there, Brendan?" There was a forced calmness to Blackwell's question, as he kept the urgency out of his voice.

"That depends, Andy. Maybe half an hour. There are drinks in the cabinet. Help yourselves."

Thirty minutes later, the car pulled up at the security gate of a large, modern office building, with well over 100 cars parked outside. Brendan drove up to the barrier, then headed to the far side of the building, and took a ramp down to the executive parking bays.

He asked his passengers to remain in the vehicle while he got out, scanned the perimeter, and called the elevator. Once the lift opened, he beckoned them to join him, locking the car doors behind them and selecting the fifth floor.

Opening a cupboard in the lift corner, he took out two zip-up hoodies and two Guy Fawkes masks and handed them over.

Both guests put them on without question.

"Occasionally we have visitors who don't wish to be recognised. Our people are used to seeing these outfits. You won't need them most of the time you're here."

"Do you have just one office in the building, or part of the top floor?" asked Blackwell, relieved that the rest of the journey had been uneventful.

"We occupy the entire building. In fact, we built it," said Brendan, pleased to note the impression his words made. "I think you're going to find today a bit of an eye-opener."

"I believe we are," said Mindy, sucking on a mint to remove the smell of whiskey from her breath.

The Spotter

The only sounds by the river were the waters rippling over the rocks further downstream, the light breeze blowing through the trees and the distant calls of a curlew. All rods were on the bank, and the group gathered by the coolbox, sipping from bottled beers as they processed Pope's account and the questions and answers that had followed. Morris knew most of the story, but Coldfront and Angus Grace only the sketchiest details.

"Thank you, Simmo." Jimmy Doyle had heard enough to convince him that Stuart Morris had spoken the truth, but had limited what he had said to protect his friend.

"Sometimes it's good to talk," Pope smiled, before taking a breath. "I know your wonderful home impressed Stuart, but he was a bit surprised by its range of defences…"

Jimmy laughed. "Fair exchange is no robbery?"

Pope shrugged. "Only if you want to."

Jimmy hesitated, then nodded. During the Seventies and Eighties, he had worked on construction projects in Northern Ireland, renting a caravan on a small farm during the week and returning to Margaret at weekends.

He kept himself to himself north of the border - willing to help someone else out, always had a joke, happy to listen and, importantly, to keep anything he was told to himself.

His workmates were a mix of faiths, plus those who didn't care for any, and everybody got on well. But time and events changed all that.

Margaret - then his girlfriend - was hurt in a bomb blast at Dublin University, sustaining injuries that gradually worsened as the years passed by. Then there were the problems at what was now The Fallen Hero. By then, Jimmy was well known in parts of the north, but never regarded as a threat by either side, which was ironic, because he was betraying both.

"I didn't care what happened around me in the north, just earned my money and then came back to Margaret," he mused. "But that changed after she got hurt, then Bobby died, and the bomb at Martin's house. It became personal."

He identified potential targets for Martin's so-called skirmishing activities. Then he would monitor the response between the different factions and report back, so the next attack could inflict maximum chaos.

"Margaret and I were on holiday when it all went wrong and young Seán got killed," he said. "Martin went completely off the rails. I was worried he'd get me in real bother, but he changed tactics. Just wanted to kill. He didn't need me for that."

Jimmy never considered quitting his job in the north - the money was too good and, despite the Troubles, the craic wasn't far behind - even when he answered a knock on his caravan door in the early hours one morning and faced a British military intelligence officer, dressed in work gear and holding a bicycle. "He was a nice guy. Introduced himself and asked if he could come in for a coffee and a chat."

The 'nice guy' explained he needed someone working on the building project to keep an ear out for any comments or rumours that might help identify future terrorist activity, or indeed, the perpetrators of any previous action.

"We know we can trust you," the officer had explained calmly. "Everybody trusts you; even Martin Kelly did until he went rogue."

Jimmy felt the name drop like a punch to the gut. He had questions to ask, but didn't want to hear the answers. He listened as the officer told him what to look out for, who was of particular interest, and how to get in touch. He was being blackmailed. He knew it; the man drinking his coffee knew it.

"I can't pay you for your trouble, Jimmy," the officer had said. "The accounts department likes to know it's getting value for money and we're not at that stage with you. Besides, they'd want invoices, receipts, that sort of thing. People might trace the payments…"

The officer didn't care what the information was, or which side it would affect.

"I just want you to help me stop innocent people dying," he said, and Jimmy had believed him.

For the next seven months, he had gone about his normal routine, but listened slightly more carefully than usual to the throwaway comments and the discussions that stopped as he approached.

If he heard a name, a rumour or a reference to an incident, he committed it to memory, then wrote it down when he was safely in his small caravan. Every Tuesday and Friday, he would scrunch the piece of paper and drop it over a dry stone wall, out of sight of anybody on his walk down the lane to the bus stop.

And then, early one Wednesday morning, there had been a knock on the caravan door. The same man, same workwear and the same bicycle.

"It's time for you to go, Jimmy," he said, handing over a small card. "Time to wrap this up. People are getting jumpy. Your name's come up. You've saved lives, mate, but it's time to save your own. If there's ever a problem, call this number."

Twenty minutes later, the officer had gone and so had Jimmy, leaving a note and some cash for the farmer on the caravan table before driving his old, battered van as calmly as possible down the lane and onto the main road, petrified of being halted at a false checkpoint just around the next corner.

"I swear to you, lads, I didn't breathe until I was back over the border. I took another breath when I got to Clonbrinny," he said, his face looking as pale and drawn as it had done that day, all those years ago.

"Did you ever call that number, Jimmy?"

"Twice. The first time was not long afterwards. I felt vulnerable. I needed to protect Margaret and myself. I don't know how they managed it, but I got a delivery - a hotch-potch of stuff, but it's still usable today."

"And the second time?"

"I called not that long ago. It went to an answering machine. I was worried Margaret would get in trouble with the Kellys, with her monitoring Father Aidan and helping Kara and all. I left a message, but I heard nothing back. It's been a long time…decades… and it sounded like someone else has the number now. Some gardener."

Breakthrough

Mindy looked out of the panoramic window of the boardroom as she made herself a second coffee from the refreshments table, having already eaten two of the nicest iced doughnuts she had ever tasted.

"What does Kay Eye Gee stand for?" she asked, spotting the large sign by the security gate.

"Kelly Industries Group." Connor wandered over to her side, concerned that the iced doughnuts were disappearing fast. He grabbed one for himself and looked at the sign. "The smaller sign lists all the companies that are part of the business. They're all registered and based here."

The writing on that sign was too small to read, but Mindy could make out twelve lines of text.

She nodded, impressed with the size and scale of the Kelly empire. If Declan's invitation had been to show them who they were dealing with, then he'd succeeded already. She sat towards the end of the twelve-seater oval table, facing the digital screen on the far wall, and pulled a notebook and pen from her bag.

Blackwell sat next to her, with Brendan and the Kellys across from them. Connor pressed a button on his laptop, and the screen on the wall sprang to life, revealing the company logo.

"We've been busy," said Declan. "I say 'we', but most of what you're about to see is Connor's work." He took a sip of his coffee, feeling nervous; conscious this might be the most important meeting ever held in the room.

"The first part of this meeting focuses on the Conclave," he continued. "If they adopt *Path Finder* as their own, then they will decide what it is, how it works and who benefits from it. If we can't stop them, there's no point in us moving onto discussing what you want *Path Finder* to be and how we might help you achieve it."

Connor couldn't wait any longer. Before Blackwell or Mindy could say anything, he ploughed into his presentation.

"We have access into Conclave," he announced.

He laughed at the looks on Blackwell and Mindy's faces before explaining his work of the previous evening.

"I'd scanned the members' various websites, just to get a feel for what might be the best way forward, but with something nagging away in my head," he said. "Then it hit me. Alexander Alcock. I did a basic search for information on his business interests and there it was - AA Enterprises."

"Noooo!" Everyone looked at Mindy, but none so curious as Blackwell, who wondered what had gotten into her. She was laughing and shaking her head, then spotted his stare. "Brendan's story yesterday? Phoenix Park Tech Zone?" Still nothing. "The parent company is AA Enterprises."

"Wow!" Blackwell almost shouted, before taking a moment to let the revelation sink in. "Well, where are we now?"

"Alcock's digital security is awful," said Connor. "He doesn't feel the need to have much. He believes the data integrity of his businesses is strong and comprehensive enough to protect him."

Mindy stood up and paced the room. "She does this when she's thinking hard," Blackwell explained to the others. "Don't mind her. Carry on."

"We accessed Alcock's private email accounts and located his passwords for access into the Conclave server," stuttered Connor, barely able to contain himself. "Security there is tight, but we're in. We can monitor activity and even access the systems of the other members."

Blackwell shook his head in amazement. "So quickly," he mused. "That's absolutely incredible."

"We were lucky," admitted Connor, "But we'd have got there, eventually."

"And now we're there," mumbled Mindy as she munched on yet another doughnut in celebration. "What are we going to do?"

"That's easy," smiled Declan. "Whatever we want."

The New Recruit

The one big problem with sumptuous banquets, quality drinks and late nights is that they all catch up with you at some stage. For Martin Barnwell, that stage was the early hours of the morning, when his bladder was about to burst and his stomach demanded all the antacids on board the ship. By the time he'd rectified those issues, he was awake enough to realise the snoring of his beloved and still inebriated wife would deny him any further immediate rest.

Instead of returning to bed, or listening to Mavis from the suite's lounge, he slipped on gym wear and slipped out for a stroll around the deck, watching the sun rise and thinking thoughts people thought when they weren't sure what to think. He usually spent these early morning wanders alone. Passengers he passed were either trying to recall their cabin's location, sneaking back to their own cabin from another, or hoping to avoid being sick, sometimes a mix of all three.

"Mister Barnwell? Good morning, sir."

He didn't even bother turning around, watching the last vestiges of darkness replaced by the first glimmers of light.

"Don't you ever sleep?" he asked. "Or is your sole task on this boat to follow me wherever I go, carrying a satellite phone and threatening to destroy my marriage?"

"The latter, sir," said the purser. "At least, that's how it feels."

Barnwell held out his hand for the phone and heard the purser sit down at a nearby table.

"Barnwell," he said.

"Martin!" Barnwell couldn't help himself. Despite the warmth of the Indian Ocean morning, he shivered. "Fancy helping us to change the world for the better, forever?"

"Are you drunk, Andrew?"

"Yes," admitted Blackwell. "I'd have put Mindy onto you, but she's been drinking since this morning and has just passed out."

"And in your respective states, how will you change the world for the better forever?"

"With the help of a Greek billionaire, the biggest criminal mastermind in Ireland, you, Mindy and possibly Simon Pope, who knows nothing about his proposed involvement."

"And the Conclave?"

"Oh, I fell out with them. They're not our people, Martin."

"And where are you?"

"Ireland. Coming home tomorrow."

"Have you spoken to any political party?"

"No, but I might do. Just to get them on board."

"Then I'm going to say no. Thanks for asking, though."

"Woah! No? To the biggest, most momentous challenge of your lifetime? Listen. I'm going to ignore what you just said and it will never appear in any memoir I may write, but I want you to listen to something Mindy wrote a few hours ago, before she started celebrating a bit too early."

Barnwell sighed. "I'll listen," he said, because his former assistant was always worth listening to, "But if I say no at the end of your speech, you must promise to accept my decision and never mention the idea ever again in my presence or that of my wife."

"Agreed!" Blackwell exclaimed, and started reading.

Half an hour later, both the phone and the purser had gone. Martin Barnwell stood at the railing and watched the glow of the sun fill the horizon, feeling the warmth on his face and the beat of his heart in his chest.

He turned and headed back towards his cabin, working out how best to tell his wife that the former chief-of-staff to the prime minister was now the Chair of a global political foundation also boasting a CEO, an ambassador to the world, a legacy founder - whatever that was - and nothing or nobody else.

A dozen steps later, discretion became the better part of valour and he diverted to the restaurant, where breakfast was just being laid out and the bar was already open.

The discussion with Mavis could wait.

Nighttime Calls

Andy Blackwell locked the car park door, walked back into the empty bar, helped himself to an orange juice with ice and switched on the television - not that he actually watched it. His mind was all over the place; buzzing so much, he doubted he would ever sleep again.

The meeting with the Kellys was a revelation. Connor's quiet search through the Conclave files resolved Declan's doubts about Isaac Delemos

Delemos was conspicuous by his absence from much of the gossip, subterfuge and malice that captivated the others - unless he was the subject of it.

His comments from meetings he'd attended since joining the group suggested a calming influence over its more outrageous plans. His personal correspondence revealed early doubts and a subsequent feeling of being trapped, with no escape from potential retaliation.

He was delighted to receive Blackwell's call and to hear the plans for *Path Finder* and his proposed role within the organisation. Blackwell had no concerns about the Conclave's activities and promised that Isaac would soon be free of any links to the group.

The call to Aston Hail - the first of the three Blackwell had made this evening - was cordial enough.

The result was as expected. Aston was keen on *Path Finder*, but felt the Conclave was in a better position to deliver what Andy wanted from the project. It was good to chat though, Andy told him, and he had appreciated the opportunity to visit Ireland and to share his thoughts with the group. The Conclave's actions reassured him that the concept had real potential, although he was disappointed that they couldn't work together on the way forward.

"You've done your bit, Andy," Hail had told him. "You can be proud that you got the Conclave involved."

Aston was surprised when Andy revealed he was still in Ireland and wouldn't be back for a few more days. Andy told him he was as surprised as anybody to read about his meetings with the different political parties.

"There really has to be a better way forward," he told Aston. "Or, at least, to try."

The call ended with each feeling it was worthwhile, and with Hail much more relaxed about the strength, or rather the weakness, of the opposition he could expect from the originator of *Path Finder*. Ironically, that specific outcome was the aim of Blackwell's call, so both men were happy.

After struggling to watch the television for ten minutes, Andy gave up, turned it off and headed towards the guest rooms, stopping on the way to put his half-finished drink on the bar. His eyes turned towards the photograph of Bobby Brennan on the wall and he raised his glass towards him.

"To you, Bobby," he whispered, "Whatever we achieve, you'll be there with us." He drank the rest of the juice, put down his glass and walked out of the bar, turning off the lights as he left.

The Hearty Breakfast

Pope looked out of the window as he heard a car crunch to a halt just outside.

"It's them," he announced.

The rest of the group, along with their hitchhikers for the day, ate breakfast as if nothing interesting was about to happen. Orla wandered in with a coffee of her own and sat down next to Stuart.

One minute later, they heard footsteps approaching through the bar area, then Westlake and Sinead appeared by the open door.

"Morning," Sinead smiled, receiving no immediate response from the seven people staring at them.

"What time do you call this?" asked her mother, face straight, but with a twinkle in her eye. Sinead's smile crumbled and her eyes filled with tears. She turned and fled the scene, racing up the main stairs to her room. Attention turned to Dave Westlake, who looked as surprised and concerned as everybody else. He was about to say something, but Orla held up her hand, then stood and followed her daughter out of the room.

Westlake cut an alarmed figure as he slumped down at a nearby table.

"What just happened?" he asked nobody in particular.

"We were hoping you could tell us," mumbled Coldfront, his mouth full of toast.

Westlake shook his head. He had no idea. Yesterday was memorable for all the right reasons. The band had been welcoming, and the audition was great. They'd tried out three traditional songs, which Sinead then performed with the band that evening. Everyone had enjoyed a great time at a restaurant afterwards. The world seemed perfect until the couple showed up in the doorway moments ago.

Pope made his friend a coffee, placing it on the table in front of him and patting his shoulder as he returned to his own breakfast. Westlake glanced at his best mate, Stuart Morris, who gave him a look that only a close friend with detailed knowledge of your history in relationships could give, and shook his head.

"Honestly Stu. It all went really well."

Mindy cleared her throat. "Maybe that's the problem." Then, realising everybody was silently requiring clarification, continued, "If the audition was bad, or Dave had been 'normal Dave', then she'd probably be unhappy but not upset. As it is, she has decisions to make, and that's overwhelmed her."

"Ah. Right. Okay…" Westlake sat still for a second or two, then stood up.

"Dave," said Mindy, "Leave it to Orla."

"Oh, I intend to," he replied, and headed to the buffet, where everyone silently watched as he loaded a plate with a full breakfast, returned to the table, and started eating.

"A hearty breakfast," announced Coldfront, "The last meal of the condemned man."

The others looked horrified, but Westlake simply shrugged. Time would tell.

Home Time

By the time the bar at the Hero opened its doors to the public at eleven, a queue had already formed outside the building. ICARUS had announced the lunchtime shindig for the Fishing Flops and those who didn't need to be somewhere else were here.

In the administration office, with Brendan standing guard outside, Connor handed over the printed airline tickets and boarding cards for Andrew and Mindy to fly from Dublin to Heathrow later that day.

"You'll travel to the airport with a friend of ours at three o'clock," explained Declan. "Use your normal passports; they'll be fine. We've also organised a car to take you home from Heathrow. The driver will hold a name board in Arrivals."

"We can't control the media," said Connor, "But they'll find out you have booked two seats on an earlier flight from Limerick to Edinburgh. Hopefully that'll throw them. If it doesn't, then that's up to you two."

"Will the media have other stories to concern them by then?" asked Mindy hopefully.

"Check the news before you board your flight, then after you've landed," smiled Connor. "I think you'll be happy."

Blackwell was unusually quiet.

Witnessing his thoughts on *Path Finder* turning into something more substantial was as exciting and humbling as it was surreal. Again, fate was taking him down paths not of his own choosing. For the moment at least, he was moving in the right direction, with serious momentum and with a substantial, incredible team alongside him.

For the first time since he had put his thoughts down on paper, he actually believed they could turn into something significant, perhaps even epoch-making.

One step at a time!

"Thank you both," he said. "I appreciate everything you've done for us, and I'm glad we're together on this journey. I never met your parents, but I'm sure they're very proud of the people you've become."

"This is just the start, Andy," said Declan, shaking his hand. "We met for a reason."

"Are you not staying for the farewell party?" Mindy asked.

"No, but we'll see you again soon," said Connor, giving her a hug. "We've got work to do."

The brothers walked out without looking back and shook hands with the Fishing Flops - minus Dave Westlake - who were by the front door to say their goodbyes.

"I feel emotional," said Blackwell as the brothers and their best friend disappeared from sight.

"You don't look it," observed his fiancée, "But appearances can be deceiving, as those men have shown and the Global Conclave is about to confirm."

"Can't wait," grinned Blackwell. "Let's grab a drink."

Breaking News

David 'Coldfront' Davies hated goodbyes, especially when everyone else was drinking and he was the designated driver. The party in the pub spilled into the car park as the Fishing Flops made their way out.

Despite the speeches and the applause by the bar, the locals seemed determined to hold on to the group for as long as possible.

Dave Westlake hugged his best friend.

"We'll be back for Clodagh's funeral, Stu. Keep out of trouble until then," he said.

Morris was about to reply, but Orla got in first.

"I'll look after him, Dave. Make sure you look after my girl."

Sinead blushed. "I'll be fine, mammy," she said. "I'll miss you."

"How will you manage that? We'll be talking every day. Now, go see some of the world."

Simon Pope was crouched down by Margaret's wheelchair, promising her they would be back soon.

"Oh, I hope so," she said, eyeing her husband standing nearby. "This place could do with livening up."

"I'll liven you up," responded Jimmy. "I'll connect that wheelchair to the mains when we get home."

Pope stood and shook his hand. "The lads couldn't have managed the other day without your help, Jimmy. Margaret's married to a genuine hero."

He turned to climb into the van, but a couple of people stood in the way.

"We never finished that conversation, Simon," smiled the priest.

"Next time, Father."

"I'm looking forward to it already."

Pope smiled and winked at Kara.

"Look after your uncle, young lady."

Kara linked her arm with Aidan's and winked back.

"Promise," she said.

Eventually, Pope and a very drunk Angus Grace joined Westlake, Sinead and Coldfront. The van lurched forward and headed down the small lane by the side of the hotel, a last blast of the horn signifying its departure.

Blackwell and Mindy had stayed in the bar, looking out of the front window. They watched the van emerge onto the high street, turn right, and disappear from view. As people drifted back in, the couple moved closer to the television, which was on but with the sound down, so people could hear the earlier speeches.

The news switched to a photograph of Aston Hail, with the caption revealing that charities in ten deprived areas of US cities had each received a $50 million personal donation from the billionaire over the weekend. A source close to the CEO of Hail Industries had suggested more donations were to follow.

"That'll explain why he was so keen to leave our get-together the other day," smiled Blackwell.

"His team should be able to trace the hack to the MisCox Crew within an hour," murmured Mindy. "MisCox won't have a clue what's happened, but won't be able to admit it. Takahashi has close links to MisCox. Aston knows that."

"So we've lit the blue touch paper."

"And now we stand well back. There may be a couple more revelations by the end of the day."

Celebrating the secret launch of their secret new political movement with a bottle of the hotel's finest champagne, the couple were interrupted from their news viewing half an hour later by the receptionist.

"Mister Morgan? Your ride to the airport is waiting for you at the front of the hotel."

After settling their bill and saying *au revoir* to Orla and Stuart and wishing them the very best of luck for their future, Blackwell picked up the bags and followed Mindy out of the front door onto the pavement, where both stopped in shock. In front of them stood a familiar-looking executive van, whose driver - an older man in a smart suit - was leaning on the side of the vehicle, arms folded, with a grimace on his face.

"I might have known," he said.

"Afternoon, Widdock," Blackwell replied, getting to the stage on the trip when nothing was ever going to surprise him again and relieved that this final stage was with a man he knew.

The journey to the airport passed without incident and, it has to be said, with little conversation.

Widdock was in the area, having chauffeured a customer to the ferry terminal, and that was all he was minded to tell them.

Despite the awkward silence, the passengers were soon in the airport departure lounge, studying their mobile phones.

"The UK's Security and Exchange Commission is urgently investigating US market manipulation, potentially involving a UK-based company," reported Mindy. "I guess they've received the emails between Alcock and Hail provided by an anonymous whistleblower."

"Have you seen EuroUptake's photos from its Rome office, showing Elena Marchetti dressed as Mussolini?"

"Show me!"

Mindy scrolled through the pictures with a huge smile on her face.

"You really are very beautiful when you smile," admired her fiancé.

"Oh? And what about when I'm not smiling?"

"I think I'll get us another drink," he announced.

"Yes. Do that," she laughed. "I have a few phone calls to make."

Avoiding The Limelight

By the time the flight from Dublin taxied to the gate at Heathrow, airport security was already having problems controlling the number of reporters and cameramen in the arrivals hall.

"From a safety point of view, we have no choice," explained the head of security to the two passengers remaining on the plane. "Your driver will pick you up here and we'll escort you to the perimeter. Then the police will make sure you get home."

Mindy understood the issue, but struggled to hide her disappointment.

Media correspondents reported that the owner of Marsh Media was, for the first time, seeking to interfere in the editorial policy of her media outlets, with insiders promising to provide more details shortly.

Technology correspondents reported that Aston Hail had ordered all his companies to replace any software applications supplied by Takahashi Technologies. He had instructed his legal team to seek an injunction against the company, and to prepare to sue for breach of contract and confidentiality. City correspondents were reporting significant global drops in the share prices of both organisations.

"We could have had so much fun," Mindy lamented when they were in their limousine, heading along the M4 with a blue-light escort, front and back.

"Let's stay out of the spotlight while they rip each other apart. We don't want to be too close to this. There'll be more fun tomorrow," replied Blackwell soothingly. "We can use tonight to complete the news statement."

By the time the first members of the press arrived outside the house, the police had done their job and Blackwell and Mindy were safely inside. Police officers guarded the front and back of the house, while another officer successfully visited the local supermarket to pick up food and drink for the homeowners and his colleagues without having his photograph taken.

Back Home

After an overnight ferry crossing and a drive in the early hours from Anglesey, across Wales and back to the Midlands, the remaining Fishing Flops plus one were understandably tired.

Dave Westlake and his new girlfriend were the first to be dropped off, and almost sleep-walked into the police officer's modern, three-bedroom terraced house. Sinead dropped her bag in the hallway and stood on tiptoe to put her arms around her boyfriend's neck and kiss him.

"Welcome home," he smiled, lifting her onto the first stair to make her more comfortable while they hugged.

"I'm pleased to be here. Where's the loo and where's the bed, in that order?"

"I thought you wanted to see the sights and work on more songs?"

"Get me to bed. Let's have a nap. Then you can show me the sights and I'll find something to work on. And bring my bag," she instructed, then marched up the stairs. The burly constable locked the front door, picked up both bags, and did what he was told.

Outside his house in Sidwell, Pope waited patiently while Angus Grace talked Coldfront through the events in his garden just over six months ago.

"So you had MI5 and E-squadron gunning for you in there?" Coldfront asked.

"Yep," Pope confirmed.

"Then one of them tried to kill you down there?" Coldfront asked, pointing further down the road.

"Yep."

"And it's all top secret, Coldfront," Angus reminded him. "Official Secrets Act. Maximum security prison. Bullet in your head. That kind of thing."

"Gotcha," confirmed their chauffeur, partly thrilled to be privy to such secret information and partly gutted to be prevented from telling anybody about it.

"I'm off," said Pope. "Thanks lads. It's been... interesting."

He waited until the van had driven off, then peered through the new railings at the neighbouring, soon-to-be-occupied house, before walking thoughtfully to his own front door, which opened as he reached it.

"Welcome home, stranger," Pippa greeted him with a smile and a hug. "Brace yourself."

A split second later, the two greyhounds careened into the hallway from the kitchen and leapt on him. Pippa threw herself out of the way as Pope fell back onto the lawn and grabbed hold of Fred and Ginger as well as he could, given their excitement and frenzied bouncing around.

"They were in the back garden," Pippa explained in a loud voice. "That's why they took a while to arrive."

"I've missed them Pip. Missed you as well."

Pippa took a handful of treats from her pocket and threw them over the lawn. In a flash, the dogs forgot the return of their owner and were on the hunt.

"Come on in," smiled Pippa. "You can tell me how much you've missed me, then we can swap news and watch it." She waited until she saw the frown appear before continuing. "They're holding a news conference at ten."

News Updates

Blackwell sat in his pyjamas, scrolling through the news on his laptop while Mindy kept writing on hers. It would be fair - although something of an understatement - to say there had been developments overnight.

Tee Takahashi was countersuing Aston Hail for damages to her business's reputation and value. Rumours suggested Alexander Alcock was negotiating a deal with the SEC to give them whatever information they needed regarding US market manipulation, although, judging by leaks from either Alcock or the SEC, they already had the information they needed.

"Looks like Aston was happy for Alexander to make some money by giving him good news before announcing it to the markets," commented Blackwell. "And he'd get him to short-sell stocks he knew were going to tank, including the Claskett Micro Distribution business that Widdock told us about."

"Did you see where Alcock gets his funds? The US financial pages have the story. He's probably the biggest money launderer on the planet. Also, you mentioned Widdock. Wasn't it a coincidence he turned up yesterday?"

"It was! Or was it…?"

"Widdock said he'd been working for Peace Castle for over eight years. Care to guess what happened just before then?"

"I'm not sure we have the time."

"The Connellys had owned the estate since the 19th century, but were running out of money. They sold it quietly to a property developer who renovated it and returned it to its former glory. Care to guess who?"

"Our new best friends?"

"Our new best friends."

"I don't know if I'm excited or concerned by that news."

"Stick with excited. Like you said, you don't have the time for anything else."

The Press Conference

At ten o'clock on the dot, Andrew Blackwell walked to his front gate with Mindy alongside him.

Facing him were four television cameras, four photographers, six reporters and four online bloggers, with one pool representative from the first three groups who would send out whatever they got to whoever wanted it.

"Good morning," started Blackwell.

"There has been some interest in where my fiancée and I have been over the past week. The answer is the beautiful country of Ireland. We went at the invitation of a group of people interested in the *Path Finder* philosophy and who were happy to make a significant donation to my charitable foundation. That donation was distributed equally between four organisations prior to our attendance at the donors' event."

He waited while Mindy handed out a list of the charities, with copies of the receipts received.

"Long story short, I can't give you any more detail about the people we met or what we discussed, but that is an irrelevance anyway, as the group won't be involved in our plans going forward."

Mindy smiled inwardly at the thought of Aston Hail's reaction to being described as an irrelevance.

"The group left quickly on the third day of our visit. I don't know why. But we were grateful for their interest and encouraged by their response to our ideas. With our meeting cut short, we spent a couple more days in Ireland to collect our thoughts away from the interest we attract over here. We decided that perhaps now was the time to talk more publicly about our plans - as basic as they are. We returned home yesterday, ready to share our ideas with everybody and, hopefully, to get some positive feedback - as rare as that is in this day and age."

Blackwell paused, imagining the numbers grunting in agreement at home and in the Westminster bubble, then continued.

"The *Path Finder* foundation manifesto - for want of a better word - will appear on our website shortly. Anybody wanting to keep abreast of developments will also be able to register for updates should they so wish. No pressure, though. Thank you for your time."

Blackwell turned to retreat into the safety of their home. A voice called out from the press pack and stopped him dead.

"What about the meetings you had in England with the major political parties, Andrew?"

Blackwell turned around once more.

"I'm sorry. I don't know what you're talking about. It's been months since I've spoken to any political leader. However, I'll be interested in their response to our ideas, once they've read them."

He took Mindy by the hand and posed for photographs, then retreated into the house and closed the door.

"Well done," she said, squeezing his hand. "Go put the kettle on. I'll publish."

* * *

"Well, that wasn't very interesting," grumbled Pippa, reaching for her laptop.

"Maybe not," Pope replied. "But he showed that every major politician in the country has lied about him over the past week, without actually saying it. And what are you doing now?"

"I'm going to read this manifesto, or whatever it is."

"How many more people do you think are doing exactly the same thing?"

"Ah," she said. "You make a good point."

* * *

"Genius," declared Declan. "He said a lot by saying virtually nothing."

He looked across at his brother, staring at his laptop. "Are you downloading the manifesto?"

"Nah, Mindy sent that over before Andy went out. I'm looking at the website stats."

Connor looked like a child in a sweetshop. "There are thousands every second getting hold of it, Dec. From all over the world."

Declan gazed at the framed black-and-white photograph on the mantelpiece; the one of the whole family together, a couple of years before things went wrong.

Perhaps this was the moment for the Kellys to shine. He stood, patted his brother on the shoulder, and wandered off to make a cup of tea.

Go To Hell

The phone rang six times before a familiar voice answered it.

"You got your man back then?"

Well, good morning Regimental Sergeant Major, and how are you this fine day?

"I think his friends sorted him out. Flew him back from Dublin last night."

"Anything to report from your last day? Get any more on ICARUS?"

"Afraid not. Not sure how that'll go down with GCHQ."

"I've talked to them. They've decided not to poke the wasp nest, but they're putting a team together to see if they can develop something similar. Anyway, welcome back. Thanks for the call."

"There's just one more thing. The person who flagged the situation in Clonbrinny. He isn't a member of the Garden Club, is he? He never was."

"What makes you think that?"

"Because he was a spotter during the Troubles. You recruited him, Pete. Actually, you blackmailed him. You warned him to get out when things became hot, then helped him before the Garden Club existed. You felt obliged to do so again recently when he left a message, even though he isn't a club member."

The silence at the other end told Pope everything.

"What makes you think it was me?"

"Let's wrap this up. Those were your words when you told Jimmy Doyle to get out of Dodge. *We can wrap this up.* Those were your words to me two days ago. You were the guy on the bike who turned up at Jimmy's caravan. And that's why you gave this job to me, because you couldn't put it through the Garden Club's books. It would raise awkward questions about how you'd helped before…"

"Quite the detective, Simmo."

"You told me this was just a recce, but it wasn't, was it? If the priest and others in Clonbrinny were in real danger, you'd have done nothing to help them. Or me and the lads who came on the trip. You'd have done nothing to help us."

"Did I ask you to take them with you?" The RSM heard the intake of breath down the phone line. "Anyway, it all worked out. You did a good job."

"We got lucky. Go to hell."

Pope rang off, then turned at the sound of movement behind him. Pippa scanned his face, then walked up and held him tight.

"Are you angry?" she asked.

"Fuming."

"Then let's get it all over with. I think I know who's moving in next door," she took a breath and held him even tighter, "Andy and Mindy."

The two dogs were dozing in the front room when the howl of rage started. They were at the bottom of the garden when it finished, staring towards the house, wondering what on earth was going on.

Author's Note

Thank you very much for checking out Good For The Soul. I hope you enjoyed reading the novel as much as I did writing it.

If that's the case, please consider leaving a rating and review on your preferred book retailer website and any relevant social media groups. Reviews mean so much to many authors and I'm one of them. It's incredibly rewarding to create and share something that others value and enjoy so much, they want to tell others about it.

Also, if you'd like to stay in touch, then visit my website **www.philrennett.com** where you'll find my blog and other bits and pieces, plus a free subscription to the occasional *Path Finder* newsletter.

Registering will also give you exclusive access to a series of prologues, where you'll learn more about the characters you've already met.

I look forward to seeing you there!

Best wishes.

Phil

Author's Books

The Path Finder Series

Paths Not Yet Taken

Good For The Soul

Where The Winds Blow
(*Coming late 2025*)